Turtles of the Midnight Moon

Turtles
of the
Midnight
Moon

MARÍA JOSÉ FITZGERALD

ALFRED A. KNOPF  NEW YORK

THIS IS A BORZOI BOOK PUBLISHED BY ALFRED A. KNOPF

All rights reserved. Published in the United States by Alfred A. Knopf, an imprint of Random House Children's Books, a division of Penguin Random House LLC, New York.

Knopf, Borzoi Books, and the colophon are registered trademarks of Penguin Random House LLC.

Visit us on the Web! rhcbooks.com

Educators and librarians, for a variety of teaching tools,
visit us at RHTeachersLibrarians.com

Library of Congress Cataloging-in-Publication Data
Names: Fitzgerald, María José, author.
Title: Turtles of the midnight moon / María José Fitzgerald.
Description: First edition. | New York : Alfred A. Knopf, 2023. | Audience: Ages 8–12. |
Summary: Twelve-year-olds Barana and Abby come together to solve a sea turtle egg poaching mystery plaguing Barana's Honduran coastal village, and learn the true meaning of friendship, courage, and community along the way.
Identifiers: LCCN 2022023295 (print) | LCCN 2022023296 (ebook) |
ISBN 978-0-593-48870-6 (hardcover) | ISBN 978-0-593-48871-3 (library binding) |
ISBN 978-0-593-48872-0 (ebook)
Subjects: CYAC: Friendship—Fiction. | Magic—Fiction. | Sea turtles—Fiction. |
Poaching—Fiction. | Honduras—Fiction. | Mystery and detective stories. |
LCGFT: Detective and mystery fiction. | Novels.
Classification: LCC PZ7.1.F57324 Tu 2023 (print) | LCC PZ7.1.F57324 (ebook) |
DDC [Fic]—dc23

The text of this book is set in 11.5-point Baskerville.
Interior design by Michelle Crowe

Printed in the United States of America
1st Printing
First Edition

To my daughters, Fiana and Brenna

Atlantic Ocean

Caribbean
Sea

La playa

Cemetery

Barana's
house

Pulpería
Gloria

Community
center

Bela's house

Centro de
Conservación
de Tortugas
Marinas

Church

Clinic

María and
Matías's house

To school →

Canal

Lagoon

N
W   E
S

PATAYA

Baula

I am from the ocean, vast and cold.
From the heart of the Atlantic.
Swimming miles away from home,
Until I return again.
I am treasure, buried deep.
Hatchlings beneath the sand.
Shifting, shaping, preparing
For the greatest march of our lives.
I am from a peaceful golden beach,
From the land of lobsters, conch, and fish.
Of rising tides and falling suns,
Where rustling wind meets shimmering sea.
I am from a hidden nest of hope;
A mother's moonlit journey.
My sisters, brothers, and I broke through:
Turtles of the midnight moon.
I am from the time of dinosaurs.
Guided by strength and spirit,
I arrived.
A la Tierra.
A la Mar.
A Mi.
Luna of the sand and sea.

CHAPTER 1

Barana

Barana woke to the crescent moon–shaped scar between her shoulder blades tingling, calling her to the beach. To Luna. She turned to face Tulu's side of the room. Her brother's body was still, his chest rising and falling in a steady rhythm.

Barana slipped out of bed and tiptoed to the doorway. She pushed the curtain aside and entered the main room of the small wooden house that teetered on stilts above the sand. Papá snored from the other bedroom. Mamá was probably cuddled up next to him with Marisol. The baby was like a tick, always attached to Mamá's body.

Nobody would notice Barana's absence.

The tingling on her back turned to a persistent prickle. She hadn't sensed Luna all season. As far as she knew, her leatherback turtle had yet to lay a clutch. Maybe tonight would be the night.

Barana slipped on her chancletas and opened the front door. The waves and crickets muffled her footsteps as she stepped off the rickety stairs and onto the shimmering sand.

The wind sang through the palm fronds, and the moon above smiled. Guided by Luna's call, the warm breeze, and the sea, Barana approached her favorite place on earth, the place where turtles roamed, where turquoise waters met the Caribbean sky—la playa.

The mighty Atlantic was three minutes from her house, and Barana knew the way to her beach by heart. She kicked off her sandals and ran barefoot through the palm trees, letting the fine sand brush against her brown toes.

The wind cooled both her nerves and the sweat upon her brow. Pataya's sweltering June weather was not for the faint of heart. As her eyes adjusted to the darkness, she paused to look up. The moon's barely visible crescent shape smiled down at her. Miles of sand stretched out before her.

The cemetery was a few minutes away, at the west end of the beach. She was in no mood to bump into ghosts or the creepy creatures of local myth, so she ran east, energized by the starry sky, the ocean, and the knowing that her turtle was nearby.

The waves lapped hungrily at her feet, the foam tickling them as she let the prickle in her scar guide her. She searched for tracks—any sign that Luna had come ashore—but there were none. She kicked the surf and wandered farther down la playa. Still no evidence of her baula. Maybe she needed to stay in one place. Her scar's tingling had become faint. Perhaps she had missed the sea turtle, or maybe Luna hadn't come onto the shore at all.

Barana sank onto a large piece of driftwood. Ten minutes became twenty. Finally, the prickle grew stronger. Luna was close. The cobalt sea glowed with green. . . . Something was stirring the fluorescent plankton. As if it had been waiting for Barana, a leathery black head poked out of the surf.

Flippers met sand as the baula's enormous body emerged— close to six hundred pounds, if Barana had to guess. Her white star-like speckles glimmered against her black body. Barana approached the majestic creature, the moon-shaped scar confirming it was her beloved Luna. Side by side, they made their way up the sloping beach, Barana carefully keeping her distance. María always reminded them that turtles were wild creatures and told them to "mind a turtle's space." Though Barana knew Luna's face by heart and could recognize the pink and white spots on her body, this turtle was not her pet. She belonged to the sea and sand. La mar y la arena.

"Hola, amiga. I've missed you." Barana's eyes teared up as she remembered the first time she saw Luna crawl ashore. She was five years old when it happened. Ever since then, when the nesting season drew near, Barana wondered if Luna would show up. Every other year, her scar would tingle, and she knew Luna had returned.

Barana rubbed her eyes and sat quietly to watch as the baula shifted her heavy body. She struggled awkwardly on the sand as she prepared to dig a pit.

Tears slipped from the leatherback's face as she pushed the sand with her flippers to form the chamber for her eggs. Barana knew the sea turtle's lágrimas were a way to rid her body of salt, a simple scientific phenomenon. But she liked to believe the mama turtle cried for her babies, knowing she'd have to leave them and their lives to fate. Both good reasons to cry.

The night was eerily quiet, and Barana had the unsettling feeling of being watched. She rubbed her neck to smooth the hairs that had prickled up. She shouldn't be out by herself. In the distance she noticed two small, distinct lights. Slowly they moved closer. And then she exhaled a sigh of relief. It was the night patrol, doing their rounds to monitor the beach for sea turtles and to record any new nests.

Still, a twelve-year-old girl had no business being out on the beach alone at midnight. She'd heard enough ghost stories to know better. El Cadejo could get you, or if the devil's dog didn't, La Llorona might. Barana turned back to her turtle and held her hand several feet above the leathery carapace, sensing that spark of connection with Luna. She wasn't sure how old Luna was, but her eyes seemed to hold decades of memories. "I'll see you again, old girl," Barana said. If this was Luna's first clutch, Barana knew she'd be back to lay another one in a week or so.

Before the turtle finished laying her eggs, Barana ran home, stopping only to rest behind a palm tree and ensure that she hadn't been seen. She didn't want whoever was on patrol to tattle to her parents. Everybody knew everybody in her village. Mamá would throw a fit if she knew Barana had been out. She'd been caught once before, and the consequences had been diaper-washing duties for a month. She'd vowed to never let that happen again.

Barana picked up her sandals and quietly crept up the stairs of her house, sprinkling a trail of sand behind her. She brushed a few grains off her toes and out of her hair and tiptoed into the casita, carefully closing the door. Before taking another step, she looked around to make sure everything was as she'd left it. There were no sounds from the other side of the flower-patterned curtain sectioning off her parents' room.

Tulu also slept soundly. Barana crawled under her soft sheet and thought about her secret excursion. Despite not being there to watch Luna go back to the ocean, it had been worth it. She promised herself that first thing in the morning she'd find out if the night patrol had marked the nest. María, who oversaw the turtle conservation project in Pataya, would know. Other people cared and helped out too, but it was María who had taken on the project almost ten years ago. She knew all of the leatherbacks' markings by heart.

A short poem formed in Barana's mind as she fell asleep.

Mama turtle tears,
Shed in sorrow,
Filled with love.
Precious cycle carries on.

She pictured Luna gliding through the water when she felt a new sensation in her scar. The gentle tickle she'd sensed earlier was replaced by a throbbing burn.

CHAPTER 2

Abby

Tap, tap, click. Picture number one, done: Aberdeen snapped a shot of the dance's welcome banner and a handful of smiling students milling about in the background. The flash on her old hand-me-down camera was working, and her mood was decent, considering she was determined to get the evening over with as painlessly—and as quickly—as possible. She wanted to be as invisible as a wildlife photographer sneaking up on a herd of gazelles.

The middle school cafetorium was decorated with blue and silver garlands, balloons, and a huge poster that said, HAVE A GREAT SUMMER! A mirror ball hung above the dance floor, reflecting colorful lights on the huddles of sixth graders scattered around the room. The music was too loud for Abby to think clearly.

She tried to ignore the sea of students and focus instead on what her photography teacher, Ms. Tenley, had asked her to do—capture a few decent pictures for the final student newspaper of the year. If she could pull it off without having to engage in any kind of socializing or dancing, the night would be a success.

Abby had hated end-of-year parties ever since fourth grade. June 16 of fourth grade, to be exact. She would never forget it. Parents had volunteered to cook food for the party. Mom had tried, unsuccessfully, to make ceviche. Abby's mouth watered every time Papi made her favorite dish from his childhood in Honduras—lime and cilantro infusing a mix of shrimp and fish with the perfect zing.

Unfortunately, Mom's version had turned out too sour, like the seafood-to-lime ratio was way off. *And* she'd used crabmeat instead of shrimp. It wasn't terrible, but Abby's classmates seemed to think the whole *idea* of ceviche was gross.

Two years later, Abby still cringed at the memory of how Thomas McDowell had reacted. "Eww! What is this, crab vomit?" he'd said, loud enough for everyone to hear.

Thomas was the most popular boy in their class, and since *he'd* disliked it, everyone else followed his lead. Mom apologized, but Thomas never did. The damage was done.

Not only had her mom's dish been a catastrophe, but a game of freeze dance had also resulted in major embarrassment. Abby kept messing up the steps to the Macarena, and everyone noticed. Apparently, she wasn't Latina enough to know the steps to a simple group dance. She became so frustrated that she accidentally elbow-jabbed Monique in the face—hard—giving her a nosebleed. Abby tried to apologize, but Monique avoided her for the rest of the party.

That was the day everyone started calling her Crabby Abby.

Ever since then, Aberdeen had given up dancing, fitting in, or having any other friends besides Fiana. Except now Fiana was gone. She'd left for London over winter break, and Abby vowed to finish sixth grade like a turtle on a stone: Invisible. Camouflaged. Silent.

She approached a group of boys from her homeroom after double-checking that Thomas McDowell was nowhere in sight. "Hey, guys, can I get a picture for the newspaper?" The boys lunged at each other and hugged. They called over a couple of missing members of their group and did the dab for the camera.

Tap, tap, click.

Another picture, done. She was grateful the boys had helped speed this dreaded night along. As they bumped around and joked, an icky mood came over her, making her skin feel prickly and warm. She watched as the boys laughed away, leaving her there with her camera dangling between her fingertips.

"Thanks," she whispered to nobody as the boys marched off to the punch bowl.

Abby wondered what Fiana was up to in London. Probably sleeping, given the time difference. She texted her anyway:

> Stuck at the 6th grade dance. Taking pics for Ms. T. Wish you were here.

She slipped the phone back into her pocket and surveyed the room for more easy targets. Three girls from her Advanced Spanish class were laughing and chatting by the snack table. She took a deep breath and bravely approached.

"Hola," Abby said. "¿Puedo tomarles una foto para el newspaper?"

"Hey! ¡Sí!" one of them replied. "¡Todas, foto!"

Abby tapped her index finger twice on the shutter before snapping the photo on the third tap.

Tap, tap, click.

"Dos más," she said. Two more, just to make sure she had a good one. She concentrated on the lighting and the angle, and on getting the perfect composition. As she looked through the lens, she couldn't help but wonder if she could ever be a part of their group. Ana's family was Mexican, and Paula's was from El Salvador. She wasn't sure about the other girl, but they'd probably never guess Abby was also Latina. Well, half Latina. Her fair skin, courtesy of her mother, didn't fit most people's stereotypes. They probably had no idea Papi was Honduran, even though she shared his dark hair and eyes.

Abby considered striking up a conversation, but she couldn't bring herself to do it. Staying behind the camera was easier. Comfortable. She walked away and stood against the cinderblock wall. Fiana still hadn't texted back.

Abby had prepared herself to take a few more photos when a high-pitched voice called out her name. "Hey! Crabby Abby, I see you've got your antique camera. Will you come take a picture of us?" It was Mean Monique.

Abby tilted her head and rolled her eyes, protesting the use of her nickname with a glare. The bubbly cheerleader smiled at her and said, "You know I'm just kidding!" Then she fake-hugged Abby around the shoulder.

Nobody else called her Crabby Abby anymore, but Monique had never let the nickname go. The words still stung enough to make Abby blush. She wanted to smack Monique with her "antique" camera.

Instead, she said, "Sure," and followed Monique over to the huddle of giggles.

Tap, tap, click.

Abby snapped a photo and then "Bailando" came on. The cheerleaders ran off to the dance floor with promises of returning for another photo shoot. The queen bee led her crew under the mirror ball, leaving Abby alone with her camera.

"Why don't you go dance with them?" a voice asked from behind, startling her.

Abby turned around. It was a boy from class, Andrew.

"Nah, I'm just taking pictures. Plus, I don't like to dance."

"I thought you were Spanish. You must like this song, right?"

Andrew was nice; he always complimented her in Señor Guerrero's class. But he'd called her "Spanish" at exactly the wrong moment.

"'Spanish' refers to the *language*. Or, if you're from Spain, then you're 'Spanish.' And I'm not from Spain. I'm Honduran, and I *speak* Spanish. And I told you, I don't like dancing."

"Jeez, don't get all worked up. I said it 'cause you're always answering Señor's questions in class." He took a sip of his lemonade. "You're, like, the best student."

"I'm not worked up; I'm just trying to correct your wording so you'll be less offensive in the future." Abby glanced down at her camera. She'd taken a total of seven pictures: the party banner and entrance, two of the boys' group, three of the girls from Spanish class, and one of Mean Monique and her crew. Was that enough to get the heck out of there already?

Andrew walked away shaking his head.

Once again, Abby was alone. Maybe "Crabby" *was* an appropriate nickname after all.

A part of her wanted to join the kids on the dance floor to prove to them *and* herself that *crabby* was not an accurate adjective to describe her. The other part of her desperately wanted to go home. She had enough photos, and she'd had enough of the end-of-year party. Again.

That's all I've got for you today, Ms. Tenley, she thought. *I am never doing this again.*

She fled to the bathroom to pass the time. There was no way she could text her mother yet; the interrogation would be exhausting if she sent an SOS this early. Instead, she sat inside one of the mustard-yellow stalls and scrolled through old photos she'd taken of wildlife around their small northern New Jersey town.

The seconds ticked by slowly, with nothing but radio silence from Fiana. Finally, Abby couldn't take it any longer. She took a few deep breaths, turned off her camera, and texted her mother.

෨෪෫

MOM'S SILVER VW pulled into the school's circular driveway. Abby braced herself for questions, but she was an expert at dodging them by now. After all, Fiana had moved away almost six months ago, and Abby had mostly succeeded at pretending life at school was fine.

"Hey," she said as she hopped into the front seat.

"Hi, sweetie."

Mom examined her face, searching for something. "So . . . you got some good pictures for the newspaper?"

"A few, yeah. I think Ms. T will be happy."

"And did you have *fun*?"

Abby considered telling her mom the truth. That she'd

been mocked by some random boy from her Spanish class for not wanting to dance to a Latin song, and that ever since Fiana moved away, she'd been unable to figure out how to even begin making new friends.

"A little." She counted the trees on their street as they approached the old farmhouse on Meadowlark Drive. *Seven, eight, nine* . . . She blinked several times to push back the tears. *Don't cry, don't cry. Ten, eleven, twelve.*

They pulled into their driveway, and Fiana still hadn't replied to her message.

As they went through the back door, Abby promised herself to play it cool when Papi asked about the evening.

"¡Hola, mi amor!" her father exclaimed from his favorite chair, the latest *National Geographic* magazine on his lap.

"Hola, Papi."

"¿Qué tal la fiesta?" Her dad's deep brown eyes and loving smile beamed at her.

"It was okay."

"Just okay, Coneja?"

Abby nodded and grabbed the magazine from his lap.

"Can I take a look?" She plopped herself on the couch, hoping the glossy, professional photos would take her mind off her pathetic life.

"It's all yours. I was almost done with it anyway." He looked her up and down like Mom had earlier. What was it with grown-ups and sizing kids up after school, after parties, after anything?

Keep a straight face and pretend you're totally okay. Focus on the magazine.

"There's a great series of photos from the Himalayas in that issue."

"Cool."

From the corner of her eye, Abby could tell Papi was still staring at her, as if waiting for more. "Listen, Aberdeen, how about you and I go on a morning hike tomorrow? We can head out to the trails off the Palisades, and you can take pictures of the river."

"That'd be nice." Abby looked up at her dad and faked her best smile. Not that she wasn't appreciative of the invitation. It *would* be nice to get outside with him again. He'd been so busy lately that they'd barely seen each other all spring.

"It's a date, then," he said.

"It's a date." She forced another smile. As much as she enjoyed their excursions, a morning hike with Papi didn't change the fact that she'd had a miserable evening. A miserable year, really. And the magazine photos of the Himalayas weren't exactly helping her forget. "I think I'll go and shower. I want to get to bed early for tomorrow's hike."

"Sounds good. Buenas noches, Coneja," Papi said.

"Noches, Papi. Night, Mom."

"Night, Aberdeen. Love you."

Abby climbed the stairs to her room and sat on the large bay-window seat to look at the sky before getting in the shower. The crescent moon smiled at her, as if trying to make her feel better. She couldn't bring herself to smile back. Papi always said the moon was magical, and that humans have always had a special connection to it, but Abby wasn't so sure about that stuff anymore. There was no magic in her life. No friend she could count on. And her photography was mediocre at best.

At least tomorrow she'd have a day outside with Papi, and she could finish her final photography project for Ms. Tenley. Just one more week of misery at Ridge Park Middle School.

CHAPTER 3

Barana

Barana stretched out in her bed as the brilliant orange sun warmed her face. Its light shimmered upon her brown skin. She sat up and scratched some of the sand off her head. Tiny golden specks fell to the wooden floor. She made the sign of the cross, praying that her parents wouldn't notice the beach in her hair and on her body.

On weekdays she awoke before sunrise, so the light reminded her that it was Saturday.

Tulu wasn't in the room. Barana figured he was out fishing with their dad or talking fútbol with the cousins over at Abuela's next door. She breathed in the salty air, put on her favorite cutoff jean shorts and tank top, and ran outside.

Mamá was wringing out a few items of clothing over their rectangular pila. The large cement container of water held a mountain of cloth diapers on the ridged surface that sat next to the spigot. Baby Marisol was wrapped around Mamá's back in a striped sling. Barana kissed her little sister on the cheek. Mamá seemed to notice Barana's sandy toes and hair but only raised an eyebrow.

Maybe her prayer had worked.

"Grab a banana from that bowl," Mamá commanded. "And wash your hair tonight. . . ." She patted Barana's head and examined the falling granules.

Barana grabbed two bananas from the tin bowl on their outdoor table. The bowl was replenished daily with bananas or mangoes. Today the bananas weren't as ripe as she liked them.

"Están demasiado verdes," she told her mother. They weren't green, but they weren't yellow enough.

"Well, they won't ripen before you can eat them. ¿Para dónde vas, Barana?" Mamá asked as she hung a diaper on the line, its bottom corners dripping.

"To the turtle office to talk to María about a nest."

"I need your help with Marisol today. And why are you going this early? Eat your banana first."

"I *told* you. It's about a turtle nest." Barana peeled a banana and took a giant bite in her mom's face.

"Come back soon. I need you to watch your sister."

"What about Tulu? Can't he do it?" Her brother never did the baby-related chores. He went fishing, played fútbol, and hung out with his friends. It was always the girls who got stuck with the boring work.

"He's out with your father, so you need to be back in an hour."

"Fine, but he's got to watch her next time!"

Barana hurried off before her mamá could reply.

Bela was next door hanging the week's laundry. Her grandmother was particular about the household chores; they had to be done on a specific day and in a specific way. Laundry was done on the weekends. Landscaping and gardening on Mondays. House cleaning on Tuesdays and Thursdays.

Bela's little white-faced monkey, Pitufo, perched on her shoulder as she worked. Barana petted him. Abuela and her monkey were inseparable. Barana scratched behind his ears and handed him one of the small bananas she'd grabbed earlier. It was too green anyway. "Here. One's enough for me."

Pitufo had been a member of their family since being orphaned as a baby. Bela had become his mother, and Barana's entire family had pretty much adopted him too.

"Help me hang this large sheet, Barana," her abuela said. "We might be having guests in the casita next week."

"But, Bela, I'm running to see María, and then I have to run *back* to help Mamá with Marisol." She took another bite of her banana and realized how hungry she still was.

"Two seconds, mija. My back's not as flexible as it used to be."

Barana reluctantly helped her abuela hang the sheet while she held the banana firmly in her mouth. When they finished, she sped off to the sea turtle office, wondering who Bela's visitors might be. Halfway down the grass-lined dirt path, she realized her sandals weren't on. It was just as well. She hated shoes anyway.

The cinder-block structure rose out of the hot sand. The paint of its leatherback turtle mural had worn off after years of erosion by the salty wind and annual rains. Still, it was Barana's favorite building. María was on the phone, her hand placed over her forehead. Barana pushed the door open a little more and poked her head inside. María waved her in with one hand and instructed her to hush with the other.

"Sí, sí, we are starting the paperwork. Aha . . . sí . . . no sé."

The person on the other line spoke loudly enough that Barana could hear the agitation in their voice.

"No, no, the storm will be here on Monday, not tomorrow. . . . Well, the money stopped coming." María shook her head. "No, he can't do that. You know how bad his health has been since the accident."

Barana assumed "he" was María's husband, Matías. He had gotten the bends a few months ago, and neither his mood nor his health had fully recovered. The local divers feared the horrible condition, which happened if they dove too much and came up from the depths too quickly; when they did, gas bubbles in their bodies expanded so fast that the divers could suffer lifelong pain. Though Matías's case of the bends hadn't resulted in him being paralyzed, he'd come close.

María stroked her swollen stomach.

Poor lady, about to have a third baby while her husband was still recovering.

María set the phone down on the table and rubbed her eyes. She took a sip from her water bottle and exhaled. "Buenos días, Barana." She massaged the back of her neck. "What can I do for you?"

"Buenos días, Señora María. Did you say a storm was coming?"

"Sí, el lunes. Possibly a big one."

"No sabía." Barana had no idea a storm was coming on Monday. It wasn't officially hurricane season, but that didn't mean much these days, with the weather so unpredictable. Big storms were never good news for her village. Though she hadn't yet been born when the last hurricane hit, she'd heard plenty of stories about the destruction it left behind.

"So, what brings you here this morning, Barana?"

"I was just wondering if any turtles came ashore last night?" Barana kept her expression neutral to hide the fact that she knew the answer. "I was curious—especially if there's a storm coming. Maybe new nests should get moved farther up the tide line."

"Good thinking, and yes, there was a nesting last night. Close to your house, actually. Here's the map Abel and Matías marked." She handed Barana a clipboard with a rough map of Pataya's beach and its landmarks.

Barana pretended to be surprised. "Oh, I see. Yes, it's right by my house! Do you want me to help you move it?"

"You go on. Take a bag, a sign, and a small shovel with you. I have to get things ready for the storm."

"By myself?"

"How old are you now?"

"Almost thirteen."

"I think you can handle it. Our nest-relocation permit applies to all volunteers, and you've done it countless times with me. I trust you."

Her mom would lose her mind if she was late, but Barana wasn't about to pass up this chance. Like María said, she'd helped with moving nests before, but to be trusted with one alone was *huge*! She grabbed a bag and a shovel and bolted out the door.

Ten minutes later, she was out of breath from running back to the spot where she'd seen Luna the night before. The location was marked by four wooden stakes with red fishing rope tied around them, forming a square. The turtle tracks were still fresh, and the sea was calm. No sign of a storm yet.

Barana dug gently. Once she'd gotten deep enough, she used her bare hands to feel around for the eggs. They were the size of Ping-Pong balls, and their shells were rubbery and soft, unlike the hard shells of most birds. *Turtles are so smart,* she thought. The flexible membranes made it nearly impossible for them to break under the sand's weight.

Before moving the eggs, she needed to find a new, safer

spot and dig a deep enough chamber. She walked up the beach, as far from the shore as she could. "¡Aquí!" she whispered to herself.

The spot was perched high above the tide line, near two short palms that bent toward each other, forming an archway. There was no way the storm surge would get this far. Barana could even see her own house in the distance.

Digging was hard work, and beads of sweat dripped from her face.

She went back to the original nest and treated each egg as if it were the most valuable of gems. Each one represented the potential for new life, a new leatherback. Only one of these might make it back home to Pataya as an adult. Or none. The odds were slim, so she took every care in the world as she moved them. She carried them in groups of about ten to be sure none got damaged.

Though the ones at the top of the nest didn't have yolks, they were just as important. They acted as buffers, protecting the ones below from nature's forces.

Time stood still, and after she had moved every last one, Barana slowly poured the sand over them like Luna had done the night before. She put four stakes in the ground and tied rope around them, forming the new square. She then staked the sign behind the nest, making sure it was firmly in place. It would alert all passersby that a treasure lay beneath the ground:

She knelt and whispered, "I'll keep you safe."

Proud of her work, Barana went over to the surf, washed the sweat off her face, and refreshed her neck with the salty Caribbean water.

"Barana!" Tulu yelled from between the two arched palms. "What are you doing?"

Barana ran to her brother, bag and shovel in hand. "Relocating a nest. There's a storm coming!"

"Mamá's been waiting for you for over an hour. She's losing her mind!" Her brother examined her work and straightened one of the stakes.

"She's at the pulpería, and a bunch of people are lined up to get bottled water. She needs your help with Marisol."

I hate bottled water, Barana thought to herself. Tulu hated it too. Every time they did a beach cleanup with their school, they'd find empty bottles everywhere.

"Coming. I have to take this shovel and tarp bag to María first. I'll go to Mamá's from there."

"No. I'll take them to Bela's. I'm meeting the primos and Jason there anyway to watch the game. You can take them back to María later. Go to Mamá now. Hurry. You know how she gets when you obsess over the turtles."

Barana shoved the bag and shovel at him, annoyed that

Mamá never thought to ask *him* to babysit their sister. She cut across the palm trees and wove around houses to make it to her mother's store quickly. Her brother got to go play soccer or do whatever he wanted whenever he wanted; meanwhile, she got into trouble for even *caring* about the leatherbacks. It was like all she could do to please her parents was take care of her sister and help with the chores. Be helpful. Be good. Be quiet.

By the time she arrived at the pulpería, Mamá was outside with Marisol, waiting. All Barana wanted was one Saturday to herself and her beach, but her parents always seemed to have other plans. If only she could've stayed by the nest all day, watching the waves for Luna's return.

CHAPTER 4

Abby

Aberdeen threw on her favorite tie-dye T-shirt and slung her camera over her shoulder. She was determined to enjoy a day of photography and fresh air with Papi, instead of dwelling on the disaster that was sixth grade.

The notification on her phone caught her eye as she tucked it into her bag.

> Hey! Sorry you got stuck at the party. Check out this pic. Took it from London rooftop yesterday. Chat later?

Abby read the text three times. She admired Fiana's photograph, but she couldn't bring herself to reply. The picture of the cityscape and sunset was beautiful, but she felt a stab of anger looking at it. While *she'd* been out embarrassing herself at the end-of-year party, Fiana was hanging out on the rooftop of her fancy new London apartment with her fancy new London friends. Abby shoved the phone back into her pocket.

She hadn't been prepared for the day her best friend moved. Fiana's dad was British and her mom was Chinese American, so she was basically the only person in school who understood what it was like to live in a mixed-up soup of languages and cultures. Like Abby, Fiana was always getting asked where she was from because of her slight accent and unique school lunches.

Now that Fi was several time zones away, her texts came at the weirdest hours. But lately they barely came at all. Out of habit, Abby decided to text back:

> Cool pic!! Heading to river with Papi! Chat later!

She ran downstairs and into the sparkling white kitchen. "¡Buenos días, Papi!"

"Morning, Coneja. You seem cheery," he said as he poured himself a cup of coffee and stared at his phone.

She didn't love it when her dad called her Bunny, even though he'd been doing it her whole life. But what bugged her more was how he didn't seem ready to go.

"Where's Mom?"

"En el baño." He didn't even look up from his device as he motioned toward the bathroom.

Abby prepared a bowl of cereal for herself. Had Papi forgotten about their plans?

"Em . . . Papi . . . ¿Vamos al trail?"

"Un segundo, hija. My boss keeps texting."

This was not good. Abby hated her dad's busy schedule. His medical work treating decompression sickness in scuba divers took him all over the world and away from her. She waited for him to say that they were leaving in a bit and not to worry, but the silence between them stretched as Papi kept texting.

"Well, I'm all set whenever you're ready." She tried to make her voice sound chirpy.

She slurped her cereal and glanced over at her dad from the corner of her eye every few bites. He texted furiously and paced the length of the kitchen. She tapped her spoon on the bowl impatiently.

"Morning, Abby," her mom said from behind her as she padded into the kitchen in her fuzzy slippers.

"Hey, Mom." Abby stuffed her face with another mouthful of O's.

"You guys heading out soon?" Mom gently rested her hand on Papi's shoulder, looking over it to spy on his phone.

Papi finally looked up, sighing heavily as he placed both his hands on the kitchen island and shook his head.

"Need to get on a work call. Looks like the big grant for Honduras finally came through, and we have to finalize our trip plans."

"Does that mean no hike?" Abby asked, though she already knew the answer.

"Lo siento, Coneja." He kissed her on the forehead and walked down the hall to his home office. *Stop calling me that! I'm almost thirteen,* Abby wanted to shout. She slouched on her stool and pushed the unfinished bowl of cereal aside as she looked out the window. A black-capped chickadee landed on their bird feeder. Maybe she'd photograph critters in her yard today . . . for the gazillionth time.

"I've got work to catch up on too, but let's watch a movie later?" Mom said.

"Fine," Abby replied as her insides churned.

She walked out to their patio with her head down and sat on a small bench by the koi pond.

The koi came up for bits of food with their pouty fat lips. She grabbed her camera and took a close-up shot of the biggest fish. It was silvery white with orange markings and had the longest whiskers.

Tap, tap, click.

Once, Abby and Fiana had caught a heron hanging out at the pond's edge, ready to snatch a tasty meal. Papi bought an expensive net and placed it over the precious ecosystem that same afternoon. Apparently, koi weren't cheap.

She looked up at the red maple and searched for a chickadee to photograph. Perhaps if she sat there long enough, the heron would return too.

"Abby, you've been out there forever," her mom said,

poking her head through a window. "Want to walk down to the park? I can take a break."

"Can I go by myself?" She needed more alone time.

Her mom considered the request.

"Fine. But take your phone and text me the moment you get there."

THE SMALL SUBURBAN park was nestled against a wall of protected forest, and the creek that wove through the back was like a buffer from whatever wildlife lived beyond. Someone had once spotted a black bear sniffing through the trash cans.

Nature and wildlife were Abby's preferred subjects; she didn't have to talk to them or ask for permission to take their picture. She could sneak up and *snap!* Her favorite photographers, Cristina Mittermeier and Paul Nicklen, were her idols. Someday she'd take pictures like they did. Someday she'd be out on a boat or in a beat-up jeep, taking the most beautiful photos of an albatross in mid-flight or a seal poking its head out of the water. Someday.

A summer breeze blew through the peaceful park. Two toddlers ran around the large metal play structure while their mom watched from a bench. Abby appreciated the little bit of noise and activity. At least she wasn't completely alone.

When her phone vibrated in her pocket, she immediately knew who it was.

> You there yet? It's been five minutes since you left! XO, Mom

Abby responded with a single "Yup" and headed toward the creek. A handful of monarchs had gathered on a purple butterfly bush. Abby snapped their photo. She already felt better.

The creek was bustling with activity. Ducks waddled in the little pool that had been created by a natural rock dam, and a box turtle sunned on a stone in the distance. Abby needed to step onto a few large stones in the water to get the perfect shot. Turtles were cool. They'd been around for millions of years and could retreat into their shell whenever they wanted, no questions asked. Sometimes Abby wished she could do the same.

As she jumped from one rock to another, a dragonfly buzzed by her ear. It flew back and forth and then around her, as if annoying her on purpose. Abby held her camera in one hand and used the other one to flick the iridescent bug away, but the flying dragon kept taunting her with its wings. Abby waved her hand wildly, and as she did, her foot slipped and she lost her balance.

Everything happened in a flash. Her elbow hit a rock and she dropped the camera; her butt landed so hard she couldn't get herself up fast enough to recover the camera before it was completely submerged in the creek. Once she managed to get on her feet, she grabbed the camera and examined the soaked device hopelessly. Water poured out of every crevice. *Stupid dragonfly!*

Nothing happened when she pressed the ON button. She tapped on the shutter, opened the battery case, and tried drying it with the one unsoaked corner of her shirt. Nada. She looked through the lens and could see that the glass was broken. Right in the middle of the lens was a curved crack shaped like a crescent moon.

She held back the tears as the swoosh of her wet shoes moved across the creek's edge and onto the sidewalk. As if testing her patience, a New Jersey Transit train blocked the access to her street for what seemed like hours. She wished she could hop on it and escape to New York City for the day. In less than an hour, she could be lost among strangers in Central Park, surrounded by tall buildings and enough sounds to muffle all the noise inside her head.

When she entered her house, her mom took one look at her soaked clothes and stood up. "What happened?"

"Fell in the creek. Broke my camera."

"Oh, honey, I'm sorry. Is your arm okay?"

"Yeah, why?"

"You're holding it funny. Thought it might be sore." Mom gently reached for her arm to have a closer look, but Abby snatched it away.

"It's fine!"

She hadn't even noticed that her elbow was bleeding and she'd been bending her arm into her chest.

"Aberdeen. I was trying to have a closer look. At least let me check your camera."

"Don't bother. It was an ancient relic anyway."

"Abby, your father's old camera was special to you."

"Sorry," Abby said, rubbing her eyes. "I know. I'm just upset." She took a deep breath and changed the subject. "Is Papi still working?"

Mom nodded. "He's been in there all day. But . . . I'm sure he'll be done soon." She grabbed a flat bag of popcorn from the cupboard and popped it in the microwave. "Go clean up and we'll watch a movie. And give me your camera; I'll put it in a bowl of rice."

"That's for phones, Mom. Besides, the lens is cracked." Abby handed the crushed camera to her anyway and turned to go to her room.

As she changed out of her damp clothes, panic crept up her spine and back down into her stomach. If the memory card was ruined, she'd have to start her final project over for Ms. T! She ran downstairs and grabbed the card from inside the camera's water-soaked guts.

She patted the card dry, then rushed to her computer, slipped it in, and waited.

Clicking frantically, she found nothing. The memory card was destroyed.

Her phone buzzed in her pocket—it was the reminder to call Fiana.

That was it! She had downloaded and emailed Fiana a few of her pictures! She could use those and at least partially salvage her project.

She went to her Sent folder and found them. Saved by an email! Her slideshow template was still in a Google document, and a handful more pictures were safely pasted into that first draft. Not all was lost.

Still, she had a lot of catching up to do if she was going to finish in time.

Her stomach grumbled loudly as her mom entered the room without knocking.

"Movie?"

"One second! Trying to save my photography project!"

"Oh! Good! But . . . you still need to eat."

" 'K. I'll be down in a minute."

Abby pasted the pictures from the email into the Google doc, closed her laptop, and went down to eat for the first time since breakfast. Maybe some food and the distraction of a movie would help turn her mood around.

AT THREE O'CLOCK Papi finally joined them in the family room. He sat next to Abby and nudged her.

"Maybe we can get that hike in this afternoon, huh? Still plenty of light left."

"My camera's ruined." Abby didn't look at him.

Her mother paused the movie and summarized the morning's fiasco. When she was done, Papi stood and shook his head. Was he upset she'd ruined his old camera?

He looked at Mom, his hand on his chin, and his eyes wide, like he'd just had an idea.

"Abby, I'm sorry about canceling our hike, and I'm sorry about what happened at the park. Come here." He opened his arms, inviting her in for a hug.

After a good, long abrazo, he pulled away. "I think I have an idea."

He gave them his "This plan could get me in trouble" look. The look he got when what he was about to say was a big deal. The look he gave them the day he announced they were all going rock climbing. The same look he gave them right before he told them he'd booked a windsurfing lesson. The "I have a wild idea" look.

"So . . . you know that call this morning?" He paused and waited for a reaction.

His work call?

"What about it?" Mom said.

"It turns out I'm heading to Honduras for two weeks. They want me to get going with this project before hurricane season goes into full swing. And they want me to leave next Sunday."

"Wow," said Mom. "That was fast."

"And I was thinking," he continued. "Abby's never been, and maybe it's time she come with me . . . you know, see where I'm from, get some vitamin *sea*?"

Abby's mom crossed her arms and breathed out a weird noise. Like a harrumph that got stuck. "You *know* my big case is this month, and there's no way I can get away!" she said.

"I know, I know. But Abby's almost thirteen, and Pataya's a small enough village that she'd learn her way around in no time. She could even join me on the dive boat!"

Abby's eyes widened, and her heart raced ten thousand miles an hour. She could hardly believe her ears. Would she finally get to go to Papi's homeland? To the little village by the sea where he had spent the first six years of his life?

"Mom, por favor, that would be amazing!" she burst out. "Please let me go. Think of how many times we've been to Michigan! I've seen your childhood home a million times!" She was begging now, giving her mom the cutest set of puppy dog eyes she could muster.

"You have grandparents and cousins in Michigan," Mom said. "It's different."

She turned back to Papi. "I don't know, Carlos. We'd only have a week to prepare and get everything ready. It feels too fast."

Papi shook his head. "Come on, you know it's time."

"Just think about it—*please, Mom*? It would be amazing!" Abby had been to Massachusetts, Florida, and Michigan.

Punto. Period. That was it. For as long as she could remember, ever since she could say *tortillas y frijoles,* she'd wanted to travel to Honduras, but Mom always had some excuse. Some wedding to go to in Michigan, some family vacation at a lake, some cousin's first communion. Or, more often, work.

Papi told her stories about Honduras, how he built sand forts on the beach and went fishing with Abuelo. Abby had never met her abuelo, and the one picture they had was scratchy and faded. Papi also told her about Abuela, how she was the reason he'd become a doctor. Papi always said he wished Abby had met her too. Whenever she asked for details, though, Papi would shut down and change the subject. Maybe it made him too sad to remember. He basically repeated the same couple of stories like a broken record, and Abby was used to it by now.

Abuela had died right before Papi graduated from medical school, so now the only family he had was Abby and her mom. He graduated with honors, an orphan doctor with a fellowship to Columbia University, where he'd met Mom. Abby imagined finally getting to visit the place she knew only from pictures and Papi's cuentos.

"Fine. Your father and I will talk about it more tonight."

Abby took her mom's reply as a hopeful sign. A maybe was better than a firm no. She hugged her tight and crossed her fingers that the maybe would evolve into a yes.

CHAPTER 5

Barana

The rooster crowed, alerting Barana that it was time to get up and get ready for school. It was still dark outside, but el gallo knew it was only a matter of minutes before the sun rose. She could hear Tulu preparing breakfast in the main room. It smelled like coconut oil and fresh pineapple. Barana wished she could stay huddled in bed, cozy under her sheet, thinking of poems and turtles. She was exhausted from a weekend of watching baby Marisol while Mom worked. The village had started preparing for the coming storm, and some people had already evacuated to stay with relatives farther inland.

Barana sat up and reached for her journal. The old notebook was filled almost to the brim with thoughts, drawings, and poetry. The words came to her in a flash:

Wind blows lightly through the palms.
A storm rages beyond the sea.

Hatchlings wait beneath the sand.
Their mother's love protects them,
A hopeful, hidden treasure.

Barana stepped quietly out of the bedroom, waving good morning at her brother before going outside to wash up. A bucket of fresh water waited for her on the pila's ridged surface. One floodlight illuminated the area. She washed her face with cool water from the bucket and let the soapy suds trickle onto the sand below. She grabbed her toothbrush from a jar and brushed her teeth while she hummed.

Back upstairs, she put on her navy blue skirt and a snow-white shirt, which Bela had freshly washed and ironed over the weekend. The little emblem on the sleeve showed the mountains and waters of Honduras with the initials *EBC,* which stood for Escuela Berta Cáceres.

Her school had been renamed after the Honduran environmentalist who fought for the protection of indigenous lands and water. Barana's village was on protected land, after all. The northern coast of La Mosquitia. Home.

She pulled on her socks and her only pair of closed-toe shoes. A neat, tight bun would do for her messy hair. Why were they even going to school? What if the storm came early?

Tulu had fetched two eggs from the chicken coop they shared with Bela; he fried them on the small gas stove as Barana devoured a piece of sweet bread, which was still fresh. Mamá had fried a couple of plantains the night before and left the slices on a plate. The napkin that lay on top of the plátanos had gathered little circles of grease. She took a bite before getting up to soak her dish in the tub of sudsy water.

"I wish we could stay home." Barana washed her plate and let the suds drip before placing it into the bucket of clean water. "We probably won't go the rest of the week, so what's the point?"

Tulu shrugged. "All we can do is wait. Makes no difference if we wait here or at school. Either way, the storm is coming." Tulu used a clean rag to dry their plates before setting them down. "¡Miércoles! I forgot to drain the tub last night."

"No wonder it looked murky." Barana examined the bucket of water. "You should do it before Mamá wakes up."

Tulu had built the makeshift kitchen sink with Papá a few years ago. A large piece of mahogany held two square plastic tubs in place: one with fresh water and the other with soapy water. Their only source of running water was the faucet of the pila outside. Tulu used the faucet to fill the kitchen buckets every night or two with fresh water. Another of his chores was to drain the sudsy dishwater into the outhouse toilet each night. (It almost made up for the fact he never had to babysit their sister.)

They walked into their parents' room to say goodbye.

Baby Marisol was nestled in their mother's arms, but Papá had left for work almost an hour ago. His fishing crew didn't wait for stragglers, and Papá was never one to be late. Barana saw him in the evenings, when he was too tired to do much more than watch soccer with Tulu or visit his own parents next door.

Barana blew a kiss to her mamá and sister and whispered goodbye.

Outside, it already felt like a hundred degrees, even though the sun was barely peeking over the horizon.

"I wish they'd let us wear chancletas to school," Barana complained, glaring down at her black lace-up shoes.

"Or sneakers," Tulu said. "I can't wait to graduate so I never have to wear these things again."

As they walked down the path away from their home and the sea and toward the dock on the lagoon side of Pataya, the village began to awaken. Pataya was perfectly situated between the ocean and a big crystalline lagoon, out of which fresh water poured into the sea. Pataya was connected by an intricate estuary system to other seaside villages, including the village their school was in.

The sun rose like a giant ball of lava over the palm trees, its light glinting off the mirror-like lagoon. A group of about twenty schoolchildren in identical uniforms walked along the main path, and pretty soon Barana separated herself from her brother, joining a couple of her classmates.

Some of the students on the path were younger than Barana, a few were in sixth grade with her, and a handful were in high school with Tulu. They waited together under the palapa, a palm-thatched structure that sat at the end of the long, crooked dock. The palapa was sturdy and well built, though every few years it needed new palm leaves on its roof. Barana looked out onto the lagoon for evidence of Nati, the pilot of their school boat.

Nati and his lancha approached slowly, trailing a gentle wake. Tulu and Jason helped him tie the motorboat to a post while the children lined up neatly under the palapa. Nati had taught them exactly how to board his "ship." The boat nearly tipped over every time someone hopped on. It was old, like Nati, and it barely had enough room for all of them, but it got them to and from school safely.

The students greeted their captain politely, just as they had been taught, and everyone sat in their regular seats. Barana liked to sit on the left side, second row.

"Buenos días, niños." Nati held the boat steady until they were all aboard.

He kept a sack of mini-bananas under his seat, and he made sure anybody who hadn't had breakfast filled their bellies before school. His callused hands guided the rusty lancha as if it were an extension of his body. Barana figured he knew the network of canals and rivers by heart.

The boat's engine sounded like it coughed up a lung before it churned down the lagoon toward the river that led them to school. The wind felt nice on her face. Barana pulled her notebook and pencil out of her satchel and doodled turtles on the way. Her brother, who was sitting behind her, interjected, "The right flipper isn't long enough." Barana gave him a look but corrected the minor error anyway. She shaded the flipper and added irregular white spots to make it look like a real leatherback. As she inspected the drawing, she chewed her pencil nervously before finally closing the notebook and shoving the pencil inside her bun.

After the twenty-minute ride, they arrived at the neighboring village, Paraíso, and once again Tulu helped Nati tie the boat up. Barana's school was a short walk up the dirt path. She waved goodbye to Tulu as he continued with his friends toward the only high school within a fifty-kilometer radius. Tulu's twenty-five-minute commute was nothing compared to what some students had to travel.

Everything looked different as Barana crested the hill. Windows had been boarded up. The land seemed barren, like anything that was once outside had been put away for safekeeping. The blue sky above would change into a deep gray before nightfall. She licked her thumb and stuck it up in the air, checking for wind.

It was eerily still.

Barana walked through the school's gate and entered her cinder-block classroom after shaking Profesora Francisca's hand. Her teacher had grown up in Pataya and was one of the few teachers who stuck around year after year.

"Buenos días, Barana. Did you have a nice weekend?"

Barana nodded and took her seat. She pulled out her social studies workbook to review the mountain ranges of Honduras, which they'd be quizzed on that morning. *Sierra de Agalta, Sierra Nombre de Dios, Sierra Punta Piedra, Sierra de Sulaco* . . . There were too many to memorize. The Honduran landscape resembled paper that had been thoroughly crinkled and then reopened, with ridges and cordilleras everywhere.

After getting half the mountain ranges wrong during the morning lesson, Barana was relieved when their teacher announced that they'd begin preparing their classroom for the coming storm. Each student was assigned to a group, and they began moving books to the highest shelves, stacking desks and chairs on top of tables, and even boarding up the classroom windows with plywood. Profesora Francisca instructed Barana's group to fill two boxes with all of the art supplies.

A year ago, Barana's class had few art supplies, but a group of Canadian volunteers had brought dozens of markers, crayons, pencils, and paint. As she put them away, Barana wondered what they would've done in art without them, or if they would've done art at all.

Back outside, the western sky was blue, while dark cumulus clouds hovered ominously in the east. Barana and her classmates were enjoying a short recess break when the first droplets began to fall.

"It's sprinkling," Barana told her friend Cynthia as she nibbled on plantain chips.

The rain fell gently at first, but the wind was quickly gaining speed. The storm had arrived earlier than expected. The teachers came out to the courtyard and instructed the children to come inside. School usually ended at one o'clock. Today, they'd be heading home immediately.

"No tenemos escuela mañana o pasado. Be safe and stay home," Profesora Francisca said.

Just as Tulu had predicted: no school for the next two days. Barana shook her teacher's hand goodbye and said a quick prayer that all would be back to normal by the end of the week. She turned back before walking down the hill. Her school looked like an abandoned building, with all the pieces of wood nailed over the windows. The planters had been put away, and not a single chair was left outside.

As the raindrops got heavier and more frequent, Barana's scar began to ache. She wasn't sure she'd have time to check on Luna's nest before the storm got serious. For all she knew, the eggs could be drenched and flooded in no time. The journal in her bag was probably getting soaked too—her drawings and poems likely dripping down the pages. When Tulu showed up at the dock, he was wet from head to toe.

"It came early!" He beamed.

"You sound excited." Barana rolled her eyes.

"I like being right. I felt the storm in my bones this morning."

"I just hope it goes by quickly." She stared out to the

horizon, chewing her pencil as she waited impatiently for the boat. There was no way Mamá would let her go to the beach when they got home.

Nati's lancha finally arrived. Barana tucked her pencil in her hair and hopped on. She and Tulu huddled next to each other on the second bench. By the time they arrived in Pataya, they were drenched.

The dirt path that led them home was now a muddy gush of clay and mud. Their parents were inside when they finally made it up the steps of their stilt house.

"¡Bendito sea!" Mamá said, hugging them both. "Quítense esa ropa mojada." She instructed them to take off their sopping wet clothes and dry off. Barana was eager to comply. Papá stood by the kitchen window, barely noticing their presence. His hands were locked in prayer, and his posture was stiff. Worry spread all over his face and body.

Barana got herself into dry clothes and hung her wet uniform on the single chair in their bedroom. She joined her papá by the window and reached for his hand. It was dry and cracked from too many years of salt water and sun.

The palm trees whipped violently, and the angry ocean waves crashed against the earth. The wind howled so loud it made Barana think of La Llorona. As if the storm wasn't enough, her scar burned, reminding her of Luna and her nest. If only she'd been able to check on it one more time before the storm arrived.

Papá must've noticed the tension in her grip because he whispered, "It will be over soon, mija."

"But it sounds so strong."

"It sounds strong, but we're stronger."

Barana wanted to believe him, but the violent storm was washing away every ounce of optimism she had left. Was Luna okay? Had she gone as deep as she could to avoid the strong currents and churning surf? And what about her nest?

Barana returned to her room and grabbed her trusty notebook. The first few pages were still damp from the boat ride home, but for the most part, it was dry. Her bag had kept it protected. She finished her poem:

> *Will it be enough? Her love, and mine?*
> *Please let it be so.*
> *Asleep beneath sand's warmth,*
> *Unaware of the deluge.*
> *Hatchlings, hear my prayer.*
> *Be still and calm within your nest.*
> *You are stronger than the storm.*

RAIN POUNDED THE rooftops, and the wind picked up steam as night fell. Around eight o'clock, they lost power, and Barana's father insisted they all run to his mother's house next door to wait the storm out together as a larger group. Bela not only had a generator, she also had a way of keeping Papá calm, and her house had survived several hurricanes. She'd prepared extra food and collected plenty of water. Her couch and spare mattresses would do for them to sleep on.

When they got there, soaked to the bone, the house still had power, and the adults gathered around the small TV to watch the news.

Once she dried off, Barana put on one of Bela's old T-shirts. She lost herself in doodles and thoughts of her leatherback turtles. She was busy finishing a drawing of hatchlings heading out to sea when her mother interrupted.

"Barana, you haven't eaten. Stop drawing and join us in the kitchen."

Irritated, Barana snapped her notebook shut and placed it on the small table by the couch. She detested it when her mom interrupted her artistic flow.

The soup was tasty, but Barana kept that fact to herself.

Bela placed her hand on Barana's shoulder and squeezed. "¿Todo bien, mija?" she asked.

Barana shrugged. "I don't know if the sea turtle eggs will survive this storm, Bela."

The light pain in her scar was still there, and it was getting stronger. Bela's grip on her shoulder eased, and she pulled the hair band from the tight bun that Barana had combed that morning.

"Nature has its cycles, Barana. Your turtles will be okay.

Here, let me braid you when you're done with your soup." She brushed her fingers through Barana's long brown hair. Barana nodded and quietly finished the last few bites of sopa de frijoles.

Her abuela grabbed a comb and pulled her hair back into a neat braid. Something about this ritual comforted her. Ever since Barana was a little girl, Bela would make the time to do her hair, and she gave her the best scalp massages too. It was as if she knew her granddaughter loved it, even though Barana never said so out loud. Bela just felt those things.

As if sensing the pain in her scar, her abuela tied the braid and moved her hand down toward Barana's shoulder blades, pausing over her scar for a moment.

Just like that, the pain went away.

Bela hadn't been there the day of Barana's accident, but of course she'd heard all the details afterward. Barana didn't think her abuela remembered that the large crescent moon scar was there, but the placement of her hand was too precise to be a coincidence.

Before she could ask Bela about it, the lights flickered, and an ominous boom bounced off the walls. The power had gone out.

Pitufo whimpered. Her grandmother's pet monkey usually slept outside in a little house that Abuelo Juan had built for him underneath theirs, but not on a night like this one. Tonight he would only be safe indoors.

"Tranquilos, let's grab my flashlight. Juan will get the

generator going." Bela tried to calm everyone down before panic erupted.

The family gathered in the middle of the room while Papá and Abuelo Juan resecured the windows and turned on a battery-powered lantern. A small puddle was forming by the front door, which shook angrily. This house was higher up on stilts than Barana's, but the rain and wind were so heavy that some of the water snuck in through the cracks and crevices in the wood.

"I'm not going outside. We have to wait until the storm calms down before I can get the generator going." Abuelo Juan had never looked so pale.

The wind howled, and the roof sounded like it would collapse any second. Its metal sheets shook and rattled. It was the most ear-splitting rain she'd ever heard. Somehow, baby Marisol was fast asleep in her mother's sling. If only Barana could curl up into her mother's arms too. She could pretend to be a baby hatchling, dreaming safely within her cozy nest.

Tulu lay on a cot, and the adults sat patiently around the living room. Barana tried to rest on the couch next to Bela as she led them through the rosary prayers. The roof continued shaking, harder than ever. Surely it would get blown away any minute, lost to the storm as the rain and wind and debris swept through the room.

And what of the turtle eggs? Would they be lost to the storm too?

CHAPTER 6

Abby

Three more days, Abby thought, walking into the kitchen. *Three more days of school, and by then, fingers crossed, Mom will have said yes to Honduras.* Ever since Papi suggested that Abby join him, she could think of nothing else. She could almost feel the salty air on her face.

Her mom was sitting in the kitchen, reading something on her phone. Abby wanted to ask about the trip, but instead she made toast, hoping Mom would mention it first.

"Morning, Mom. Are you taking me to school?"

Her mom looked up for less than a second. "Hey, Abs. Didn't see you there. Yeah, looks like I am. Papi went for a bike ride."

A long silence followed, and Abby could tell her mom was more distracted than usual by her device. Abby wanted to probe. Maybe she was looking at flights to Honduras. . . .

"Anything interesting going on in the world?" Abby asked.

Her mom shook her head in silence and sipped her tea. She lowered her reading glasses and looked up. "It's not good news, Abby. Nicaragua and Honduras were hit by a storm last night." Her eyes went back to her phone, moving rapidly from left to right as she held the clunky device in her hand. "It went right over the coast."

"But it's just rain, right? Plus, the trip's not for another week. The storm will have passed by then."

"Looks like it was more than just rain. I'm not sure it's a good time for either of you to go down there."

"Mom, that's ridiculous. Because of a storm? A storm that's over already?" Abby threw her toast on her plate and crossed her arms tightly.

"Easy there. Don't take it out on your breakfast," her mom said.

"Is Papi still going?"

"No sé. It was a Category 1 hurricane before making landfall. Fortunately, it weakened to a tropical storm before it crossed over Pataya and the rest of the coast. Still, Abby. It looks like there was some damage."

"Let me see." Abby grabbed the phone and fact-checked her mom.

The footage of the devastation made her worry that perhaps her mother was right; the conditions would be too rough. There was flooding and debris everywhere. And yet she desperately wanted to travel to Honduras with her father. As she feverishly scrolled through news outlets and pictures, Papi walked through the back door, muddy and red-faced from his bike ride.

"Sure is somber in here," he said. "Why all the long faces?"

"We're reading about the tropical storm in Central America, and I told Aberdeen I don't think it's a good idea for her to go."

"Jessica, a storm doesn't change the fact it's still a great opportunity for her to see where I grew up." He grabbed a paper towel and wiped the sweat off his brow.

"Wait—were you guys going to say yes?" Abby followed her father across the kitchen, demanding an answer with her eyes.

"The plan was to check ticket prices and book your flight today. We thought we'd surprise you over dinner."

"How does this storm change things? A little water, a little damage. I can deal with it."

"Abby, the community will be overwhelmed with rebuilding and cleanup. The timing isn't right," Mom said.

"Do you know how Pataya fared?" Abby asked Papi. "Almost all of these pictures are from other places, mostly Nicaragua, miles away from where you're going."

"There was some flooding, a few roofs were damaged, but it wasn't as bad as Mitch in '98," Papi said. "The locals and relief organizers will be cleaning up all week, but the international airport is already up and running! I talked to my colleagues down there, and they said that the training is still a go. We're bringing new equipment and helping them set up sustainable traps—casitas—to minimize the risks these men take." He gave Abby an empathetic glance.

"Mom, please. This is important to me. If Papi's going, I can go too."

"Abby, you're twelve. You don't understand. Your father will be busy. I'm not sure he has a plan for what *you'd* be doing down there for two whole weeks."

"Taking pictures! Swimming! Reading! Come on, Mom, I'll be thirteen this summer. And *you're* the one who doesn't understand. I've wanted to visit Honduras for as long as I can remember. To see where Papi grew up, to practice my Spanish. You always said that being bilingual was a gift I would one day appreciate. Well, let me finally appreciate it!" She threw her hands up and walked out of the room, wishing there was a magic wand she could wave to convince her overprotective mom. She wished she could skip school the rest of the week too. What was the point of going for the last few days—so Monique could make fun of her? She could just as easily email her final project to Ms. T and be done.

In the family room her parents argued in whispers. Papi would try to convince her mom again, but Mom ran the show, and what she said was the law in the Durón household.

"I want Papi to take me to school today!" Abby yelled.

"Fine by me!" her mom yelled back.

Abby texted Fiana:

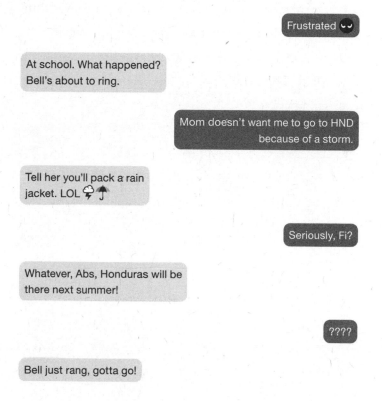

> Frustrated 😔

> At school. What happened? Bell's about to ring.

> Mom doesn't want me to go to HND because of a storm.

> Tell her you'll pack a rain jacket. LOL ⛈️☂️

> Seriously, Fi?

> Whatever, Abs, Honduras will be there next summer!

> ????

> Bell just rang, gotta go!

Abby couldn't believe it. Fiana had always understood how important a trip to Honduras was to her! How important it was to her dad! *Or had she?* Fiana had heard the whole story: Although Papi had immigrated to America over thirty years ago, he returned to Honduras every couple of years to work and contribute in whatever small way he could. His parents' deaths had nearly closed the door to him ever returning. And yet something kept him going back, like a migrating monarch or a sea turtle. One night Papi told Abby and Fiana that leaving Honduras had been hard for him. It was home, and he'd traded it for a new life in America.

Now it was time to join him there. Her heart told her so.

But if Papi couldn't convince her mom, Abby wasn't sure anyone could.

CHAPTER 7

Barana

It was noon when Barana woke, and the storm had finally passed. She must've fallen asleep at the crack of dawn. Her chest tightened in anger—nobody had thought to wake her up. She needed to get to the beach and check on Luna's nest.

The destruction around Pataya was evident the moment she walked outside. It was as if a bunch of bandidos had gone out with machetes, slicing branches and palm leaves off trees. She could barely make out the main path that crossed through town, and already her entire family was outside picking up trash and other fallen debris.

Barana stood on the porch in a state of shock. She watched as her father, Tulu, and her abuelos piled stuff in a clearing. Everyone was there except Mamá. Even Tulu's best friend had come over to help. The damage to Bela's small inn was minimal, and Barana's house looked equally intact, but there were branches and wreckage to dispose of. Where had it all come from?

"¿Dónde está Mamá?" Barana asked her father as she came down the stairs.

"En la pulpería con Marisol. You should walk over there and help her."

Barana turned toward the beach. It would only take her a few minutes to see if the nest had survived. She just needed to sneak over there before going to help Mamá.

Inhala, exhala. Breathe and focus.

"Barana, ¿Me escuchaste?"

"Yes, I heard you. I was thinking."

"No time for thinking. There's too much to do. We're lucky our house is okay, but Mamá's pulpería isn't. Rápido, hija. Hurry over there."

The roof of Mamá's little store was not as sturdy as the one on their stilt house. Opening Pulpería Gloria had taken years of saving and hard work on both her parents' parts. Barana feared it could all be gone now. But she had to go to the beach first. She needed to know if Luna's nest had made it.

"¿Puedo ir a la playa primero? There's something I need to check on. ¿Dos minutos?"

"You're *never* out there for two minutes. Go with Tulu and see how you can help Mamá. It'll take everyone working together to get our lives back to normal. You need to do your part."

Barana glanced in the direction of the nest. Her scar

burned a little. She'd have to wait to find out if the storm surge had damaged the eggs until after doing her daughterly duties. Papá called Tulu over and instructed them to do whatever was needed at the store.

They squished through the mud and hopped over the puddles on their way to the pulpería. Once on the main path, they couldn't avoid the chocolate-milk lagoons that blocked their way. Barana walked on the outer edge of a humongous puddle. The clay was too wet and sticky, and she got soaked to the ankles. At least the sun was high in the sky and shining brightly, giving her hope that some of the damage would be fixed by the weekend.

They passed the sea turtle office, and she ran to have a closer look. It looked abandoned, like a relic from the past.

Her brother kept walking. "Hurry up."

She examined the one-room building. A windowpane had fallen out, and a foot of water surrounded the cement structure like a moat. The ground had become so saturated that the water had had nowhere to go and pooled up inside the office.

"That's why Papá built ours on stilts," Tulu said, as if reading her mind. "Vamos, hermana, we have to hurry."

Barana caught up with him. They jumped over fallen branches, passing homes that had lost their roofs. They could see the lagoon in the distance, and more boats than usual clustered around the small docks. People had come from far and wide to help.

Mamá was sitting on a small bench outside the wooden building, talking to her best friend, Chiqui. The two women were shaking their heads as they spoke. Mamá looked somber and disheartened.

Barana could see why. A corner of the pulpería's roof was missing. The sheet metal had been blown away. At least the walls were intact. Papá's handiwork had held strong. The floor was muddy and wet, covered by several inches of water.

"I need to empty it out and see what's worth keeping," Mamá said.

"Barana and Tulu will help you," Chiqui replied. "I'll take Marisol to my house and make sure she gets a nap."

Chiqui was like family, but she'd never had children of her own. Her paintings were her children. The only artwork in Barana's house was Chiqui's. Her favorite was a landscape of La Mosquitia with the ocean in the background. Barana thought her art was great; her brushstrokes were bold and thick, and she had a way of making even the most boring objects, like a fruit bowl, look special. Alive. Chiqui went to the market in Lempira the first weekend of every month to sell her paintings, but Barana wasn't sure she made much money, because so many of them adorned the walls of Bela's house and her own.

Barana and Tulu pulled the waterlogged merchandise out of their mother's store, creating a "keep" pile and a "discard" pile. A few members from their church arrived with cleaning supplies. Papá also joined them and cleared the debris from around the building with the help of their primos, and before they knew it, the sun was low on the western horizon.

Her scar had burned faintly but persistently all afternoon. And each time it twinged, she thought of Luna and her nest.

As the family sat outside the pulpería and passed around water and bread, Barana planned her escape. Everyone was exhausted. The light would be gone soon, and she needed to check on Luna's nest.

It was now or never.

"Mamá, tengo que ir al baño," she said.

"Okay, mija, you can go home. Bela is there. Help her with dinner."

After five straight hours of working, Barana *did* have to go, so technically it wasn't a lie. She was just omitting the route she planned to take.

Once she'd gotten far enough away from the group, she detoured toward the beach, weaving through trees and bushes, hopping over piles of wreckage and praying she'd find her nest intact. She made her way toward the two arching palms, but the sun's light was quickly fading.

When she finally arrived, the palms stood strong despite a few missing fronds. But the nest markers were gone, and the beach was almost unrecognizable after the storm surge. There was driftwood where there'd been only sand, algae had been deposited a few yards from the high-tide line, and even palm leaves and trash were scattered by the wind and water. The debris filled Barana's once-pristine playa as far as the eye could see.

She retraced her steps, determined to find Luna's nest. Finally, under a large banana leaf, she spied the toppled stakes. She cleared the spot and dug around. She moved the sand carefully until she felt the first few eggs underneath. They were still there!

Her scar stopped throbbing, and she smiled for the first time all day.

Barana covered the hole with sand and cleared a large radius around it. She used the old stakes to mark the nest again, vowing to protect the eggs until the hatchlings emerged, about seven weeks from now. She searched for the sign and finally found it several feet away amid a large tangle of sea grape leaves, branches, and weeds. She staked it back in place to let everyone know that treasure was buried deep.

As she started to walk home, a shadow behind a palm spooked her. She couldn't make it out, but whoever—or whatever—it was, it was tall. She moved away from the figure to see it from a better angle. As she approached the row of palms where the figure stood, it jumped out and ran toward her.

Barana screamed.

Her brother laughed and clapped, proud of his childish joke.

"*Tulu?* Stop it! I'm not in the mood for your ghost scares!"

"Mamá went to Chiqui's to pick up Marisol's bag and told me to come home to meet you and help with dinner. I showed up, and Bela had no idea where you were. I figured you'd be out here frolicking with your turtles."

"I was checking on a nest," Barana replied, her heart still racing.

"And? Did it survive the storm?"

"Sí, they're okay."

Tulu shook his head. "You can't think of anything else, can you?"

"It's like you with soccer."

Her brother rolled his eyes.

They left the beach quietly, both collecting rubbish along the way—Pepsi bottles, runaway plastic bags, an old shoe. By the time they made it to Bela's, the large trash bag Tulu carried was half full.

"See, I checked on my nest and you collected a bunch of trash. Win-win." Barana smiled at him.

Tulu glanced over his shoulder and smiled back.

"Remember: family comes first, even before the baulas. Mamá told Chiqui they might not be able to reopen the shop for at least a couple of weeks, so things are gonna be tough. Papá doesn't know when they'll get the materials to fix her roof," Tulu said.

"Don't tell them you found me at the beach, okay?"

"What am I supposed to tell them?"

"Just say I was by the turtle office talking to María or something. Besides, nobody will even ask."

Barana's parents didn't support her turtle obsession. In fact, they barely tolerated it. Whenever Mamá caught her doodling a sea turtle, she'd roll her eyes or ask Barana to help in the kitchen. There was always something else to do. Papá was too busy fishing or hanging out with the guys to care about anything Barana was interested in.

"Fine. I won't say you were at the beach *this* time," Tulu said. "But stop sneaking around."

Tulu didn't understand, either. Nobody did.

The leatherbacks were like family too, in their own way, but no one seemed to get it.

Keeping it secret was her only choice.

That nest was her responsibility now. And she'd stop at nothing to make sure the little hatchlings were safe.

At Bela's, Tulu kept his promise, lying about where he'd found her. They helped set the table. Bela was quiet, and Barana wondered if she suspected they'd taken a detour before coming over. Dinner was simple. Rice and beans and fried plantains. Bela had cooked them in the clay stove outside, since the electricity had yet to be fully restored. Their generator was strong enough to power a small refrigerator and a few lights, but not enough to illuminate her indoor kitchen fully.

Her grandmother's beans were second to none. They were simmered in coconut oil and seasoned with the perfect amount of salt. A combo of sweet and savory that melted in your mouth. Barana noticed that Mamá wasn't eating much, and she wished the storm had never happened.

"Will the doctor and his crew still come this Sunday?" Papá asked Bela, breaking the uncomfortable silence.

Bela looked up slowly, her eyelids heavy. "I don't see why he wouldn't, unless the landing strip is still a mud pit," she said. "I hope he's still planning to come. We could use the money from renting our casita."

They were lucky her grandparents' guesthouse hadn't been damaged by the storm. Abuelo Juan had built it years ago, and he took pride in how nicely it had turned out. He was a talented carpenter. His hands were wrinkled, with dozens of light brown age spots, but they were still strong. They could still build anything.

"Gracias a Dios, it wasn't damaged," Abuelo Juan replied, his hazel eyes twinkling. Her abuelo was not a man of many words; he was a man of work and faith. Whenever something bad happened, he said they needed to trust God's plan. Barana wondered if God had a plan for her sea turtles.

Also, she didn't understand the commotion over this doctor visitor. As far as she was concerned, the work he did with all the lobster divers was irrelevant. Nobody in her family was a diver or lobster fisherman, and getting the bends wasn't something she had any experience with—except for María's husband, who had been grumpier since his accident. Maybe the doctor could help him.

"Barana," Bela said, interrupting her inner rant. "He said

he might be bringing his daughter along! You'll be in charge of taking good care of her, if she comes. Show her around, make her feel at home."

"What? Who?"

"You heard me. Dr. Durón might bring his daughter."

"I don't have time for more babysitting, Bela." Barana's chest felt like erupting. She breathed and tried to calm down. One babysitting job on top of another babysitting job was not going to happen. Marisol was enough.

"He'll be busy with the fishermen, and we'll be busy working. If his daughter joins him, you'll be her host. You will be welcoming. End of discussion." Bela lifted her chin and squinted at Barana, daring her to challenge the request.

"But I want to help María with the turtle project. It's almost the end of the nesting season. Just one more month and the leatherbacks will stop coming ashore!"

Bela nodded slowly. Perhaps she'd make Tulu do it.

"Maybe *she* can help you," Bela said. "I bet this American girl would enjoy taking care of the turtle nests and patrolling the beach with you."

Ugh! The last thing Barana needed was a tagalong.

Barana prayed that the local airstrip would remain an unusable soup of mud, that this girl would not come after all, and that the doctor would cancel his trip altogether. She wanted to focus on protecting any remaining nests, logging new mama turtles, and helping María at the office as much as possible. The project needed a plan for the rest of the season. María was due to have her baby any day now. Who would replace her when she was out? Having an unexpected visitor would complicate all of Barana's plans. She couldn't allow a complete and total stranger to ruin the last month of nesting season. No matter what Bela said, the American girl was on her own.

CHAPTER 8

Abby

That Aberdeen had pulled together her final photography project was a miracle. She'd dug up just enough photos and completed the portfolio slideshow close to midnight the night before it was due. Though her latest pictures had been lost in the creek catastrophe, she felt okay about what she was turning in. It was better than nothing.

The theme for the final assignment was "Home." Ms. Tenley had given them a lot of freedom, and Abby had, of course, chosen nature as her subject. Local trees, flowers, birds, and a handful of squirrels, fawns, and fungi. She even snapped pictures of her koi in the pond at the last minute when she realized she was short a few photos. Her phone's camera was terrible, but she added a filter and made the best of it.

She hoped Ms. Tenley would like the way she took close-up shots of the bark and played with the lines and light. The only problem was, she had struggled to explain how the collection tied into the theme. She figured that since she'd taken shots of the critters' home environments—maple and oak trees, mostly—she could claim that these trees represented "home." How an old photo of a fox and another of random birds fit into the theme, she'd leave to Ms. Tenley to interpret.

It was the last full day of school, and the rest of the week was going to be a hodgepodge of half days, field days, and end-of-year locker cleanup. What was the point of even going? When the last bell rang, Abby walked over to the visual arts room. On the way there, Ana and Paula from Spanish class were hanging out by the photography bulletin board, and they waved her over. *Why?*

"Abby!" Paula said. "Did you take this one?" She pointed at a black-and-white print of a woodpecker. Underneath it was a little index card that said, ABERDEEN DURÓN, *WOODY.*

"Yeah," Abby said shyly.

"It's cool!" Ana said. "We're thinking about taking this elective next year."

"It's my favorite class," Abby said. She thought she should probably say something else, but it was like she'd forgotten how to act when people were being nice to her. How had Fi managed to make all those new friends in London?

"Anyway!" Ana said. "You'll have to show us the pictures from the party sometime."

Paula nodded and grabbed Ana's hand. "Maybe we'll see you around this summer!"

They waved goodbye and ran off. Abby turned nervously

toward the door to Ms. T's, wishing she'd told Ana and Paula the party pictures had been ruined and wondering if they really wanted to see her around this summer. . . .

Inside the classroom, Abby found her teacher organizing materials into neatly labeled plastic bins. The room was like an art museum and artist's studio combined. She knocked lightly on the door.

"Ms. Tenley?"

"Hey there, Abby, come on in."

"I wanted to thank you for being so understanding about the party pictures getting messed up."

"Don't worry about it. I've been there many times," Ms. T said. "The newspaper still came out nicely, don't you think? A few kids shared pictures from their phones, so we made do."

"It turned out great." Abby cut to the chase: "Hey, Ms. T, how'd I do on my final project?"

"Honestly, Abby, I haven't had a chance to look through them carefully. The end of the year has been nonstop. Want to have a look together?"

Abby nodded politely.

Ms. Tenley walked to her desk and opened her laptop. Her desk always intrigued Abby. It was covered with beautiful photographs, museum postcards, and trinkets from around the world. Her desk was like a colorful collage of a cultured life.

One picture caught her eye. It was a full moon over the ocean.

"Where is this from?" Abby asked, pointing at the photo.

"Oh, that? Just a photo I took on the beach right here in New Jersey. Believe it or not, I didn't even use a telephoto lens. My Nikon P900 did the trick because of its high magnification capacity. I just zoomed in!"

Ms. T is pretty cool, Abby thought. "It's awesome."

Ms. Tenley smiled her genuine smile and kept clicking through files on her computer.

"Ah, here's your project," she said. "Yes. I remember glancing at it this morning. Lots of trees and critters."

"Did I do okay?"

"Abby," her teacher said, looking up at her. "I can tell you love wildlife photography, and you captured some lovely images here. Your use of light and symmetry is intuitively good." She scrolled through the photos. "I love this close-up of the bark! Also, this one of the tree from the bottom up was clever. It reminds me of one of my favorite Georgia O'Keeffe paintings. I get how you wove in the trees for your concept of home. . . ." She paused awkwardly at the end of her sentence, as if there was more she wanted to say.

"But?" Abby said expectantly.

"There's no but. Every photographer has their preferred subjects. I guess my feedback would be that you start experimenting a little more. You've chosen nature for every project this year."

Abby pretty much only photographed animals and landscapes, and Ms. T was onto her.

"If you choose to stick with my Photography and Digital

Media elective next year, I'd encourage you to dig a little deeper with your photos. Take more risks," she said.

Dig deeper? Take risks? What did she want, for Abby to climb the trees and photograph them from the canopy?

"How do I do that?" Abby asked.

"Maybe see what it feels like to take portraits, for example. Include people in your photos, or even find ways to put your *own* life into the pictures. Right now, you're removed from your subjects. There's nothing wrong with what you did, but my job is to push you to keep growing as an artist. See what it's like to take pictures of people in *your* life. Catch them doing real-life things too."

Like who? And doing what? Her mom on the computer? Papi pacing the kitchen on his phone? Her idols were *wildlife* photographers—Cristina Mittermeier, Paul Nicklen, Beverly Joubert. She couldn't name a single photographer who wasn't a wildlife one.

"Thank you, Ms. Tenley. I'll remember that. And yes, you'll definitely see me in class next year." She tried not to look disheartened.

"Have a great summer, Aberdeen. And keep taking pictures!" Ms. Tenley said.

"You too," Abby replied, turning toward the door.

"Oh, and, Abby?"

She looked back to see Ms. Tenley waving her over.

"You know, I usually only tell my rising eighth graders about this," she whispered, "but you seem very motivated in your photography for an almost-seventh grader." She handed Abby a slip of paper. "It's information about an exhibit happening this August. If you send me your best picture by mid-July, I'll enter it in the competition. Every summer they feature young photographers from our county schools at the New Jersey Performing Arts Center." She winked. "There's even a prize!"

Abby thanked Ms. Tenley, but as soon as she was in the hallway, she shoved the paper into her bag. Her mouth was dry, and her heart was heavy. She walked over to the water fountain and pushed the button. Water sprayed all over her face and up her nose. Go figure. She didn't even have a camera anymore. There was no way she would enter the stupid photography contest, not after her favorite teacher said her final project basically stunk. She wiped her face and went outside to wait for Papi.

As he pulled up to the school parking lot, he honked and waved Abby in excitedly. "Let's celebrate the start of summer with some ice cream!"

Abby's spirits lifted ever so slightly as she hopped in the car. Though she wasn't in the most celebratory mood, ice cream sounded perfect.

INSIDE THE AIR-CONDITIONED ice cream shop, Abby sipped a thick chocolate shake. Papi sat on the stool next to her and enjoyed a caramel cone.

"How was school? Anything fun happen?"

"Fine, I guess. I talked to my photography teacher about my project, and she gave me some good advice," she said, half lying. She couldn't bring herself to tell Papi that school was terrible, her final project was no good, and she was ending the year with zero friends.

"That's nice. What was her advice?"

Abby thought quickly. She had to give him something.

"I think she wants me to take portraits for a change. Too much wildlife and nature in my pictures. But she said she likes how I balance the lines and angles, and that I have an 'intuitive sense' for lighting."

"So maybe you can take pictures in Honduras and put your teacher's advice into practice," he said, a cunning smile on his face.

Abby almost dropped her milkshake. "Wait—what did you say? Did you just say in *Honduras*?"

Papi nodded. "I convinced Mom to let you come with me. Told her you'd be well taken care of by our hosts, and maybe threw in a few white lies for good measure."

"Wait up! What do you mean, 'white lies'?"

"Well, that there was a bathroom in your room with running water, for starters. And that we'd have reliable Wi-Fi."

"There's no bathroom? Or Wi-Fi?" Abby asked.

"The bathroom might be *outside* our room."

"But there *is* a bathroom?"

"Of course!" he said. "It's just . . . outside."

She gulped her shake, worried that her persistence had come back to bite her like a mosquito.

"But Pataya's on the beach, right? I can swim and read and relax?" She held her breath. Summer meant she got to set her own schedule, and she was hopeful it would be no different in Honduras.

"Yes. And take pictures. We'll be right on the beach."

"What exactly are *you* going to be doing?" she asked.

"Pataya is a fishing community; for decades, lobster divers there have suffered decompression sickness. A local team and I will be training them, bringing new equipment, and introducing sustainable traps called casitas. We've partnered with community leaders to make sure everyone is as prepared and well equipped as possible. This is the first trip of many."

"Sounds amazing. Papi, gracias. I can't believe I'm going with you!" Her heart expanded. She could already feel the warm sea breeze.

"I can't believe it, either, Abby." He smiled and took the final bite from his cone.

"What about the storm?"

"They're still cleaning up and rebuilding. It means we'll have to help and do our part to be gracious guests."

Abby took the news in. Now that it was happening, her stomach and mind were doing somersaults, and she had a million questions.

"So, is Mom really fine with this?"

"Let's just say she respected the arguments I made."

"That works for me."

They chatted about the trip the whole way home. Abby would skip the last day of school, which was a half day anyway, to get any vaccine boosters she was due for, followed by a visit to the mall for a new bathing suit and other travel essentials. After a less-than-perfect day at school—a less-than-perfect year, really—a summer in Honduras was exactly what Abby needed.

CHAPTER 9

Barana

Sunday morning began like every other Sunday morning: Barana's family got ready for church. Barana put on her best dress, which she was close to outgrowing, and she packed her notebook in a small satchel, just in case she got bored and the service went long (which it usually did).

The sun was bright, and the heat of the past few days had mostly dried up the liquid evidence of a storm. Still, the piles of debris scattered outside reminded Barana of all they'd lost.

Despite her many efforts to excuse herself from family gatherings, endless chores, babysitting, and homework over the last four days, she had failed at making it out to the beach in search of Luna. Mamá couldn't open the pulpería until Papá completed the roof, so she'd spent all her free time hovering around them, offering to help with this and that and everything in between. Their house had never been tidier, and neither had Bela's.

Barana had walked by the sea turtle office on her way to and from the school-boat dock when classes resumed. Nobody was ever inside. It looked as if they didn't plan to reopen, and she didn't like it.

Papá had been busy fixing the store's roof and had gone out fishing only once; Barana could tell he was worried about finances now that the pulpería wasn't bringing in any money. One night, he'd told Mamá he was considering joining the lobster divers. Apparently, a few of his friends had suggested it.

"You'll dive over my dead body. I'd let Tulu drop out of school to work before I let you join that crew," Mamá said. Mamá valued their education above everything, so it was a bold statement for her to make.

"Your education is insurance for your future," she would say anytime they whined about homework. But Barana had never heard her mamá voice these fears about diving.

As the family walked down the path from their house, past the empty turtle office, and through town, Barana wished more than ever that the storm had never happened. Mamá would still have her store, Papá wouldn't have to consider lobster diving, and María would be in the turtle office, finishing the nesting season.

They walked into the white-and-pink chapel and sat in their regular pew. Marisol squirmed as she was passed from parent to sibling to abuelos and back again. Barana half listened to Pastor Pablo, who, despite being her abuelo's best friend, was sometimes a bore. Besides, she was distracted by her thoughts of Luna's nest and what was in store for the remainder of the season. At least her scar hadn't been hurting.

"Let us begin by giving thanks that the storm weakened when it made landfall over our territory," the pastor said, raising his hands to the heavens. "The damage was minimal, and no lives were lost, thanks be to God."

"Amen," the congregation replied.

Mass continued, but all Barana prayed for was that Mamá would stay and socialize after the service and that Papá and Tulu would go watch Sunday fútbol. If she bolted to the beach fast enough, maybe she'd even find fresh turtle tracks.

The sermon finally ended, and Barana thought she was free to go, but then Pastor Pablo said someone had requested to make a "community announcement."

They'd been there over an hour. Patience had never been Barana's strength. She remembered to breathe.

Inhala, exhala.

The pastor beckoned someone to the altar.

Much to Barana's surprise, her very pregnant turtle protector and mentor, María, waddled over to the pulpit. She was about to pop. Her belly bulged out of her shirt, and she held both her hands behind her hips as she made her way down the center aisle, but it was the hopeless look in her eye that most caught Barana's attention.

María fiddled with the microphone, bending it down to her height. She cleared her throat and fixed her long dark hair. Her gaze was focused on her husband, Matías, whose beard was looking scruffier than usual. Both their kids sat next to him. He shushed them as María started to speak.

"Buenos días," María said.

"Buenos días," the crowd responded.

"I asked Pastor Pablo to give me this moment to share some difficult news with you. La playa is no longer safe for patrolling. Two nights ago, my husband and I were threatened by poachers from the islands. They were armed, and we were instructed to stay off the beach after dark, or they'd hurt us and our loved ones." She stared into the congregation, blinking as if to hold back tears.

Everyone was quiet. Then the faint sound of *oohs* and *aahs* echoed throughout the church. Barana's chest tightened, and she felt like she might faint.

"What about the conservation project funds? Will they go unused?" someone said from the back row.

"We didn't receive any funding for this season yet, and the government said they were reallocating money toward storm repairs."

"We are cursed!" a woman yelled.

"Hush!" a familiar voice responded. It was Nati, Barana's school-boat pilot. "We need to be safe, and now is not the time for hysterics. Remember what happened in the Cayos?

We must stay calm and do as they ask. Stay away from the beach at night, for now, and focus on getting our village up and running again."

"But they'll ruin this year's nests," a patrol volunteer said. "And what if they keep returning year after year?"

Barana wholeheartedly agreed. If they didn't defend their baulas now, there might be no new nests to protect. The poachers would think they had free rein of the beach and keep coming back for a quick score. She took several deep breaths to keep her lungs from popping out of her chest.

Inhala, exhala.

The townspeople erupted into conversations.

"We've lost enough because of this storm! Let's not risk getting hurt by these ladrones. The nesting season will be over soon anyway," a man said from the back.

No one seemed too happy about things. Some people started getting up and moving toward the door. Others gathered around María to bombard her with questions.

Speaking into the microphone, Pastor Pablo reminded everyone to stay hopeful. "Juntos," he said. "Together we can come up with a solution. Remember that we are here to help and support each other." He started saying something about forming a committee, but by that point hardly anyone was listening.

Barana's family got up. Mamá and Papá shook their heads and made the sign of the cross, but Barana couldn't move.

The weight of the announcement pushed her down into her seat with a force she couldn't overcome. Tulu tugged at her hand and helped her off the pew.

BARANA'S PARENTS KEPT a watchful eye on her after María's announcement, but soon enough Mamá drifted over to the community center next to the church with her friends, and Papá and Tulu went off to the field to watch fútbol. Nobody questioned Barana when she said she was going home.

At the site of the nest, all that remained was an empty hole.

The wide-open gash in the sand revealed what she had feared the most. Luna's nest had been poached. All the eggs were gone, and only a few empty shells had been left behind. She was too late. She had broken her promise to Luna.

Her legs gave out. The moon-shaped scar on her back burned. She toppled over and sat next to the empty chamber. Her fists gripped the sand. She kicked the fine grains in all directions, releasing her anger and frustration.

She remembered to breathe and tried to calm herself down enough to allow her lungs to get some oxygen. Her chest felt like she'd been buried under pounds and pounds of sand.

Inhala, exhala. Inhala, exhala.

She stood slowly and walked to the sea, dipping her toes

in the surf. Her scar stung like a moon-shaped flame, and she lay down right there, where the sand met the sea, hoping the water would soothe her back.

She let the salty foam flow over her clothes as she stared into the sky. There was a rhythm to the coming and going of the waves. It was predictable, and it comforted her a little. A pelican soared overhead, and she spotted a few others gliding farther up in the atmosphere. Their ease in the sky reminded Barana of what it was like for her turtles in the sea.

Effortless.

She wished she could fly with them, or swim deep in the ocean with Luna and the leatherbacks. Either place would be better than Pataya.

When she got up, refreshed from the water, she had no idea how much time had passed. She walked home under the blazing sun, hoping nobody would be there to notice the state of her drenched church clothes.

The yard between Barana's house and Bela's was quiet. The two hammocks hung empty and still beneath the palm trees, and her grandparents were nowhere to be seen. Even Pitufo seemed to be napping inside the little house Abuelo had built for him.

Laundry dripped from the long cables strung between two fence posts. Barana was walking through the property and toward her house when her grandmother called out.

"Barana, where are you coming from?" she said from underneath her stairs.

Her abuela used the area under the stilt house for everything from an outdoor kitchen to a small chicken coop. She even let Tulu have a makeshift workshop, where he kept a stash of recyclables and whatever usable scraps he found lying around town. Miraculously, it had all been spared by the storm.

"¿Qué te pasó?" Bela said.

"I decided to go for a swim after the service."

"In your *clothes*?" Bela squinted at her, searching for the truth. "You know you shouldn't go swimming by yourself in the ocean. ¿Estás bien, mija?"

"I didn't swim, just got in the water up to my ankles and then lay down so the water would cool me off." Barana hoped this explanation would be enough. She didn't want her abuela asking any further questions.

"Go dry off. Our guests might be arriving in a few hours."

Guests! Barana had forgotten about the unwanted visitors and the random gringa she was supposed to take care of. The girl probably didn't even speak Spanish.

"They arrive today?" she said.

"Yes," Bela said, nodding.

There had to be some way out of this obligation. With the tourist girl hanging around her all week, she'd never find time for Luna. One nest was already lost, and there was no way she was going to let that happen again.

She needed a plan. She couldn't afford any setbacks, especially not with poachers on the prowl.

"Abuela, por favor. Can't Tulu be in charge of her?"

Bela grabbed an empty condensed milk can with a few cuttings of white mar pacífico flowers prettily arranged inside. She gave Barana the glare that always made her stomach flutter.

"She will be *your* responsibility. You know this village and beach like the back of your hand. It's all been arranged. You'll take her with you to school tomorrow and make her feel welcome. Her father has a lot to do, and I promised him his child would be in good hands." She gave Barana the flower can. "Here, take these and put them in the guesthouse. Then get out of your wet clothes and be back here in an hour."

Barana wanted to tell Bela about the poached nest she'd just found. She wanted to run to María's house and convince her to confront the poachers. And yet there she stood, hopeless and powerless, unable to say a word. Worst yet, her scar felt cold on her back, something that had never happened before. She had no tears left, and her mouth was dry. All she could do was nod at Bela, who seemed unaware of her despair.

At home, she poured herself a cup of water and changed into dry clothes. Then she sat on her mattress and looked over at Tulu's empty, unmade bed. *No era justo.* It wasn't fair that he got to be out playing fútbol and doing whatever he wanted, and she was forced to help with the gringa.

As soon as I can, I'm ditching her.

Barana let out a few good screams into her pillow. She was

miserable and alone. The thing she loved most was threatened, and she had no idea what to do. So she did the only thing that ever seemed to help—drawing and writing feverishly in her notebook. A picture of the empty hole took shape on the page, as well as the footprints around it and the few broken shells left behind as evidence. After adding some details, she shaded the scene of the crime. It was somber and dark, just like her mood. She wanted to write a poem about the darkness she felt inside and the ice-cold feeling in her scar, but the words didn't come. Instead, in her best script, she wrote a simple line underneath the drawing:

I will bring these thieves to justice.

CHAPTER 10

Abby

Aberdeen felt a hand on her shoulder. It was such an ungodly hour that even the sun wasn't out of bed.

"Es hora," Papi said as he turned on her bedside lamp.

"¡Papi! Not nice. Turn it off!" Abby grumbled and rolled back on her pillow. It was painfully early.

He laughed, in a nice way, and reminded her they had three flights to catch. Missing the first one would result in postponing the trip until who knew when. "Rápido, hija. The car will be here in ten minutes."

Que tortura. She squirmed and stretched her arms out, taking in the pitch black outside her window. It looked like it was still midnight, with a quarter moon shining through her window. Abby wasn't used to early mornings, but she got up anyway. Honduras was waiting!

With her big suitcase in hand and a backpack over her shoulders, she gently closed the door behind her. She'd started packing her bags the day Papi told her she was going, and she could scarcely believe the time had come.

In the kitchen, her parents immediately stopped whisper-chatting when she entered. Her mom could barely bring herself to say goodbye. She still had reservations about the trip. Yet somehow Papi had won the battle.

Her parents saw the world differently. Her mom had grown up in a small town in Michigan and hadn't left the state until she went to law school in New York and met Papi. Her idea of travel was a road trip to the big lake. Her lens was zoomed in.

Papi, on the other hand, was a world traveler. He'd left his first home at the age of six to live in the city and then immigrated to America shortly after. His lens was wider. Zoomed way out.

"Can I try some coffee?" Abby asked, hoping to show her mom just how mature she was. "I think I'm going to need it today."

Her parents looked at each other in disbelief, but Papi poured her a small cup anyway. Her mom grabbed the hazelnut creamer from the fridge and added a generous splash.

Abby took the first sip and let the sweet, nutty flavor distract her from doubts about her ability to "rough it" in Pataya. Too bad the aftertaste was not appealing. She gave the beverage a second chance, but not a third.

"I'm good," she said, and handed the mug back to her mom. Coffee was not her cup of tea.

Mom's phone buzzed. "The taxi is outside."

"Well, this is it," Abby said, looking at Mom.

"Call me as soon as you can, okay?" Her mom squeezed her tight. The warm embrace eased Abby's nerves.

"I will. Promise." As they hugged, a small part of her wanted to stay right there in Ridge Park, where things were predictable. But the other part of her wanted to pull away and finally travel with Papi to Honduras.

Her mom broke away first and kissed her on the forehead. "I'll miss you," she said.

"I'll miss you too, Mom," she replied.

As the black car took off, Abby looked back at her dimly lit home until they turned the corner away from Meadowlark Drive. They headed toward the Palisades Parkway, zooming steadily, with no traffic to skirt around. Across the Hudson River, New York City awoke with the rising sun.

In the back of the air-conditioned cab, Papi pulled out a black case from his oversize backpack and gave it to Abby. "An early birthday present from Mom and me. She wanted me to surprise you in Pataya, but I couldn't wait."

Abby opened the case to find a shiny new black Nikon digital SLR camera with three lenses. It was heavier than her old hand-me-down, but with the same point-and-shoot features. It was perfect!

"I thought I'd be taking pictures with my screen-cracked phone! This is amazing, Papi! Thank you! It even has a wide-angle lens!"

"We couldn't let our young photographer visit Honduras without one. You have a special way of seeing things, Coneja. A photographer's keen eye. Mom and I can't wait to see the pictures you capture down there."

Nothing could have made Abby happier. "Can I try it out?" she said.

Papi nodded. "We charged it last night. It's all yours to play with," he replied.

Abby turned the camera on and got familiar with her new gift. She looked through the lens and snapped a picture of the moving trees outside as they sped down the highway. The blurred image on the display screen gave her a funny feeling, like déjà vu, or a premonition.

Like this camera was important.

THEY MADE IT to their gate without a glitch and boarded their flight to Miami. Abby considered texting a picture of her camera to Fiana, but they hadn't spoken much all week. Fiana had minimized the storm and Abby's excitement for the trip. Plus, she'd declined Abby's call yesterday, knowing full well that she was leaving this morning. None of it felt right. Abby put her phone on airplane mode and fastened her seat belt.

"Don't worry if the plane shakes a bit," Papi said. "It's normal. And if your ears pop, just do this." He pinched his nostrils and popped his cheeks. "You cover your nose and breathe out. That way your ears equalize. We do the same when we scuba."

He double-checked her seat belt and tapped her knee.

The plane shook as it rose. Abby gripped the armrests tightly while clenching her jaw. Her stomach felt like it might come out of her mouth. She was nervous. And nauseous. Until finally, the plane steadied above the clouds.

Papi pulled out his laptop and worked on a fancy slide-show presentation with bar graphs of health data. If it weren't for the loud buzzing air above her and the strange popping and unpopping of her ears, she would have asked him about his childhood in Honduras.

He never talked much about Pataya or Abuelo's death; all he ever said was that it had been related to scuba diving. Abuela had outlived her husband, but he didn't share much about her, either. Abby knew they would both be proud of who their son had become, though.

While Papi worked, Abby pulled out the magazine in the seat-back pocket; the professional, glossy photos reminded her of what Ms. Tenley had said. Her words still stung a little. How could she bring *herself* into her photography? What *was* her unique lens, anyway? And what the heck did she mean by "take more risks"?

As she turned a page, the centerfold picture of a whale staring straight into the camera mesmerized her. The scuba-diving photographer's silhouette floated peacefully next to the whale's enormous body, like two friends saying hi. The picture was full of emotion. Right then and there, Abby decided she'd show Ms. Tenley that she could simply include portraits *in* her wildlife photography. She'd find a way to highlight the connection between humans and the environment—the bond between people and the natural world. It was possible. The proof was right there in front of her, in one of Cristina Mittermeier's stunning photos.

~ ~ ~

MIAMI INTERNATIONAL AIRPORT was wide awake when they arrived, and the quiet of dawn had transformed into a loud and busy morning. Passengers rushed around, and little electric carts with white-haired people whooshed by them. The hunger pangs in Abby's belly gurgled.

After grabbing a couple of breakfast sandwiches, they sat at their gate and waited for their second flight.

"Papi," Abby said, "do you like going back to Pataya?"

"Of course. It was my first home."

"Why did it take you so long to go back—after medical school, I mean?"

"You know the story." He took a bite of his sandwich.

"Tell me again." Abby never got tired of hearing Papi's stories.

"Your abuela wanted me to reach for my dreams. She sacrificed a lot to help make that happen. She brought me to the city so I could continue learning, and after my father died, she moved mountains to get us both to America. I finished my studies, went to medical school, met your mom, and the rest is history."

"But your father hadn't gone to the city with you, right?" Abby said.

Papi nodded. "He preferred a simpler life by the sea."

Abby wanted to tell him she was sorry, that it must have been hard to lose his father so young and grow up with only his mother, but the words felt stuck in her throat like a lump of clay.

"That's all in the past, Coneja. They are both with us in spirit. And now you get to go see their home."

"And your first home." Abby wanted to ask more questions, but Papi got up to answer a call on his phone. He didn't like talking about the past much anyway.

THREE HOURS LATER Abby could see Honduras outside her double-paned window. Mountains rose along the coast in the distance. The ocean waves crashed in slow motion against miles and miles of sandy coastline. She noticed an archipelago of islands ahead, surrounded by turquoise water and white beaches. It was like a painting that contained every shade of aqua.

Tap, tap, click.

"Those are the Cayos Cochinos," Papi told her. "Where I did most of my fieldwork during graduate school."

"It's beautiful," Abby replied.

"We'll visit one day. Or maybe Roatán, the biggest of the Bay Islands. Best snorkeling you'll ever do."

Her ears popped as they descended, and it felt like the aircraft was gaining speed. She braced herself for landing.

After the plane came to a stop, the passengers clapped in celebration.

"It's kind of a thing here—we clap after we land," Papi said.

Abby joined in, putting her hands together with the rest of them.

They exited the airplane directly onto the tarmac. The sticky, hot air was a relief after hours in the cold, recycled air-conditioning. Abby got through customs without having to utter a lick of English. She surprised herself with her fluency in Spanish but somehow felt more American than ever.

After calling Mom to let her know they'd arrived, they boarded their third and final flight. Sweat dripping down her forehead, Abby took her seat and fastened her buckle tightly, double-checking it for good measure.

The "airplane" was more like a washing machine with wings. It was tiny, loud, and old-looking, like something out of a World War II movie. Only six passengers fit inside, plus the two pilots. The engine roared so loudly that she couldn't even listen to music.

"Veinte minutos, and we'll be there," Papi said, tapping on her knee.

Assuming this flying appliance can stay in the air for twenty minutes . . ., Abby thought.

The miniature airplane shook and rattled, and Abby wasn't sure the worn-out seat belts would do much to protect them if they crashed into the rain forest below. The mountains were so close she could practically reach out and touch them. The landscape became flatter but no less green as they began their final descent.

The "airport" was a long runway of packed dirt, with a small wooden building off to the side. Puddles of brown water sat unmoving on its perimeter, evidence of the storm. The surrounding area was like something out of a Jurassic Park movie, where any moment a giant reptile might come crashing through the bushes.

Abby hopped off the plane, and her feet hit the softest earth she'd ever stood on. A flock of colorful macaws flew overhead. A lagoon shimmered at the end of the landing strip; it was a pool of sapphires. She immediately pulled out her camera.

Tap, tap, click.

She captured a scarlet bird as it flew across the sky, its wings outstretched above the water.

Just then, they were approached by a group of big, burly men. Papi was greeted by one of them, who happened to be heavily armed. *Jeez, what's the gun for?* A friendly woman and her son also approached them. They each carried a box filled with bags of fruit. Fruit felt better than guns. Abby turned her attention to the friendly-looking vendors.

"¿Quiere lichas?" the woman asked. "¡Un dólar!"

Papi gave Abby a nod. "Get me some too."

"Yo tengo mangos," the boy said. "Un dólar también."

Abby pulled two dollars out of her backpack and purchased a bag of rambutans and one of mangoes. The boy's smile was contagious, his brown eyes deep and joyful.

Take risks, she thought. "¿Les puedo tomar una foto?" Abby was shocked at her bold request to take their picture. The mother and son held their bagged fruit and nodded. They'd be her first portrait.

Tap, tap, click.

"Gracias." Abby's heart fluttered. She waved goodbye to the boy and his mother and followed Papi and the three men onto a narrow dock. A white motorboat, no bigger than a small school bus, was waiting for them. It would be their final transport to Pataya. The pilot welcomed them with firm handshakes and a wide smile.

The lancha's engine revved, and they sped away from the landing strip and toward the maze of mangroves.

Despite the cooling breeze, Abby could feel the freckles forming on her nose as the sun beamed down on them. The top of her head was as hot as embers, her dark hair absorbing the heat like an iguana sunning on a stone.

She replaced the lens on her camera, steadied her grip, and captured two huge herons on the shrinking shoreline. One of them took off as she clicked the shutter, and its reflection was perfectly projected onto the mirror-like water below. Papi explained that the area they were in was protected land and a "mecca of biodiversity." Abby could tell that was true, even though she wasn't sure what *mecca* meant.

The sky was the brightest blue she'd ever seen. Palm-thatched huts on stilts rose above the greenery like a floating, magical village. Here and there, a rickety dock jutted out into the water. As far as she could see, there were few power lines or telephone cables. No streets. No cars. Just water, nature, and boats. Could she really make it without the amenities of a modern life for two whole weeks?

Suddenly, the lancha jerked backward, and the captain shut off the motor. The instant silence surprised her. Were they in Pataya already? They were feet from the shoreline, but there was not a dock in sight, only mangroves and jungles and sky.

Then the pilot hushed them all. "¡Silencio!"

Papi leaned over the side of the lancha and waved frantically for Abby to come see something in the water. She scooted toward him and looked over the boat's edge. There was an enormous creature in the estuary.

A manatee, grazing on the grass below, floated a few feet away. It was like a giant potato bobbing by the mangroves. They admired the shy, peaceful creature, and the locals explained how it was not uncommon to see manatees in this part of the canal system. They were in the estuarine zone, a mix of salt water and fresh water, where marine life thrived. She quickly changed the lens once more.

Tap, tap, click.

Tap, click.

Click.

Click.

Click.

Her new camera was amazing. She snapped several photos of the sea cow, determined to get as close as possible. It was time to channel her inner wildlife photographer. But the animal did not move, and Abby could barely see its face. She couldn't figure out how to capture the magic. The angle was wrong, the water was painted with the shadows of the mangroves and clouds, and the manatee never turned its face toward the camera.

"Isn't it great?" Papi said, beaming.

Abby looked up from the camera's viewfinder and nodded. It *was* great. She might not have gotten the perfect shot yet, but she couldn't agree more with Papi.

And they'd only been in the boat for ten minutes.

The pilot pushed off a mangrove branch and rowed them out of the manatee's home. He turned the engine back on once they'd established a good distance from the innocent mammal. The river wove and spun until it finally opened into a large lagoon. They approached a village—Abby figured it was Pataya—and the landscape changed. Papi showed her how rows of cacao and banana trees lined the shores. There were more houses now, tall ones and short ones. Many stood high above the ground. A group of grazing horses hung out by a rickety old fence.

"¡Caballos!" Abby said.

Her father nodded, and his eyes twinkled. "The locals get around on horses or bikes when a boat can't get them where they need to go." He reached over and squeezed her shoulder. Abby could tell he was happy, but her brain could barely keep up with all the questions she had.

Horses, manatees, and fresh fruit on arrival? Everyone was so welcoming, and Abby had yet to see any major destruction from the storm.

"Abby," Papi said, "I've got a meeting today with the local fisheries and diving committee."

Abby nodded, unsure of what his point was; she already knew he was here to work.

"Our hostess arranged for her granddaughter to show you around until I get back for dinner. She even offered for you to join her at school tomorrow morning while I work. I thought that could be fun for you, so I said yes."

The excitement about arriving in Pataya fled in an instant. Her stomach did that sinking thing, like she'd swallowed a stone. School while on vacation? Being babysat by a stranger? Why hadn't Papi told her this sooner?

"I don't need a babysitter! Can't I explore on my own? Besides, you said the beach was right outside our cabin."

"Abs, it's fine. She'll take you everywhere. You can't gallivant around Pataya by yourself. It'll be more fun for you to have a friend while I'm working than for you to join me in boring meetings."

Why didn't he let *her* decide what would be more fun? She grunted and crossed her arms.

"I'll be done by dinner and will join you then. Be a gracious guest, all right? Besides, there'll be plenty of time for us to be together. Today and tomorrow will be my busiest days. After that, things will settle down, and we'll explore together. I promise."

Abby's mood deflated. How could she enjoy Pataya with a strange girl hovering nearby? Worse yet, how would she find time to work on her photography? She'd have to find a way to ditch her, even if it meant being rude to their hosts or upsetting her father.

They arrived at a wooden dock with a gazebo at the end. Fishermen were cleaning their catch in its shade. Papi unloaded their luggage as they hopped off and thanked their pilot.

A man in a wheelchair was waiting for them, and another man stood behind him and greeted them as they got off the boat. Abby knew immediately that the man in the chair had suffered from the bends. Papi approached him as if he'd known him his whole life.

"Julio, esta es mi hija, Abby," he said.

"Mucho gusto," the man replied. "Este es mi amigo Matías." Julio pointed at the gentleman behind his chair.

Matías forced a smile. He leaned against the wheelchair as if using it for support. Maybe he'd also gotten the bends, just not as bad as Julio. They all walked up the dock together. Matías pushed Julio's chair toward a dirt path lined by fruit trees and palms. Two small barefoot children rushed up to Abby, hugging her and pulling her by the hand.

"These are my kids," Matías said softly. "They are excited to have visitors."

Abby's father motioned for Abby to walk on with the kids. "I'll be right behind you," he said. "Need to firm up my plans with Julio and Matías."

Abby walked up the path with Matías's son and daughter. They gripped and tugged her excitedly. A few yards from the camino was a simple waterfront house. It was built on stilts. The wood was weatherworn, and part of the metal roof was missing. Abby assumed the storm was to blame. A set of steps led to a small front porch, where a cute mutt wagged its happy tail.

As Abby petted the dog, the children's mother came out of the front door. Her large, pregnant belly reminded Abby of a bright full moon.

"Buenas tardes," Abby said, trying to be polite.

The woman didn't reply. Her gaze was distant and sad.

"Me llamo Abby," she told the children.

They smiled and giggled innocently, blurting out their names in the middle of bouts of laughter. "Take a picture of us!" they yelled, tugging on the camera hung around Abby's neck.

"¿Puedo?" Abby asked their mother to make sure it was okay.

The mother nodded, and a hint of a smile almost crossed her lips.

Tap, tap, click.

Abby took several shots of the children, some with the dog and some without. They smiled wide for the camera. Matías walked up the steps slowly, and Abby wondered if he and his wife would be okay with a family portrait. *Take risks,* she told herself. She wanted to capture all four of them in the afternoon sun outside their house, but she froze in place, unable to say anything.

As if reading her mind, the kids invited their parents over. "¡Todos!" they said together. They wanted a family portrait. "All of us!"

Both Matías and his wife were unimpressed by the request, but they did it anyway, and Abby snapped their picture as quickly as she could. She thanked them and ran to join Papi, almost tripping over her feet on the way down the stairs.

The picture she'd taken of the young family reminded her of those old-time photos she'd seen of her mom's parents from before she was born. They'd posed with serious expressions, making for a vintage and almost haunting portrait. Matías's wife had stared off toward the horizon with a look that Abby couldn't quite place. Was she depressed? Worried? Or just plain sad?

"So, where exactly are we staying?" she said.

"Up the road a bit. A couple here owns a small bed-and-breakfast of sorts. Like a mini-hotel."

"What are their names?"

"Bela and Juan, though I think her name is really Lisette. Everyone's always called her Bela. It's short for Abuela. She's like the village grandmother, so the nickname suits her."

Abby nodded as they walked farther away from the lagoon and Matías's house. "What happened to Julio? Why the wheelchair?"

"Bad case of the bends." Papi took a deep breath. "Matías had a close call too. He used to make a living diving for lobster, but he had an episode a few months ago and has been too scared to dive since. He and Julio are helping me with the big presentation on Friday."

"What are you presenting about?" Abby said, genuinely interested.

"Our main goal is to help transition these men to fish for lobsters using sustainable traps called casitas—like Bela's rental house. Our hope is that they spend less time underwater and have quality equipment for when they do dive."

"Why do they dive so much?"

"It's the only way they can make a living. Unfortunately, until the government invests in programs that provide other jobs for them, they have no other choice. In the meantime, we'll do our part to make their livelihoods a little less dangerous."

"Whoa," Abby said.

"We also train the community doctors on how to best treat these divers if and when they fall ill. But we have a long way to go to really make a difference."

"Wow, I had no idea you did all that," Abby said. Papi was saving lives, and she'd never been prouder of him.

They walked down the grass-lined dirt path, and locals popped out of their casitas every now and then to wave hello. When they reached the bend, a large soccer field filled with children stood before them. The boys and girls ran toward Abby and invited her to play. The circle of sweat on her back doubled in size just thinking about fútbol. She politely declined.

The kids laughed and ran back onto the patchy field.

Tap, tap, click.

She captured an action shot of the kids running toward the slightly deflated ball, some sporting big smiles and others with looks of steely determination.

"You'll play before we leave," Papi said. Abby shook her head dramatically. He nudged her and winked. "Either that or maybe I'll get you to dance merengue with me."

Neither of those two things sounded appealing. Then again, this place was full of surprises. There was just one unwelcome surprise she needed to get a handle on, and that was the matter of the babysitter Papi had arranged. She had to find a way to get out of the situation with Bela's granddaughter so she could explore her father's homeland on her own terms.

CHAPTER 11

Barana

"Your grandmother is calling you," Mamá yelled across the room.

Barana rubbed her eyes and rose from her mattress. She'd been drawing and writing and must've dozed off mid-poem. She gave her body a good stretch and walked out to the main room. Mamá sat on a dining chair with Marisol, and Papá lay on the couch, napping.

"Barana, rápido," Mamá insisted. "Bela called you over. The doctor and his daughter will be here soon."

Barana placed her notebook on the tiny stool by the door and quietly put on her chancletas.

"Do I *have* to go?" She held the door ajar, hoping Mamá would let her off the hook. She wished she could just disappear.

"Yes, mija, go. Your abuela is counting on you. She's

excited to finally have guests again. She has a whole menu planned for them and everything." Bela's B&B was the only "hotel" in town. Barana wondered if that would ever change. A few bigger hotels had popped up by neighboring beaches, but so far Pataya remained a quiet village, mostly tourist-free.

Barana stomped out the door, her forehead wrinkled with annoyance. Bela was sweeping the steps to the screened-in comedor. Pitufo was perched on her shoulder. The dining area was sparkling. Abuelo had spruced up the landscaping too, clearing debris and pruning the foliage. Things looked almost as good as they had before the storm.

"Que bueno. You changed out of your wet clothes! I think they're almost here," Bela said. "Your abuelo says he saw the boat pulling up when he was walking home with Pastor Pablo."

"And what am I supposed to do with her again?"

"Be a good host, take her for a walk, and show her around. I've got fresh coconut bread that your mamá baked this after-noon too. Chiqui's secret recipe."

"Fine," Barana grumbled. "I'll wait right here." She let the entire weight of her body collapse dramatically onto one of Bela's outdoor chairs.

"It won't be long," Bela said. "Just be nice."

In the distance, Barana spotted the guests as they turned off the main path. The girl was about her height, with brown hair down to her shoulders and pink, sun-kissed cheeks. Her father looked Honduran—his skin was brown and his features dark—but Barana concluded the girl's mom was white because her skin was fairer than his. The doctor approached with a smile, but the girl looked nervous.

Barana got up from her chair. "Bienvenidos," she said.

"Gracias. ¿Eres Barana?" the doctor asked her.

"Sí." *Guess they know my name.*

"Esta es mi hija, Abby." He placed his arm around his daughter. "Tiene doce años."

"Mucho gusto," Barana said in a raspy voice. Why did this girl need babysitting if she was twelve—the exact same age as Barana?

The friendly doctor thanked her for agreeing to show his daughter around, and Barana didn't have the heart to say anything rude. She forced herself to smile and took the guests over to their casita as they awkwardly rolled their suitcases along the uneven ground. She could tell the girl was impressed with the plants and flowers everywhere.

The girl had yet to speak, and Barana wasn't about to talk first. The sooner she could show her around, the sooner she could ditch her and focus on the sea turtles.

Bela joined them at the door, hugging the doctor and the girl before they all entered the guesthouse. After the visitors placed their big, fancy bags inside their room, Bela and Abby's father retreated to the main house, where he would be setting up a makeshift office for whenever he wasn't at the clinic or out on a dive boat.

"You show Abby around, and be back before nightfall

for the welcome dinner," Bela told Barana. "Take some of Chiqui's fresh pan dulce to share."

Barana broke the bun and gave Abby the bigger piece. They ate in silence until the girl finally spoke up.

"¿Tu nombre es Barana?"

Barana nodded, deciding not to bother asking for hers. It was something with an *A,* but she didn't really care to get it right.

After another awkward pause, the girl spoke again. "I'm happy to explore on my own. If you point me in the right direction."

Her Spanish was quite good, despite the tinge of an accent.

Barana considered the girl's idea. On the one hand, she could tell Bela that it had been the girl's idea to cancel the guided tour. She'd *asked* to explore on her own. On the other hand, Bela would be furious with her for agreeing, and besides, she already knew Barana hadn't wanted to be the tour guide and hostess. Ditching her now might make ditching her later impossible.

She decided to offer a short tour of la playa and hoped that they'd be done well before dinner. She needed alone time to plot her next steps with the poachers and the sea turtle project.

Maybe the ladrones had left something behind on the beach, a clue that would help Barana figure out who they were.

"It's okay. I promised my abuela that I would show you around. Vamos." She got up and started walking west, where the graveyard and canal met the sea. She figured it might be amusing to see the girl's reaction to the creepy gravestones. Or better yet, maybe she'd want to call it quits and return to the safety of the guesthouse early. Cemeteries scared most people.

Much to Barana's disappointment, Abby not only wasn't scared of the cemetery, she seemed to be fascinated by it. She photographed the tombstones from all kinds of angles with the fanciest camera Barana had ever seen. She swerved around them, got down on her knees, and even lay next to one to take a photo. Her camera reminded Barana of the time a professional photographer came to their village. He worked for some magazine up north, and they were doing a big project about La Mosquitia and its biodiversity. He was most interested in the birds.

Abby's sandals also caught Barana's eye. They were made of thick rubber and fabric, and they didn't flip and flop the way Barana's flimsy chancletas did.

The minutes dragged on. Barana hung around impatiently, watching Abby crouch down to capture photos of nothing but relics and grass. Barana walked toward the canal, making sure she could keep an eye on her odd guest. She worried about Luna and whether she'd return this month. Would the magical beacon that led her home each year somehow warn her of the danger that awaited if she came back?

"Barana!" the girl called out, joining her by the water.

"Sí, Annie? Or is it Allie?"

"Abby," the girl corrected her. "It's so beautiful here. You must love living by the sea."

Barana nodded. She did love it.

"Seriously, I remember how to get to your grandmother's house. I can head back on my own after taking a few more pictures. You don't have to stick around, if you don't want to."

Maybe this girl wanted to be alone just as much as Barana did.

Still, Barana didn't want to get in trouble with Bela or her parents. The responsible thing to do was to take her down to the beach, point out a few important spots in town, and get her home safely and on time. She needed to be on her family's good side if she was going to find a way to stop the poachers.

She needed her family to trust her.

"But I haven't even taken you around town yet."

"I don't need to see the village today. I can see it tomorrow after school."

"Okay," Barana said. "We can walk along the beach some more if you want."

Abby gave her two thumbs-up, something Barana had only ever seen on TV.

Perfect. Maybe she could take Abby to the site of the poached nest and check for clues while the girl was taking pictures. That would be a win-win. She'd look for evidence *and* be a responsible hostess, just like her abuela wanted.

"Wow! This beach is endless!" Abby said when they arrived. "I've never seen anything like it. Es bello! Where I'm from, the beaches are completely crowded with people. Here, there's not a soul in sight."

"Except for the ghosts." Barana raised her eyebrows.

"Ghosts?" Abby said.

"People say the ghosts come out at night—you know, near the cemetery. Some people say they've heard the wails of La Llorona too . . . and my brother swears he saw El Cadejo."

"What's that?"

"The dog of the devil. But I don't believe Tulu. He likes to scare me."

"Well, I'm more scared of live humans than dead ones," Abby replied.

Thinking of the poachers, Barana couldn't help but agree.

"There are no big hotels around here, right?" Abby said.

Barana shook her head in answer. Pataya's shoreline belonged to the sea turtles, and she was grateful there were no resorts. She had heard that the only thing big hotels did was damage the ecosystem. She loved her beach as it was. Empty, quiet, and home to dozens of leatherbacks.

Barana walked ahead of her guest toward the scene of the crime. Abby followed closely behind and resumed taking pictures near the water's edge. The aquamarine waves reminded Barana of what mattered. She breathed in the salty air.

Inhala, exhala.

The sea was always her antidote to a lousy day.

They moved along the seashore slowly. Abby stopped to examine a crab and a washed-up jellyfish. She tapped and clicked while Barana gazed along the coast, looking for any sign of poacher activity.

At the site of the old nest, nothing was amiss since she'd last been there. The ladrones had cleared all the evidence, except for a few empty eggshells—a depressing reminder of what could have been.

Abby was busy photographing a pelican when Barana noticed the sun was starting to set. It was time to go. She called Abby over from the surf, waving her hands.

"It's time to go already?" Abby said.

"Yes, the sun is setting soon. We should start walking back."

Abby pointed at the ground. "What are those?" Barana hadn't thought to pick up or hide the handful of empty eggs the poachers had left behind. "Are those eggs?"

Barana nodded. "Leatherback sea turtles."

Without asking for permission, Abby took a picture of Barana and the broken shells.

"Hey! What are you doing?" Barana covered her face.

"Oh, sorry. I'm so sorry. I should've asked. I'm a little trigger-happy with my new camera. I'll delete it if you want."

Barana's scar started to burn a little. She felt more alone than ever, and yet here she was with this new girl hovering around with her camera and her questions.

"It's okay."

"What happened to them?" Abby pointed down at the eggs again.

"There was a nest here, but it was taken."

"As in eaten by an animal?"

"No. Stolen." This girl was way too curious. "We should go. The sun will be gone in ten minutes, and my grandmother will never forgive me if I have you out here at night."

"Why? What's the big deal about being out past sunset? The *ghosts*?"

So. Many. Questions!

Are those eggs?

Are there hotels around here?

Are there ghosts?

The one question Abby should've asked was, *May I take your picture?*

"It's not safe out here at night, and it's not because of the ghosts," Barana said. "Poachers have been roaming the area, stealing sea turtle eggs and threatening people."

To avoid an interrogation, she gave Abby a summary of the week's events. She told her about the storm, about María and how the poachers had scared her, and how the village feared islanders were to blame.

"Sounds like these poachers are out for blood."

More like out for fast money, Barana thought. She had heard how valuable fresh sea turtle eggs could be on the black market. She wasn't sure why people liked eating them, but they did, and they were willing to pay good money for them.

"The eggs are worth a lot. Apparently they're a 'delicacy' for some people. But if you ask me, it's just as bad of a crime to eat their eggs as it would be to kill a full-grown turtle."

Abby's eyes got as big as the full moon. "Oh, wow. So the eggs are literally like buried treasure waiting to be found."

"Exacto," Barana said.

Barana kept a quick pace as they wove through the palm trees toward Bela's. The last sliver of sun began to sneak behind the horizon. The sky was purple, and Barana feared it was already too late. Then she spotted a shadow lurking behind a thick, stubby palm tree. She stopped and motioned for Abby to hush. She'd get Tulu this time.

"Tulu, is that you? Stop with your tonterías. I'm not in the mood for your jokes."

They watched as the tall figure stilled and then moved over to the next palm tree. It was too dark to make him out.

"He knows we saw him." *He'll try to sneak up on us from behind later.* "Follow me," Barana whispered.

"Who do you think it is?"

"It's my brother. He likes to jump out and scare me, but we're going to make a run for it, and he won't have the chance."

As they got closer to the area where the silhouette had been, it turned and sped toward the sea grapes. The figure was tall, slightly slouched in his posture, and wore a backward cap. He carried a large empty bag in his hand, but it was too dark to make out any other identifiable features. Barana's scar prickled—she had a sneaking suspicion that whoever it was, he was up to no good. Tulu wouldn't run off like that. Though his body shape and height were similar to this stranger, Tulu always jumped out and scared her . . . he never ran away.

They hid behind a tree and waited. Barana's heart was beating faster than a jaguar's. She didn't like it. If Abby hadn't been with her, she would've followed him toward la playa. When the figure was gone, the girls began to move.

"Que miedo," Abby said.

"Yeah. That was very creepy."

Barana's moon-shaped scar throbbed the rest of the way home.

CHAPTER 12

Abby

They walked in silence the rest of the way to Bela's. Abby hadn't seen the inside of her hosts' house yet, but the quaint outdoor lights strung around the deck were a bright and welcoming sign. Their twinkling eased the discomfort that sat in the pit of her stomach. Her belly ached with hunger and nerves, and she craved her mom's mac 'n' cheese.

Like the humid heat of Pataya, the exhaustion of the long trip overcame her. She wanted her bed. She wanted air-conditioning. She wanted an ice-cold drink. Plus, that shady encounter with the tall figure on the beach had left her spooked.

Barana led her up the stairs, through a rickety turquoise door. There was an assortment of colorful chairs and tables arranged like a restaurant on the deck. Papi, an older gentleman—probably Barana's grandfather—and two other men waved them in.

Papi got up, introduced everyone, and immediately asked

them how the tour had gone. Abby was about to tell him everything, but Barana glared at her and interrupted.

"Your daughter took beautiful pictures at the beach and cemetery, but we ran out of time to see the rest of town. I'll give her the full tour tomorrow after school," she said. "It was nice—right, Abby?" She gave her a big-eyed stare and didn't blink until Abby nodded in agreement.

Abby could tell that Barana didn't want her relatives to know about their encounter with the shadowy dude. "It was awesome. I got some cool shots of the graveyard!"

"Can't wait to see them," Papi said.

Bela pushed open a swinging door and came through with a tray of drinks.

"¡Justo a tiempo! Right on time, girls," she said. "Take some fresh jugo de tamarindo. It's ice-cold."

She handed the seafoam-colored cups to the girls. They were filled to the brim. Abby had never had tamarind juice before. She tried to sniff it secretly, but Bela caught her in the act.

"It's tart, but I add the perfect amount of azúcar," Bela said. She laughed and gestured for Abby to drink. Bela's eyes twinkled, her big laugh was joyful and contagious, and her cheeks glistened with hints of peachy pink. She was like a Honduran Mrs. Claus.

Abby sipped the juice slowly and puckered her lips. Bela was right—it was tart, sweet, and ice-cold. Different, but yummy.

Barana snuck inside with her drink, and Abby was relieved

to have a moment alone at the table. She pulled out her camera and scrolled through the new photos. The cemetery ones were her favorite. The gravestones looked awesome, with the Caribbean Sea in the background and bits of blurry green and brown speckles from the beach. Her eye was drawn to one tombstone, which appeared in the background of several photos. It was lonely and small and covered in vegetation. She zoomed in and tried to make out the name.

"R. Durón." She squinted to make sure she was reading it right.

That was *her* last name.

"Sit down with our guest," Bela said, startling Abby. "And get to know each other." Barana was standing next to her abuela looking annoyed. Abby shared her sentiment. She wanted to get through dinner speaking as little as possible and then go to sleep.

Getting to know Barana was not on her to-do list.

But Barana did as Bela instructed and sat next to Abby. Much to Abby's surprise, Barana placed a hand on her shoulder and smiled. "Thank you for not saying anything about that strange man. I don't want to worry my family."

Abby nodded and smiled back. "¿Por qué quieres guardar el secreto?" she asked.

"No es eso. It's not that I want to keep it secret. I just didn't want to ruin the night my grandmother planned. She's been excited about having you here. . . . No need to bring up suspicions about poachers. Besides, we don't even know if that guy is involved. He was probably just some chavo going out swimming."

"It's okay, I get it. And I agree. It was probably nothing."

They sipped their tamarindo drinks quietly as more people arrived. Barana gave Abby the lowdown on who everyone was: her tidy and hardworking mamá, her expert-fisherman papá, her loud primos, and her clingy baby sister. Everyone welcomed Abby and Papi with hugs and smiles.

"What about your brother?" Abby asked.

"I don't know where Tulu is. That's strange, he should be here by now."

Just then, a tall, athletic-looking boy showed up carrying a set of plastic bins. Next to him, another boy with deep brown eyes and ebony skin held a soccer ball.

"It's like he read our minds. *That's* Tulu. And his best friend, Jason. Tulu's the tall one with the recycled drums. My brother takes junk and makes stuff out of it," Barana said. "The fact that he cleans up so much litter around town is the only reason I put up with him."

Before Abby could be introduced, Tulu's best friend blew into a large conch shell. The sound was so sudden that the tamarind juice went down the wrong pipe and almost made her choke. Then Tulu and Jason sat and played their plastic bins—drumbeats.

The music's energy filled the room. It made Abby tap involuntarily on the table. It was enchanting. *Tum, tum, ta, ta, ta, tum, tum.* The adults stopped their chatter, and Barana's mom started dancing with the baby still in her arms. She moved her hips while everyone clapped to the rhythm. The beats seemed improvised, like jazz, but the sound was different.

"What's this called?"

"Punta," Barana replied. "It's the dance of the Garifuna people, like Jason and his dad—they taught Tulu how to play. And my mom's best friend, Chiqui, is also Garifuna. She's the best dancer in town."

"I like it!" Abby was mesmerized by the speed with which Tulu's hands moved, by the smile on his face and the sweat dripping from his brow. His friend Jason's ebony hands struck each drum in perfect synchronization with Tulu's. "Do you think your brother will mind if I take a picture of them?"

Barana shrugged. "Eh, just do it. They love performing together and probably won't mind."

Tap, tap, click.

Tap. Click.

Click, click, click.

Then, as the music died down, the smell of something co-conutty filled Abby's nose. She wished she could capture the aroma in her photographs. She wished Mom could be there with her, listening to the music, feeling the sea breeze, seeing the palm trees sway. Abby didn't want to forget any of it.

"¡Ya está la sopa de caracol!" Bela said, inviting them to line up for dinner.

"What's sopa de caracol like?" Abby whispered to Barana as they both stood.

"It's a coconut-milk broth with some lime, cilantro, and fish. Oh, and conch—caracol," Barana said. "The conch is a bit rubbery, but you get used to it."

"It also has yuca and plátanos," Bela said. She poured Abby two heaping scoops. Her face was radiant, and clearly she would not take no for an answer. It wasn't Mom's mac 'n' cheese, but it smelled good.

As she sipped the soup, Abby realized it was the perfect way to end her first day in Honduras. Papi took a seat in front of her and winked as if agreeing.

Best. Soup. Ever.

"Abby, how about we take a picture?" he said.

He pulled out his phone and asked Bela's husband, Juan, to snap their portrait. Juan grabbed the smartphone and fiddled with it a little before figuring out how it worked. Abby sat before her empty bowl while Papi hugged her. She realized how relaxed Papi was, how he seemed right at home. She wondered if he missed living in Honduras, or if he longed to move back.

"Cheese!"

Abby wanted to take Papi's portrait with her new camera too, to remember this moment with him on their first night in his homeland. She turned the camera on and asked if she could take his photo. He nodded. As she looked through her lens, it was like she was seeing him for the very first time. Or maybe she was seeing him in a new way.

It was the first picture she had ever taken of her father. Ever.

After the soup pot was emptied, Papi thanked their hosts for the evening. It was finally time to get some rest. As Abby got up to go, Bela insisted that she go inside her kitchen to help Barana with the dishes.

"I'll send her over to your cabin when they're done," Bela said. "She can meet Pitufo. Our little mono."

A pet monkey!

"See you in a little bit," Papi said. He kissed Abby on the forehead and walked toward their cabin. There really was no arguing with Bela. She was the boss.

"See you soon," Abby said.

Inside the kitchen, the girls quietly dried the bowls as Pitufo perched himself on Abby's shoulder. "He's so cute," she said. The pet monkey was adorable. He had a permanent grin on his face and big, bold eyes that begged to be photographed.

"Mind if I give him to you for a second? I want to take his picture. Maybe with Bela too?" How far she'd already come since arriving in Honduras. The awkward anticipation of asking people for a photo was shifting into a new feeling, creative instinct taking over.

Barana took Pitufo and called her abuela over. "Bela, la Americana quiere una foto," she said.

Bela walked over from the kitchen table and took Pitufo and held him in her arms.

"Say cheese!" Abby said.

As she looked through the camera, it was as if time was frozen in place. She felt safe. She could frame the world exactly as she wanted it. She focused the shot on Pitufo's eyes.

Zoom. Closer. Perfect!

Tap, tap, click.

"I love animals. Thanks, Bela," Abby said as she placed her camera on the counter.

"Of course, niña. You are our guests! I hope you take many beautiful photos while you are here."

"¡Muchísimas! Lots and lots!" Abby beamed. By the end of their trip, she hoped her new camera would feel like an old friend. And that her pictures would prove she could take risks.

"Barana can take you to the beach tomorrow after school—right, Barana?" Bela looked over at her granddaughter as she dried the last of the soup bowls. "Barana, why the long face?"

Abby hadn't noticed, but Bela was right. Barana looked like she'd seen a ghost.

"Nothing. It's just . . . I overheard Papá is going on the boat with the doctor tomorrow. He wants to learn the lobster trade. Is that true, Bela?"

"Sí, mija. Times are tough, with your mother's shop still closed. He'll just need to be careful and disciplined."

"I can't believe Mamá is letting him."

"Has he ever done it before?" Abby asked.

"No, never. He's always been a fisherman and helped Bela and my mother with their businesses when he wasn't out on the water."

Abby thought of her own abuelo and the fact that she'd never met him. Anytime Papi went diving, she worried he'd suffer the same fate as his own father. She dropped a cup, and it clattered loudly on the floor.

"Are you okay?" Barana asked.

"Yeah, I'm fine," Abby replied. "I was thinking about my grandfather. He was a fisherman too. I never met him. My father wants to help divers be safe because of him. He swore that he'd work to help make the conditions for fishermen and lobster divers better."

"Did your father grow up here?" Barana asked.

"Until he was six. Then he moved to the city. And then to the States, with his mother. But she died too, right before he graduated from medical school." Why was she sharing so much with this stranger?

"Sorry you never met them."

"It's okay. Anyway, I should probably get going. Looks like we're done with the dishes."

"Buenas noches," Bela said. "Barana, please walk her over."

Abby tried not to think about the grandparents she never had as Barana escorted her across the half acre of palms and flowers that led to the casita.

"Buenas noches," Barana said, and she disappeared into the darkness.

Papi was reading in bed when Abby walked in. The room had two twin beds—one on each end—with a small table between them. The beds each had a mosquito net cover, and the crisp white sheets looked fresh. The floor was made of rustic wood and had woven petate rugs all around, giving the room a funky vibe. The cabin was simple and cozy.

"What do you think of this place?" Papi asked.

"It's different," Abby said.

"In a good way?"

She nodded. "I think I love it here."

"You won't find friendlier people anywhere," he said.

Abby smiled. She sat on her bed and looked through the photos on her digital display.

"Papi, where is Abuelo buried?"

"Buried? What made you think of *that*?"

"I don't know. Barana took me to the cemetery. There was a gravestone with the name 'R. Durón' on it."

"Must be a distant relative. I told you once my mother wanted their ashes scattered. Besides, I'm sure there are lots of Duróns in Honduras."

Abby sensed something different in his voice but couldn't quite place what it was.

She was too tired to probe.

"Where's the bathroom?"

"Just around back. There's a solar-powered motion detector light. Want me to go with you?"

"No, that's okay."

"Hope you're okay with no hot water," he said. "At least there's *running* water now. Took the government decades to get that set up here."

"Cold water is perfect in this weather," Abby said.

The outside bathroom and lack of a water heater were the least of her concerns. At dinner, Abby had overheard the adults talking about power outages and recent issues with the internet at the community center. Plus, who knew how dangerous these poachers were? Mom would flip out if she knew about them.

But none of that mattered. She loved being in Pataya. She'd perfect her wildlife photography skills. She'd incorporate portraits and prove to Ms. Tenley that she could take risks too. She'd take her most beautiful photos yet.

She grabbed her toiletry kit and made her way toward the door.

It was quiet in Pataya. No car noises. No sirens. No trains. Just nature. It would take some getting used to. The crickets and bullfrogs had started their chorus when Abby stepped outside to wash up. The crashing waves roared in the distance. The moon was directly above her and shimmered in a way that was almost magical. It was the clearest night and brightest moon she'd ever seen.

Abby brushed her teeth and washed her face underneath its safe and soothing light.

PAPI WAS SNORING when she entered the room. He'd left one small bedside lamp on. Its dim light guided Abby toward her bed. When she finally lay down and hugged her pillow, something firm pushed up against her hand. It was an object about the size of a walnut.

It was a small totem.

She inspected the object carefully, holding it in the palm of her hand. The wood was the color of honey. The little figure was a perfectly carved leatherback sea turtle, and a crescent moon had been whittled along its back. Its flippers were smooth and symmetrical, and its head was slightly rounded at the beak.

She held the sea turtle in her palm, lay back down, and closed her eyes.

She thought about Barana's story, and about María and the poacher problem. She remembered the leatherback eggs stolen from their home. She had the sudden urge to see one of these prehistoric creatures for herself. Maybe even photograph one.

Her finger glided down the little charm's back, following the moon shape back and forth and back again. Its surface was warm to the touch, and the longer Abby held it, the warmer it seemed to get. The charm had an unexplainable energy that she couldn't ignore. When Abby opened her eyes, the moon on its back seemed to glow . . . it was shimmering. The totem's warmth and light intensified as she held it between her palms.

Who had placed it under her pillow, and why?

CHAPTER 13

Barana

Barana tossed and turned in bed, unable to shake the feeling that the man hiding in the trees had something to do with poaching Luna's nest. Few people fished in the evenings, and who would go for a sunset swim after María's announcement?

It had been a week since she had seen Luna come ashore, and there was a chance she would soon be back to lay another clutch. Barana focused on her scar, willing it to tingle and tell her Luna was nearby, but nothing happened. No tingle. No burn. Nada.

Still, the urge to keep checking the beach was irresistible.

Tulu had asked to spend the night at Jason's. Perfecto. With Tulu away, sneaking out to la playa would be a breeze. Her parents were tired from the long week of cleaning and rebuilding, not to mention the busy day they'd had helping Bela get ready for the visitors and then socializing with them. They'd probably sleep right through Barana's excursion.

The trouble was what to do once she got out there, where dangerous ladrones lurked about. She needed a plan for how to react if she saw them. Or worse, if *they* saw *her*. Run? Scream? Hide? Confront them?

She imagined the mystery man digging away at fresh egg chambers, stealing what was never his, disrespecting the mothers who had made the long and difficult journey to Pataya from across the seas. The leatherbacks swam thousands of miles each year, only to return to their place of birth. Their precious eggs were not his for the taking. They were not his for the selling. They were not there to be eaten by people who considered them a "delicacy."

What made him think he could snatch them right out of the ground?

Her scar throbbed for the first time that night. She was filled with rage, and the pain was blistering. She had to go out and try to beat the poachers at their own game.

La playa was several kilometers long; there was a chance she'd never even run into them. All she cared about was protecting her turtles. Protecting Luna.

If she found a fresh nest or a nesting leatherback before they did, she could camouflage all evidence of the clutch and prevent them from finding it. It was risky, but she knew the beach by heart, and her legs could outrun almost anyone. Except Tulu.

Vamos. It's now or never.

Barana snuck outside. This time, she threaded her way

slowly through the palms, stopping every few feet to make sure nobody was around. A chill went up her spine, as if danger lurked in the darkness. But she pushed through. By now her scar was throbbing.

Inhala, exhala.

She walked west, past the gravestones, to an ancient gumbo-limbo tree that would provide cover if she needed it. The waves were gentle, and the breeze cooled her nerves, disentangling the anger crunched up in her chest.

The reflection of the quarter moon shone over the water. She squinted to check for turtle tracks and looked out as far as she could for anything that resembled a baula.

Nada. Just an empty beach. She waited.

Her eyes got heavy, and she leaned back on a piece of driftwood, rubbing them. She was on the verge of heading home when, out of nowhere, two faint lights appeared in the exact direction she needed to walk. She thought fast. If those were the poachers, hiding was step one. Identifying them was step two. She looked for a place to hide.

The lights got closer, but the men were still too far off for her to see their faces. She was almost sure that one of the men was the same one she and Abby had seen in the shadows earlier. He wore a backward cap and had the same slouchy posture. He was tall. The shorter man carried a bag. They were still too far away!

They pointed their flashlights at the ground, making

their faces completely unidentifiable. Clouds hid the moon now, making it even more difficult to see.

Barana stayed behind the tree, her knees shaking and her lungs ripping through her skin. And then, as if things couldn't get worse, one of the men turned off his light and disappeared. Where had he gone? Had he seen her somehow? Impossible. She hadn't moved an inch and they were still far away.

The light came back on farther down the beach, and the shorter man pulled a small motorboat into the water. They'd left it perched high above the tide line. She squinted to see it, to make out its markings or color, but it was too dark and the boat was too far away. Everything looked black. Nothing but silhouettes.

The men pushed the boat into the water and vanished beyond the waves.

Barana wanted to follow its wake, to see if they went inland toward the canal or out toward the ocean, away from Pataya, but the impulse to run home took over. Her scar was cold, and her palms felt like ice. She'd seen her enemy and was no closer to an answer. She ran as fast as her legs could take her.

WHEN BARANA FINALLY reached her house, she felt queasy, and her chest was pounding. She stopped to catch her breath and wipe the sweat off her brow. The sky above twinkled, and the safety of her favorite palms swayed above her. She was okay.

She leaned against the stair rail, panting and dizzy.

Then the front door creaked open, and Papá stepped outside. Glaring icily, he motioned for her to come up the stairs. He'd only ever spanked her once, but he'd had that same look on his face that day. As she faced him on their porch, he said, "We keep this between us. The storm has been enough to deal with."

"Papá, lo siento."

"Cállate y escúchame." He raised a hand. "This little obsession of yours with the baulas stops *now*. Focus on school, help Mamá with Marisol. That's it." He got his temper under control and shook his head. "Por Dios santo, Barana."

When Papá said "for God's sake," that was it. Barana knew she was in trouble.

There would be no reasoning with him tonight—or ever—about protecting the leatherbacks. No talk about poachers or right and wrong. There would be no listening to her side of the story. She'd get the silent treatment for a few days too. There was no way to make him understand how much this meant to her. Even if she knew how to explain it, he wouldn't listen.

"I do help Mamá." It was all Barana could say to defend herself. Her throat was stuck, and her scar throbbed again.

"Nah. Every chance you get, te escapas a la playa. See some turtle. Hide some nest."

He didn't get it. He was too busy working or watching fútbol with Tulu to care. Besides, he wasn't entirely wrong. Any chance she had to be at the beach, she took. Why was that so terrible? It was because her needs always came last in her family. Behind Tulu, behind Marisol, behind her parents' work.

She was the odd one out, and now she was also the one in deep trouble.

Papá mumbled something under his breath, and she only managed to catch the last part.

"What matters more, eh? ¿Nosotros o las tortugas?"

There was only one answer he would accept, and Barana wasn't sure she could say it.

Her heart was torn.

Before she could reply, he opened the door and motioned for her to enter.

"Don't ever do this again, Barana."

When he disappeared into his room, Barana realized her scar was still ice-cold, and she didn't know how to will the pain away. For now, sleep was the only solution she could think of.

Feeling around her room in the darkness, she reached under her pillow for the T-shirt she liked to sleep in. When she lifted it, something fell onto the mattress, startling her. It was glowing. She picked it up and tried to make out what it was.

A figurine. A turtle.

It was wooden, and the details were carved delicately into its shape. She rubbed its carapace, flippers, and head. Along its back were the familiar ridges of a leatherback. As she moved her fingers down, she made out an odd shape etched in the wood, right where the faint glow was coming from.

She stroked it with her index finger and realized what it was. It was a crescent moon. Just like hers. And just like the one on Luna.

The burning in her scar completely went away as she held it.

It was a sign.

It was hope.

The totem confirmed what she already knew: the sea turtles were her purpose. Even if her family demanded otherwise. Even if they didn't understand. She held the wooden turtle between her palms. It got warmer and warmer the longer she held it. She lifted her hand to see it in the darkness. She couldn't believe it. The moon on its back glowed with an even brighter silvery light.

The magic was undeniable. It had been placed there for a reason.

She was on the right track.

And she would stop at nothing to protect Luna and her babies.

CHAPTER 14

Abby

It was a good thing she'd gone to bed early. Papi woke her up before sunrise, for the second day in a row, so they could go to Bela's for breakfast, and Abby was not pleased. She'd slept nine hours, but waking up at six-thirty was *not* her idea of a vacation.

"Is this normal?" She rinsed her teeth with the bottled water Bela had left for them by the outdoor sink. She wiped her face off with a small towel. "Seriously, who has breakfast at this time on a weekday? The sun's not even up!"

"Camarón que se duerme se lo lleva la corriente. That's the motto here. You sleep in, the current takes you away like a shrimp. Besides, you slept plenty. Come on, we need to get a move on. You've got a boat to catch."

"Well, I'm not going to school the rest of the week. I'll go today, 'cause I'm up and you have a busy day. Seriously, Papi,

I'm on summer break. I've got photos to take and books to read and major relaxing to do." Maybe Papi should've been clearer about this whole school thing, because there was no way she was spending the entire week rising at the crack of dawn for class.

"It'll be a great cultural exchange opportunity," he said, ruffling her bangs. "You'll get to immerse yourself in the local life."

Couldn't she immerse herself in the local life *after* 10 a.m.?

They walked across the garden to Bela's main house. She'd prepared eggs and refried beans, with a side of papaya all cut up and arranged beautifully on the plate. The papaya was sweet. Not too firm and not too soft. Abby squeezed a little lime juice over it. Papaya ceviche.

She double-checked her backpack to make sure she had everything she needed, especially her camera. Inside the front pouch, the mysterious little sea turtle charm glowed. The moon on its back gave off a silvery glint, and she couldn't help but wonder once again how it had ended up under her pillow.

"You sleep well, child?" Bela asked as she poured water into her cup.

"Sí, gracias, muy bien." Abby had slept like a baby.

"Well, good. Eat up, and you let me know if Barana isn't an attentive host today, okay?"

"Sí, señora."

"Call me Bela." Her eyes sparkled.

Abby smiled. She offered to rinse the plates again, but

Bela insisted they get going. They each had a boat to catch. Papi would be heading out on the dive boat, and Abby would be on a boat to school.

"Will I have internet at some point today? I want to email Mom." A week ago she might've also wanted to reach out to Fiana, but that email would have to wait. Abby wasn't sure what she wanted to say to her friend just yet.

"It was working fine yesterday. We'll check out the community center this afternoon, and I'll get you logged on." He held her hand as they walked. The sun was barely poking above the tree line, and the salty air was already sticking to Abby's skin.

Abby thought she and Barana would walk together, but she hadn't seen her on the way out of Bela's. As she and Papi walked farther down the camino, a small, one-room building caught her eye. There was a faded turtle mural on one wall and a barely visible sign that said, CENTRO DE CONSERVACIÓN DE TORTUGAS MARINAS DE PATAYA. Abby figured whoever worked there might also be trying to stop the poachers, like Barana.

Tap, tap, click.

She took a picture of the weathered building. Dawn's light had an eerie effect on the photo, reminding Abby of ancient ruins. She'd have to remember to take another one in broad daylight.

Some people were already up and working outside their homes. A few villagers even waved at Papi like they knew him, saying "Buenos días, Doctor!" as they passed by.

Papi walked differently here. Prouder and taller. Like he belonged.

Abby didn't know where she belonged.

Tap, tap, click.

She snapped a photo of her father's profile as he waved to an older gentleman who wore a big straw hat. The back side of Pataya—the southern edge—was quieter. The ocean sounds had faded away, and the lagoon was like a quiet mirror lined with small wooden docks of different lengths. Abby could see the canal that had brought them here from the airport, and there was another small canal on the opposite side of the lagoon that curved toward the ocean.

Barana was sitting on a bench underneath the palm-thatched structure at the end of the dock. Abby forced a smile. She might as well try to be nice. "Good morning," she said.

"Buenos días," Barana replied.

"Morning, and thank you for keeping Abby entertained today," Papi added.

"De nada, Doctor. I'll do my best," Barana said.

"What time will we be back?" Abby asked, hoping it wouldn't be too late.

"Una y media," Barana replied.

"Wait. *What?* One-thirty? Seriously? What time does school end?" Abby was confused by how early Barana said they'd be back.

"One," Barana said.

"Is it a half day?"

"No, that's just the schedule. Start early, end early."

Abby needed a minute to process this fact. What she wouldn't give to be done with school by one o'clock every day. To have an entire glorious afternoon for herself!

"You're so lucky," she said.

Barana raised her left eyebrow. "I'd prefer it if school started later, but I guess I'm used to waking up in the dark."

Abby wondered which was better. Wake up later and stay at school until three . . . or wake up early and get home early?

"The boat is coming," Barana said, pointing at a motor-boat that was approaching from beyond the lagoon. The pilot shifted into reverse as he eased toward the dock. The lancha sounded like it could use a new motor. It coughed like a sick smoker.

"Sit with me in the front. It's less noisy there," Barana said.

Abby nodded and watched as Papi waved and walked toward a group of men, including Barana's father. It was true. Barana's dad would be giving the lobster-diving thing a shot.

"Are you okay?" Abby said as they took their seats.

Barana shrugged indifferently. "Why do you ask?"

"You know—the diving? ¿Tu papá?" She pointed at the group of fishermen.

"Oh, that. It's fine. He says it will be good to learn the trade."

Abby could tell Barana's words didn't match how she felt. Her eyes expressed worry. Concern. Hesitation.

"My dad will take good care of him. He won't let anything bad happen to any of the divers. He's going to teach them how to set up special trap-like structures called casitas so they don't have to dive as much."

Barana nodded and smiled. "Gracias."

The boat sped down the river, and Abby held her backpack tightly against her belly. The turtle totem was getting warmer. It was as if there was a hot stone in the front pocket of her bag. But something about it made her feel calm and safe. Like a friend.

"Hey," she said, breaking the silence between her and her host, "did you tell your parents about the guy we saw last night?"

Barana shook her head.

"Do you think you will? Later maybe?"

"I don't think so. They don't care about the baulas. I don't think many people do right now."

"But *you* care. Maybe that's enough?"

Barana leaned in close to Abby's ear and whispered, "I snuck out last night. And Papá caught me when I got home."

"You *what*? Isn't that dangerous?"

"I wanted to catch them. Or maybe see Luna, my special leatherback, and hide her nest before the ladrones could find it."

Barana was more determined than Abby had thought. Abby had never snuck out of her house before, not once, and Ridge Park was one of the safest small towns in New Jersey.

She and Fiana had talked about sneaking out in the middle of the night to take pictures at the park, maybe get a photo of Foxy the red fox or other nocturnal animals out and about, but they'd always chickened out.

"What did your father say when you got home?"

"Estaba *furioso*."

Abby imagined so. Whose father wouldn't be furious? Just then, Tulu interrupted their conversation with a tap on Barana's shoulder. He and his friend had taken their seats on the boat behind her and Barana. Abby wondered if Tulu knew what his sister had done.

"Hermana, these are from Nati." He handed Barana two small bananas and mouthed, "Barana Ba-Na-Na" with a smirk. "Good morning, Abby," he said before turning around.

Barana stuck her tongue out at the back of his head but took the fruit anyway.

"I hate when he calls me Banana," she said, turning to Abby. "He used to call me that when we were younger. I would chase him with a banana and smoosh it on him whenever he did. Here, take one. They're from our captain, Nati, back there. He likes to keep us healthy. Says bananas are great for our growing minds and bodies."

Abby turned her head, and the pilot smiled at her. She peeled the banana and smiled back. She tried to picture what it would be like if the school bus drivers in Ridge Park handed out fruit to kids every day. It'd probably be illegal. Yet here she was, riding on a boat through mangrove forests in the middle of a tropical paradise, going to school. There was a magical wooden totem in her bag, and she'd met a girl who was just as obsessed with saving the turtles as Abby was with photography.

With two whole weeks left of her trip, she could hardly begin to imagine what else was in store.

CHAPTER 15

Barana

Maybe having Abby around wouldn't be as bad as Barana had thought. Abby's Spanish was better than she'd imagined, and during math she'd told the class about New York City and about her town in New Jersey, which everyone loved because it made them miss most of the lesson. It was worth having Abby hanging around if it meant missing math. Abby even asked the teacher if it was okay to take a picture or two. Barana noticed she'd been shy about it, so at recess, she made some introductions. By the end of the day, Abby was photographing everyone and everything.

After school they walked down the grass-lined path to catch the boat back home. The weather was hot but not unbearable, and Barana's scar hadn't hurt all day. Nati and Tulu talked about a recent soccer game while other high school students waited on the benches.

"Is your brother a senior?" Abby said. "He's even taller than the boat pilot."

"Yeah, he's very tall. He has one more year left, though."

"When my father left Pataya, there was no secondary school nearby," Abby said.

"That makes sense. Tulu's high school has only been around for about ten years. People donated money to build it. It's really good, because Tulu didn't have to leave Pataya to keep learning."

"Will he go to college?"

"No lo sé." Barana shrugged. *So many questions!* "Come on, let's get on the boat so we can get the best seats." She didn't like to think about what was next for Tulu. Even though he annoyed her to death, he was still her big brother. They'd always shared a room. He looked out for her. If he did leave for the university, she hoped he'd return every year, just like her leatherbacks did.

WHEN THEY GOT to Pataya, Abby asked if they could wait by the dock for the dive boat to return. She said she wanted to see the lobsters they'd caught and tell her father all about school. They sat under the palapa overlooking the shimmering lagoon.

While they waited, Barana reached in her bag and rubbed her turtle charm's moon. She'd brought it to school for good luck, and to remember her purpose. The small leatherback totem warmed up instantly. A few seconds later, her scar began to tingle.

Luna was nearby.

"Mind if we get going? I can show you the town and Mamá's pulpería. I want to ask her if we can take a walk on the beach. I have a feeling we might see Luna."

"You think so? But what about the divers?"

"They're usually gone all day. Some boats even go out for weeks at a time. Besides, the weather is perfect to be out on the water. We'll see them afterward. ¿Vamos?"

"Okay," Abby said. "Vamos."

The girls clambered up from the wooden boards of the dock. Barana quickly took off her shoes and socks and placed them in her bag. Barefoot was better. She led Abby up the path toward her mother's store, but she couldn't help looking over her shoulder to check for any signs of the dive boat one more time before they reached the bend.

The pulpería was almost ready to reopen. Mamá was busy cleaning, and the roof was almost done. Marisol was in her hand-me-down playpen, napping in the corner behind the register, and Chiqui of course was there, gossiping away the day.

Barana grabbed a bag of platanitos to share with Abby. "Mamá, can Abby and I take this and go to the beach?"

Abby smiled and held up her heavy-looking camera. "I want to take pictures, if that's okay."

Good. This whole tour-guide thing *would* work in Barana's favor.

"You can go if Tulu goes with you. He was supposed to come here after school anyway."

Tulu wasn't there, though, and Barana didn't want to wait.

"Where is he? I want to take Abby now, while there's still plenty of light, so we can get home early to do homework." There. That would help convince her mother. She was being responsible.

"Wasn't Tulu on the boat with you?" Mamá asked.

"Sí, but we stayed at the dock for almost half an hour. What's taking him so long?"

"No sé, mija. You know your brother. He's always got something going on. His projects and his fútbol. Espera unos minutos."

"I don't want to wait a few minutes. When he gets here, just tell him to meet us en la playa."

Mamá refused. She waved her index finger back and forth and said, "No, not with the threat of poachers looming. I don't want you out there alone, even in the middle of the day. It's too desolate. Too risky."

That's what Barana loved about her beach. How desolate and quiet it always was. Besides, nothing ever happened in broad daylight. The ladrones wouldn't dare steal a nest while fishermen were out on the water, in sight of the beach. She crinkled the bag of platanitos and put a few in her mouth, then stomped to the wooden bench outside Mamá's store. Abby sat with her, and they waited for Tulu.

Her moon scar was still prickling persistently when Tulu finally walked up with a large empty plastic bag in one hand and a soccer ball in the other.

"¡Por fin!" Barana said.

"What? I was over at Jason's, playing fut. Were you waiting for me for something?"

"Your sister wants to take our guest over to the beach. It's a nice day, so I told her they could go if you went with them and kept an eye out," Mamá said.

"¿En serio, Mamá?" Tulu said. "It's the middle of the afternoon. They can go alone."

"No. I need them home before sunset, and last time Barana was out there with Abby, they stayed out too late. Go with them. You can do your beach cleanup while you're at it."

Tulu's class had led beach cleanups since fourth grade, and her brother had never stopped. Barana respected that about him. Tulu dropped his pelota and kicked it toward the beach. "Fine. But I have homework, so we're not staying until sunset."

They darted through the palms, kicking and passing the ball as they wove around them. Abby seemed to enjoy running up the small hill toward the beach, but she hesitated to kick the ball with them at first. Finally, Barana got her to kick it a few times before they crested the hill and headed down toward the water. The sand was warm, and the ocean's sounds grew louder.

Barana even let Abby take pictures of them—because this time Abby asked.

They ran through the last row of dense palms and arrived at la playa. The Caribbean Sea was like medicine. Its effects were instant. Barana couldn't help but smile every time she stood before its magic and mystery.

Abby took pictures, and Tulu stayed behind to pick up the little piles of plastic junk that beckoned him.

Finally, Barana could look for Luna.

The tingling was different this time. It came in waves. Like the sea itself. Maybe that's what Luna was trying to tell her. She was still in the water but she'd come ashore tonight.

Barana stood in the surf calf-deep. Not deep enough for the waves to knock her down or get her uniform skirt wet, but deep enough that she felt closer to her special leatherback. It was a hot day, and the soft seawater was too good to resist. She could see the light brown sand beneath her toes. The water was crystal clear.

She took another step.

"Barana, mind if I take another picture of you?" Abby said.

Barana gave her a thumbs-up, like she knew Americans liked to do, and stepped deeper into the water. Her blue skirt got splashed, but she didn't care. She turned around to face Abby and motioned for her to snap a photo.

Abby waved her hands frantically, as if trying to warn her about something. Before Barana could turn around, a wave crashed into her back. She lost her balance just enough to fall face-first. She stumbled a few times from the jolt and got up, laughing uncontrollably. Abby came closer to the surf, and she burst into laughter too.

"Did you take pictures of that?" Barana said.

"I think so! Are you okay?"

It was a good thing she'd left her backpack on the beach—her notebook and totem were dry and safe. Standing where the waves broke, water to her knees, Barana realized she couldn't remember the last time she'd laughed like that, from deep in her belly.

"Barana . . . behind you," Abby whispered.

Barana turned. A few feet behind her, a leathery black head poked out from the waves, followed by an enormous body. The leatherback stood almost motionless next to Barana, unbothered by the surf swooshing up and down over her carapace.

"It's *her*."

Abby stared and pointed her camera at the leatherback. "She has a big scar on her back."

They watched as the baula pushed up the sand to find a spot for her next clutch of eggs. Tulu joined them with wide eyes. He lay his bag down at the top of the high-tide line, and they all watched as the sea turtle made her way up la playa. It was a slow but beautiful process.

"I've never seen one during the day," Tulu said.

"That's because it hardly ever happens!" Barana replied. Why had Luna come ashore in broad daylight? Did she know the night was no longer safe?

"Don't go any closer," Barana told Abby. "She's a wild animal, and we need to respect her space. I call this one Luna. She's my favorite."

"She's huge!" Abby said. "I can't believe she's out in the middle of the afternoon!"

The creature was humongous. She probably weighed twice as much as the three of them combined.

"I want to zoom in on the moon-shaped scar. I had no idea there were sea turtles like this, without a hard shell."

"Barana has the same moon-shaped scar on *her* back," Tulu said.

"You do?" Abby looked at Barana, her eyebrows high.

Barana nodded. "I do. Our scars are identical."

She hadn't shared the cuento with anyone in years, but something told her it was okay to share it with Abby. She explained how she'd been learning to swim with Mamá when it happened. "Mamá preferred to swim in the lagoon, but I loved the sea. I convinced her to take me to the beach. And that's where it happened. I went out where the waves crashed and was tumbled. Badly."

"When she fell, her back hit a sharp, broken conch shell sticking up from the sand," Tulu added. "It was the strangest coincidence."

"I bled pretty badly. My mom wrapped me in her towel to try to stop the bleeding. Later that same night, Luna came ashore. That was the first time I saw her."

It was like she and Luna had cried together that day. Barana had asked Mamá if Luna was crying because she was also hurt, and Mamá explained that Luna cried because she'd never get to see her hatchlings. That sea turtles left their eggs hidden in the sand, having to trust fate.

But Barana didn't tell Abby that part.

"Can I see it?" Abby asked.

"Maybe another day? When I'm wearing a bathing suit," Barana said.

"Totally. Makes sense." Abby's cheeks got red.

"Trust me, their scars are identical," Tulu said.

By the time Barana had finished her story, Luna was digging a body pit for herself before starting to dig the deeper chamber that would become her babies' sacred nest. They all sat a respectful distance away as her flippers scooped the sand again and again.

It always amazed Barana how the turtles got into a dreamlike state when they laid their eggs. The effort was so difficult there wasn't room for thinking about anything else. Their focus was otherworldly.

As Luna worked, a new poem hatched in Barana's heart:

A mind in sharp focus,
Like a photographer's camera.

What is she thinking
As tears fill her eyes?
Now is my time.
Pat, kick, dig.
A job must be done.
Lágrimas de protección.
Inhala, exhala.

Barana wanted to make sure they camouflaged Luna's nest before leaving. Leatherbacks did a decent job of hiding their own treasures, making false tracks instinctively, but with poachers out and Luna's other nest stolen, Barana didn't want to take any chances.

She told Tulu and Abby to grab palm fronds and erase all evidence on the sand. They helped smooth out the area around Luna's pit after she'd begun her slow descent back toward the water.

"Abby, take a picture of the exact spot where the eggs are buried. Get as much background as you can." She wanted the nest to be so hidden that even they would need a photo to locate it again. Abby pointed her camera at the site and snapped a photo.

"We need to go," her brother said. "This is good enough."

Barana looked at the sand around her and nodded. It wasn't perfect, but they'd done their best. The night would help hide the treasure even more.

Abby put her hand on Barana's shoulder as they watched Luna get closer to the waves. "Barana, I think I understand it now. Luna and the leatherbacks are worth fighting for."

Tulu stood a few feet behind them, his hands on his hips and the hint of a smile on his face.

"They've been here longer than we have. We have no right to take from them," Barana said, admiring Luna as she marched toward the sea. "Did you know that only about one in a thousand of the hatchlings will make it to adulthood?"

Abby shook her head. "The more hatchlings we can help make it to the ocean, the more mamas can return here years later to start the cycle again."

"Exactly!" Barana said, putting her hand on Abby's shoulder.

"I'll help you make sure this nest stays safe," Abby said. "Promise."

"The only way to do that is to catch those ladrones before it's too late." Barana crossed her arms and stared at the spot where Luna's clutch lay. She wanted to stay and guard the nest for seven weeks straight, to stay put, to make sure Luna's babies were safe. She'd even sleep out on the sand if she had to.

But that wasn't possible. She needed to believe they'd be okay on their own, like Luna believed they would.

Beyond the waves, the majestic leatherback finally disappeared, and so did the tingle of the moon on Barana's back.

She was certain Luna understood her promise: that she would keep the nest safe.

Still, something made her chest tighten.

Inhala, exhala.

She breathed.

"It's time to go," Tulu said.

CHAPTER 16

Abby

After Luna's rare and unexpected visit, Barana, Tulu, and Abby went back to Bela's and devoured a tray of baleadas. An early dinner. The soft bean-filled tortillas were Abby's second-favorite Honduran dish, after ceviche. When she was nine, Papi had taken her to the Bronx for lunch at his favorite Honduran restaurant. She'd loved the baleadas so much that she'd begged to go back the next month. And the next. Until it became a monthly tradition.

If the baleadas in New York City were five stars, Bela's were a solid six. Her flour tortillas were thicker and warmer, and the refried beans melted in Abby's mouth. Bela had even arranged sliced avocado all around the plate and decorated the edges with little pink flowers. But there was something else about them, something beyond taste and appearance. Bela had a way with food, and Abby wished she could somehow capture all the flavors in her photographs and keep them in her memory forever.

After savoring the baleadas, Abby suggested they go outside to wait for their fathers. She wanted to curl up inside one of the hammocks and take a nap. The late-afternoon heat and full belly had made her sleepy.

Abby and Barana sat on the hammock together and took turns pushing off the sand to rock it back and forth. Abby's eyes relaxed with the swaying. She wasn't sure how much time had passed when the muffled sounds of men's voices approached them, waking her from her afternoon siesta.

"They're back!" she said.

Barana was chewing her pencil nervously when Abby alerted her that the fishermen had arrived. She put the chewed-up pencil back in her tight bun and jumped out of the hamaca. The hammock was so large it swallowed Abby's body whole when Barana got out. Abby had to roll over and lean forward to finally get her body to defy gravity and cooperate.

She ran to catch up with her friend.

"Hola, niñas," Papi said. He set down his backpack and hugged Abby. He smelled like the ocean.

Barana's father put his hand on her shoulder and smiled. "Dr. Durón is a good teacher."

"Maybe one day you girls will learn to scuba dive too," Papi said.

"Yo? ¿Una *niña*?" Barana said.

Abby was also taken aback. She'd never heard her own father suggest she learn to dive.

"Por qué no?" Papi replied. "Anybody can learn to scuba dive."

Abby wondered if local women ever took up diving, or if it was something reserved for men.

"Barana, maybe one day we'll dive together. I could get an underwater camera and take pictures of you in the ocean with Luna!" Abby had never imagined herself scuba diving, but for some reason saying it out loud to Barana didn't feel scary. If she wanted to be a legitimate wildlife photographer, underwater pictures were a *must*. Learning to dive suddenly became . . . important.

Barana stared at her like she'd never considered the possibility, either.

"I think that sounds like something we can arrange one day," Papi said.

And just like that, Abby could imagine herself taking underwater pictures. It was a before-and-after moment. Before this moment, she'd not once considered underwater photography or scuba. After this moment, both became a possibility.

At the bottom of Bela's stairs, Barana asked her father what it had been like beneath the waves' surface. He explained that the new divers had to watch and learn about equipment safety before putting on a tank and diving.

"We laid out a few new casitas too," Barana's father said.

Papi nodded. "And you'll dive with the crew in a couple of days," he told him. "You did great today!"

Abby wasn't surprised. If anybody could teach someone to scuba dive well and to do it safely, it was Papi.

"Guess what we saw at the beach?" she said as they walked up the staircase.

"Crabs? A washed-up jellyfish? A giant conch?" Papi said.

"Nope! A leatherback sea turtle!" Abby beamed.

"Coneja, that's amazing! She came ashore during the day?"

Abby nodded. "Barana said it's super rare for that to happen."

"It is. I hope you took lots of pictures," he said, pushing the door to Bela's dining deck.

"Duh! Best moment of the trip so far! I need to email Mom and show her my pictures."

"Barana's father and I have a few things to discuss over dinner, but I can't wait to see the pictures too. We'll go to the center tomorrow. Did you eat already?"

"Yup. Bela made baleadas! They're even better than the ones back home!"

Papi rolled his eyes back in his head and licked his upper lip.

He and Barana's father went inside to eat and talk while Abby and Barana once again helped with dish duty. When they finished, Barana invited Abby to school again the next day. Papi insisted Abby take her up on the offer. In fact, he said his first few days of work in Pataya would be so busy that it would be a good idea for Abby to join her at least through the end of their first week.

The nerve!

Then Abby thought about it. She was starting to like Barana, and they could use the time together on the ride to school to talk about how to protect Luna's nest . . . and maybe plan a way to catch the poachers. After all, Barana was starting to feel like her first new friend in years. Though Barana had a one-track mind for the sea turtles, Abby respected her determination.

Abby didn't feel friendless anymore, and she was having the best time she'd had in a long time.

The weight of the camera bag over her shoulder reminded her of Ms. Tenley and the whole risk-taking business. Maybe her camera could help them record evidence and track down the poachers somehow.

She was more than just a "critter photographer." Maybe her pictures of Luna, the beach, and the people of Pataya could convince Ms. T that wildlife photography was not only about capturing photos of animals and nature—it was about showing connections. It was about conservation. It was about people *and* the planet.

Later that night, Papi lay in bed and asked for details about the leatherback sighting. Abby showed him a few pictures on her camera's display screen, but she left out the close-ups of Luna's scar. She'd keep that (and the whole poacher problem) between her and Barana.

"I remember seeing the baulas as a kid," Papi said.

"You do?"

"Just a couple of times, but I'll never forget looking at their eyes and seeing so much wisdom and magic!"

Abby scratched her head. Magic and wisdom in a sea turtle?

Papi nodded. "Tell me about school, and Bela's grand-daughter," Papi said.

"School was actually fine. And Barana's nice. I like her." It was true. Something about Barana was different. Special. She was brave. She'd snuck out in the middle of the night to spy on criminals. She cared about something important. She'd been nice, even when Abby had wanted to ditch her on the beach.

"Abby, you held a *monkey* last night. That was unexpected, no?"

"The cutest monkey!" Abby couldn't believe the last twenty-four hours. Manatees. Monkeys. Sea turtles. School in Spanish. What was next?

Papi put his book on the small table between their beds and turned off the lamp.

"Let's get some rest, Abs. The sun and sea wore me out, and we need to be up early again."

It was nice bonding with Papi in Pataya, talking before bed and stuff. Abby smiled to herself in the darkened room.

"Noches, Coneja. Love you."

"Love you too. Night, Papi."

Early to bed was easy when you had no screens to glare at and the sun had worn you out. Within seconds, her father was snoring.

Abby figured it wasn't just the sun and sea that had tired Papi out. He'd finished his first intense day with the divers too. She imagined that was also exhausting. Still, she could tell he was happy and comfortable in Pataya. And when you're comfortable, you relax and sleep better. After all, this was her father's first home. He was upbeat, his shoulders were relaxed, and he smiled at everyone. Back in Jersey, he worked all the time at the hospital, taught twice a week, and rose at the crack of dawn just so he could exercise.

Life in Pataya was different. Less noisy. Less distracting. Less rushed.

Their guest room smelled like coconut sunscreen and bug spray, and the hot Mosquitia air wrapped around her like a toasty hug. She was grateful for the mosquito net canopy that hung from the ceiling and over her bed. That morning, there'd been more than ten dead bugs stuck in its mesh, species of insects she'd never seen before—not just bloodthirsty mosquitoes. Though she couldn't see them in the darkness, she could hear them zipping all around her, trying to get a nibble off her skin. She tried to shake away the image of bugs surrounding her from all angles and reached under her pillow for the turtle totem. Thankfully, the bug spray and net were doing a fine job so far, and the fan provided just enough of a breeze to allow for sleep.

The mystical charm glowed brighter and stronger than before. Once again, its moon shimmered a silvery white, and its light was soothing. It reminded Abby of the seashell-shaped night-light she had in her bathroom back home. As she held the charm between her palms, its warmth intensified. She tried to make sense of it. Who had carved it and left it there for her to find?

Whoever it was, they possessed some kind of magic.

Papi always said that some things in life were without explanation, that some things were simply meant to be.

Maybe her meeting Barana was one of those things.

AT DAWN THE next morning, Abby and Barana sat on the second bench from the left as they waited for the rest of the kids to board the school boat. When they sped off, Abby pulled her camera out and took a picture of its wake, with Pataya in the background. It was a warm Tuesday morning, and she was determined not only to have a positive attitude but to intentionally document the rest of her trip with Ms. Tenley's advice in mind. She had dozens of pictures to sort through and edit already. And she wanted more. She wanted to leave Pataya a better photographer than when she arrived.

"I still can't believe I saw Luna," Abby said.

"It was a sign. You were meant to see her."

"You believe in that stuff? That things are meant to be?" Abby said.

Barana smiled. "Of course. I believe we all have a special purpose. Sometimes I think I believe in magic too."

Abby reached in the front pocket of her bag and grabbed her turtle totem. She tried to put together the series of events that had brought her to that moment: on a school boat, next to a kid with a special connection to the leatherbacks.

A week ago, she'd been home in New Jersey, stressing over her photography project and angry at the world for her miserable life. Now she was in a tropical paradise, surprisingly happy to be joining a girl exactly her same age to go to school in the village where her father was born.

She kept her hand in the bag and stroked the moon on the charm's back. There was no denying it. The object warmed up immediately. Did she believe in that stuff too? Life had been so magic-less and crummy last year that she couldn't be sure.

"What do you have in there?" Barana asked. She leaned over to peek inside Abby's bag.

Abby panicked. She wasn't ready to show the totem to anyone. Besides, what if it belonged to Barana? After all, she had found it on her grandparents' property, and the girl was obsessed with sea turtles. It wasn't out of the realm of possibility that it was hers.

Abby didn't want to part with it.

"Nothing." She reached deeper into the backpack pocket and pulled out the first thing she could find that wasn't the totem. A crumpled piece of paper would be a good distraction. It was the one Ms. T had given her about the exhibition. "It's this photography competition my teacher said I could enter." Abby reread the information about the exhibit and for a split second considered participating.

"You should! You love your photographs like I love my drawings. Maybe you can win!"

Abby nodded and smiled. She carefully folded the paper and placed it back inside the pouch. That was a close one. And no, she was not going to participate in the photo competition.

The crystalline water shimmered as they made their way to school. Being on the boat, riding through estuaries and breathing in the warm, salty air, felt right. She spotted a group of black howler monkeys in the canopy above. She adjusted her camera and cleared her mind. Time to capture La Mosquitia's beauty.

Tap, tap, click.

They were too far away to see clearly, but she zoomed in and took several photos of them anyway.

Focus.

Channel your inner wildlife photographer. Frame the photo. Look for the best lighting.

Tap, tap, click.

Barana showed her a spot where the boat had once stopped to see a pod of dolphins.

"Seriously? Dolphins on your way to school? This place is wild in the best way possible! I've seen more amazing animals in a couple of days than I have all year." Honduras was a wonder. And Abby was beginning to understand why La Mosquitia was worth protecting.

"What do you want to do about Luna's nest?" Abby asked. She had to stop taking pictures as the boat sped up and bounced around.

"Keep it safe. Protect the eggs. . . . Will you help me?" Barana whispered.

Abby nodded. She wanted to help, but she didn't know how. Without nightly beach patrols or eyes on Luna's nest at all times, there was no way to make sure it was safe. "¿Qué hacemos?" she said.

"I'm not sure, but there has to be a way to stop them."

"Why don't we start by writing down what we know?" Abby opened her bag and realized she didn't have pencil or paper. She wasn't exactly the best detective, but she was willing to give it a try for her new friend. And for Luna.

Barana reached into her bag and pulled out her journal. As she flipped through its pages, Abby could see that it was filled with scribbles and sketches of turtles. There was some writing too, and from the way the lines moved down the page, Abby could tell it was poetry.

Barana pulled a small chewed-up pencil from inside her bun. On a clean page, she wrote:

CLUES

Two men

Tall one wears a baseball cap and carried a bag

They have a boat

Might've come from far away? Islanders?

Barana handed the notebook and pencil to Abby. "¿Qué más?" she said.

Abby tapped the pencil on her chin. They didn't know much more than that. She paused and then added:

María = eyewitness

"We should talk to her," Abby said.

Barana shook her head. "She's *really* pregnant." She put her hands out in front of her stomach to show how big María's belly was. "She hasn't been to the turtle office in days. I'm not sure she can help."

Abby wondered if it was the same pregnant woman from her first day in Pataya.

"But she *saw* the poachers! They threatened her. If we can get her to tell us more about them, we can go to the police and at least give them a physical description. Besides, why aren't the police getting involved? Shouldn't they be patrolling the beach?"

"The police are useless. They don't care about the sea turtles, or the environment. Trust me."

"Well, still, María might know more than you think, and maybe she'd like to know about yesterday's nest too."

Barana exhaled loudly and closed her journal. She tucked it in her bag and put the small dented pencil back in her hair. "Okay, fine. Let's go see María. Even one clue from her could be helpful. But let *me* do the talking. And if her husband is home, we are not staying. No me cae bien."

"Why don't you like him?"

"He's just grumpy. He got pretty sick from diving last year and hasn't been the same since."

It *was* the same pregnant woman, then. Her husband had had the bends, and he'd definitely seemed a little grouchy. "I think I met both of them the first day I arrived."

"They live right up from the big lagoon dock."

"Yes! That's them! I feel bad for that family. Seriously. The bends are no fun. But that's why my dad's here, to make sure the cases continue to go down until there are none."

"I'm glad he's here, especially now that Papá is joining them," Barana said.

"Nothing will happen to him. Papi's an expert. I just wish he could've helped María's husband in time. He said that the reason so many divers get the bends is because the faster they can come up, the faster they can go back down for more lobsters. And that means they can make more money." Yet many were still willing to risk unbearable pain, paralysis, and even death. . . . Or perhaps they'd never known they had a different choice.

"It's been hard for him and María. It could've been worse, though. At least Matías can still walk. A few local divers haven't been as lucky," Barana said.

Abby couldn't imagine the pain. The bends were not something she wished on anybody. Not even Mean Monique. Or Thomas McDowell, the ceviche hater.

"We'll talk to María after school. But we must go check on Luna's nest immediately after," Barana said.

"Perfecto." Abby liked that they had a plan. First, interrogate María. Second, go check on Luna's nest.

Everything was coming into focus.

CHAPTER 17

Barana

Barana couldn't wait for school to be over so they could visit María and then bolt to the beach to check on Luna's nest. She chewed her pencil nervously and thought about her sea turtle during every single lesson until the recess bell finally rang and they could go outside to the courtyard.

While Abby took pictures, Barana drew Ping-Pong-shaped leatherback eggs, shading each one and adding a tiny moon on their shells, like little stamps. As she shaded one of the moons, a poem came to her:

> *From different worlds,*
> *Friends seeking truth.*
> *Guided by the magic of a totem.*
> *Its golden glow—hope.*
> *Chasing shadows of la luna.*

Mama turtle knows . . .
The answers are within.

Her scar suddenly burned. It was bearable but enough to make her worry about Luna and her nest. Abby joined her on the bench and showed her the pictures she'd captured of the colorful school courtyard: kids pushing each other on swings and playing landa and chiminicuarta, and quiet moments of friendship over hopscotch. Barana had never given her schoolyard much thought, but Abby's pictures helped her see that her school was beautiful in its own way.

After recess, the pain in her moon scar grew stronger. Mamá wanted her to check in at the pulpería after school, and she prayed that it wasn't a ploy to have her babysit Marisol. That would ruin everything. Her pencil was almost chewed to the core when the last bell rang. She grabbed Abby by the hand, and they ran to the dock.

They were the first to board Nati's boat. Barana's scar continued to remind her that something wasn't right.

The rest of the students got on, and the engine revved. *Finally.*

"Nati needs to give the motor a checkup. Sounds like my uncle Charlie in Michigan. He smokes a pack a day," Abby said.

It was true. The lancha was in desperate need of a tune-up.

As they rode the winding river back to Pataya's lagoon, Barana wished she could go to the beach first, but it made no sense. María's house was right up the hill from the dock.

She'd stick to the original plan: ask María only the important questions and get out of there as fast as possible. They needed a lead, some useful bit of information to guide them in the right direction. Someone was behind the crime, and Barana was determined to find out who that was.

Inhala, exhala.

"Mamá wants you to check in at the store right after school. No se te olvide," Tulu said from behind her.

"I won't forget. But I'm going to visit María first. Can you let Mamá know?"

"I can't. I have a game."

There he went again. Free as a bird. Able to go off with Jason and their cousins and roam on his own, play soccer, and do whatever else he pleased. She was only three years younger than Tulu, but everyone acted like he was a grown-up and she was still eight.

She didn't want to stop by the store at all. Maybe she wouldn't. Maybe she'd skip it in protest. She didn't have time to get stuck watching baby Marisol. Not today.

She winced—the scar was burning again.

Nati slowed the boat down and maneuvered it toward the dock. Tulu and Jason jumped out first, helping the pilot secure the boat to the posts. They ran off with their soccer ball and disappeared beyond the bend.

"Vámonos. María's house is this way." She led Abby up the hill, her back throbbing. She knew they had to hurry.

Everything was quiet at María's. Drips of water fell from

the laundry that was hung on neat wires in their yard. They walked up the wooden steps, and Barana knocked. María opened the door. Her long dark hair flowed over her narrow shoulders, and she wore a tight orange T-shirt that made her belly look like a plump naranja.

"Hola, niñas," she said, pulling her hair into a low ponytail.

Her mutt ran and jumped straight into Abby's arms.

"Hey, little guy! You must remember me." Abby looked up at María. "Thank you again for letting me take your portrait the other day."

María nodded as her two kids poked their heads out of the door and asked if they could play outside. She shooed them down the stairs toward the yard and instructed them to stay within her sight. She closed the door behind her and stepped outside, holding her hips and slowly sitting on a stool in the corner of her porch. She wiped her hands on her skirt, leaving a dusting of flour on it. She must've been preparing tortillas.

"What brings you two here?" she said.

Barana cleared her throat. "We wanted to ask a few questions about the night you saw the poachers."

María's face changed. She looked both scared and sad, like she'd seen the ghost of someone she loved. Her jaw clenched, and her big brown eyes got watery. "Not much I can say. They had weapons. Guns, they claimed. They said they'd hurt us if we were out patrolling the beach. They said the eggs were theirs until the season was over."

She shook her head and looked at her feet. Her heels were

peeled and cracked, and the red nail polish on her toes was mostly chipped off. She seemed to prefer being barefoot, just like Barana did. Barana wondered if her feet would one day look like that, all dried up and cracked like a desert.

"But did you see their faces? Or which way they went?" Barana asked.

"No. They hid their faces with pañuelos. But they definitely went north, away from Pataya."

Of course they had covered their faces with handkerchiefs. That's why María hadn't recognized them. So far, this visit was providing zero new clues.

"Did you go to the police?" Abby blurted out.

Barana rolled her eyes. There she went with the policía again.

"La policía here won't be of any help," María said. "They're probably in on it and taking a cut of the profits for themselves."

It was true. The chepos were known for being dishonest. Tulu once said they took money from criminals in exchange for keeping quiet.

"How many ladrones were there?" Barana asked. At least a number would help. She wanted to know if the two men she'd seen in the distance were the same ones who had confronted María, or if there were more than two.

"Dos. There might've been a third man in the boat, but I was too scared and can't remember clearly. Matías and I ran off as soon as they let us go."

"I'm so sorry that happened. It sounds so scary. How can we help?" Abby said.

"There's nothing you can do. Our village is too small and remote to get the support we need." She got up and rubbed her belly, looking out toward the lagoon. "Same thing happened to the ones protecting the scarlet macaws farther inland. Nobody's helped them stop the illegal trafficking."

Barana was getting impatient, but María was speaking from the heart, and she didn't want to be rude.

"Conservationists have been hurt before. Barana knows that about our country. We're blessed with nature and wildlife that others only dream of, but we're also cursed because of it."

María was right. Even the name of Barana's school, Escuela Berta Cáceres, was a constant reminder of that fact. Cáceres had been one of those environmentalists María was referring to—a protector of water and indigenous lands. Her outspoken opposition to hydroelectric dams had gotten her killed.

"Protecting the environment comes with a price tag here. Sometimes that price is your life. You need to promise me you'll stay away from la playa," María said.

"But all those eggs. The hatchlings. Thousands of them. This beach belongs to the turtles, not the ladrones. There has to be something we can do." Barana paced the porch. She was ready to go. The scar on her back was screaming at her.

"Look at me, Barana." María turned and stood in front of her. She reached out both her hands and held Barana's. They were ice-cold. "I'm about to become a mother again. I can't take this on. And you shouldn't, either. We must wait. The nesting season will be over in a month. We can plan for next year after that, when our beach is safe again."

Barana disagreed. Even the weekend felt too far away. She needed to protect Luna's nest *this* season. Now.

She reached for the turtle totem in her pocket as a reminder that there was still magic and goodness in the world. She stroked the wooden charm and the etched moon on its back.

Inhala, exhala.

Abby placed her hand on Barana's shoulder and smiled encouragingly.

The totem got warmer. It kept Barana from giving up. Its magic reminded her of her purpose: to protect Luna and the beach, no matter the cost. She held the charm and breathed. Though her scar still burned, at least she had air in her lungs again.

"What about the people on the islands—the ones who protect sea turtles there? Didn't they deal with poachers a few years ago on Roatán and the Cayos Cochinos? Maybe they could help." Barana remembered what Nati had said at church after María's announcement. She wondered if María knew what had happened to those criminals, if they'd been caught or if they'd left the islands and gone looking for other turtle nests. Somewhere like Pataya.

María held her belly and winced, pursing her lips tightly. Was she having a contraction? Finally, her face relaxed, and she exhaled. "Their names might be in a file at the office. But I can't take you there today. Too much to do as it is. Barana, to be honest, I don't think they'll be able to do anything."

The situation was growing more hopeless with each passing minute.

Inhala, exhala.

Her scar throbbed. It was time. Luna was calling, and it wasn't good news.

Barana and Abby thanked María and ran down the steps toward the sandy, grass-lined path. They'd gotten nothing more than a confirmation of danger looming over her beloved beach. If María had given up, the chances of reviving the project before the season ended were slim. For a split second while María spoke, Barana had considered calling it quits too. But she couldn't. The turtles needed her. The warm totem in her pocket was a reminder of that. There had to be a way to stop the poachers before it was too late.

THE FIVE MINUTES Barana had intended to stay at María's had become twenty. As they rounded the bend near her mother's store, she stopped in the middle of the camino. "Espera." She put her arm out to keep Abby from taking another step.

"What are you doing?" Abby said.

"We'll take a shortcut to the beach."

"What about checking in with your mom after school?"

"No importa. I'll tell her you needed me to escort you home first. I need to get to Luna's nest. We'll cut across to the conservation office and go to the beach from there. Mamá will have to wait."

They ran uphill through a dense patch of banana trees, arriving at the turtle office just as they crested the top. Tulu was standing outside, and he wasn't alone. But Barana didn't recognize the young man he was talking to. Tulu held something out, which the stranger then put in his pocket. They shook hands. His friend got on a bike and disappeared down the path. Her brother then started walking toward their house. He didn't see Barana and Abby coming from the other direction.

"¡Tulu!" Barana yelled. "¿Qué estabas haciendo?"

He ignored her and kept walking. Barana ran after him, leaving Abby behind. "¡Espérame! ¿Hermano, quién era ese chavo?" Though her scar was still throbbing, seeing Tulu outside the office piqued her curiosity. She slowed to listen and catch her breath.

"Nada. It's private. Don't be so nosy, metiche. And why

aren't you helping Mamá with Marisol? Have you even gone to the store?"

"Never mind that. I'm going to the beach to check Luna's nest first. Why were you outside the office? What did you give that guy?"

"Te dije, nada. I didn't give him anything."

Other than the two times she'd snuck out to the beach, Barana had never kept anything from her brother. She always assumed he'd never kept anything from her, either.

Out of breath, Abby caught up with them. "What's going on?" she said. "I thought we had to get to the beach right away."

"You're taking your friend to the beach and haven't even gone to Mamá?" Tulu said. "Classic."

Barana's scar turned ice-cold. There was no time to explain things to Tulu.

She turned on her heel and ran to the beach, faster than a jaguar, leaving both Tulu and Abby behind. She didn't care if they joined her or not. She didn't care if her mother grounded her forever and forced her to wash her sister's diapers. All she cared about was making sure Luna's baby turtles were okay. As she ran, the moon on her back told her what she didn't want to know: that they weren't okay at all.

When she got to the site of the nest, an empty hole surrounded by piles of sand had taken its place. A couple of cans and a few footprints completed the scene of the theft. Barana's chest heaved. She fell to her knees by the side of the open gash in the sand, tears streaming down into the spot where the turtle eggs once lay. It should have been impossible for the poachers to find them. They'd camouflaged the nest. It was hidden.

More tears fell into the empty chamber below. Her scar became numb.

A hand squeezed her shoulder gently. When she turned, Abby was standing behind her, looking just as shocked as Barana was.

"Oh, Barana," she said.

Tulu had followed Abby and stood a few feet behind her. He also shook his head in disbelief.

"I don't understand. We hid it perfectly," Barana said.

Tulu knelt next to his sister. He picked up a cigarette butt. "Looks like they were smoking."

"And they like soda," Abby said, grabbing a can.

Tulu took the can from Abby and put what was left of the cigarette inside it. Abby bent down too, and the three of them stared into the crevice, where just one day ago they'd witnessed the mystical cycle of life. Now before them lay nothing but an empty nest and empty dreams.

"How is this possible?" Tulu said.

Abby's face changed. She fixed her eyes on Tulu. "*You* tell us. *You* were the only other person who knew the nest even existed."

"Are you accusing me of poaching, gringa?"

"Maybe," Abby said. "Who was that stranger you were talking to just now? What'd you give him?"

Tulu scowled at her. "How dare you accuse me," he said.

"Basta. Los dos. Abby, Tulu would never get involved in a poaching scheme. Right, hermano?" Barana looked into her brother's deep brown eyes for an answer, but he turned and walked toward the water.

"Barana, was your brother home the night you snuck out and saw the men in the distance?"

Barana shook her head. Her scar burned. A warning. What was Tulu doing with that boy at the turtle office? What was he hiding?

Tulu *wasn't* home the night she snuck out and saw the poachers in the distance.

Tulu was tall.

Tulu had secrets.

No. Her brother would never.

"You said the thieves were too far away to identify, but one of them was tall. Look at him! Your brother is taller than most grown-ups around here. Think about it. There's no way anybody else could've found that nest."

Barana didn't want to believe that Abby had a point, or that her own blood would betray her in that way. "I don't think he would do it. Besides, the poachers might have secret ways we don't know about to help them find the nests. Like dogs that sniff out their location. I would've recognized my own brother, right?"

Even though she didn't want to consider her brother a

suspect, she tried to think back to that night and the shadow behind the palms. She remembered Tulu showing up late to Abby and the doctor's welcome party, his obsession with beach cleanups. Were the bags he claimed he used for litter actually for keeping illegal turtle eggs and somehow transporting them to a buyer?

"Barana, you're finding complicated excuses. The simple answer is that Tulu knew where the nest was. Period. Even if he's not one of the poachers, maybe he told them its location. That guy was probably involved too, which is why he rode off on his bicicleta before we could get a better look at him."

"But what did my brother give him that he put in his pocket?"

"Money? His cut of the egg sales, maybe. Or a piece of paper with information on it. Who knows!"

"Espera. Let me think." Barana got up. Her knees were getting sore. Tulu stood by the breaking waves like a statue. She breathed deeply, willing the tightness in her chest to dissipate.

Inhala, exhala.

She reached into her pocket to hold her little totem of hope and tried to reason through the problem. She tried to picture what the taller man looked like, his coloring, his clothing, but nothing came. He'd been too far away.

"Can you take a picture of the empty nest?"

Abby shook the can until the cigarette butt fell out and

placed both pieces of evidence next to the empty hole in the ground. She pulled her camera out from her bag and tapped on the shutter. "The more clues the better."

Tulu didn't smoke, at least not that Barana knew of. But some kids in his school did. She had seen them. He liked soda, but pretty much everyone did. That clue was useless. She continued to watch him standing there, unmoving, as teal-blue waves crashed into his legs. He was acting like nothing had happened.

"It can't be Tulu. You don't know him," she said. Her mind and heart battled inside her.

"At least ask him where he was that night, and why he won't tell you what he was exchanging with that guy."

"No. I know my brother." *Did she?*

"You have to admit it's possible. It makes sense. That nest was invisible. Why are you being so stubborn?" Abby huffed and marched toward the surf. She stood where the bubbles covered her ankles and kept her distance from Tulu.

Barana needed to feel the ocean too. She walked to the soothing sea and stood as far away from both of them as she could. The waves were small but steady, and the warm seawater calmed her down. *Inhala, exhala. Inhala, exhala.*

Barana knew she'd have to confront her brother and ask him where he was that night. She needed him to come clean about what he was doing outside the office too.

The waves came and went, just like the doubt in her heart.

As the bubbles of seawater rose and fell over her toes, she

took her sea turtle totem out of her pocket and held it in her hands. It burned just like her scar. The carved moon twinkled like diamonds as the sun shone down on its back.

After what seemed like hours, Tulu walked up to her. Without looking her in the eyes, he said, "I'm going home. You should go to Mamá. She's probably still waiting for you."

Abby joined them near the surf. "Can you drop me off at the cabin on your way?" she said. "We need to talk."

"Fine," Barana replied. It was a quick detour. She could even change into her favorite shorts and a comfy T-shirt before meeting her doom at Pulpería Gloria. It would be a good excuse for being late. She could say she had to drop Abby off at the guesthouse, they got distracted, and then she decided to change out of her uniform.

Barana walked with Abby in silence, several steps behind Tulu. The walk home felt like she was pushing through tar. Every step was heavy and sticky.

"Barana, I know you're upset, but we can get to the bottom of this. We might be closer than we think."

"Because you think it's my brother."

"I mean, we should explore that possibility."

"Then *you* do it. *You* figure it out. But I'm not accusing him of anything!" Barana huffed away from Abby's cabin toward her house. She was disheartened to the point of wanting to give up. María had been of no help, and they'd been too late to the beach. She had failed Luna.

She was mad at Tulu for keeping secrets.

She was mad at María for giving up.

She was mad at Abby for judging Tulu.

But the truth was, she was angrier at herself for knowing deep down that Abby might be right.

She stood over the pila and splashed cool water on her face; she couldn't wait to head upstairs and get out of her uncomfortable uniform. Then, from the top of the stairs, Chiqui called out to her. What was Chiqui doing in her house?

"Barana!" Chiqui beamed from their porch.

Barana walked up the steps, confused. "I was just dropping off my friend and going over to the pulpería to help Mamá. Are you here with Marisol?"

"Sí, mi niña. Your mamá needed you to put her down for a nap. She was waiting for you, but you never showed up."

Oh, that was not good. Barana would get an earful later about how unreliable and irresponsible she was. "Thank you for watching her, Chiqui. I'll take over. Was my mother mad?"

Chiqui winked and smiled. "Just be prepared to explain why you didn't do as you were told." She examined Barana's face and body, probably noticing the sand on her legs and her puffy eyes. "¿Estás bien, mi niña?"

Barana realized new tears had fallen. She wiped them with one stroke and nodded. "I got in a fight with Tulu. I'm fine."

Chiqui kissed her on the head. "Marisol will be up any minute. Tranquila, mi chiquita. You and your brother will work things out." Chiqui had a way with words. Barana figured it was why Mamá loved her so much.

Chiqui closed the door behind her, and her heavy body rattled the entire house as she walked down the stairs. Before Barana could call after her from the porch to ask if Marisol had gone number two, her baby sister's wails echoed through the entire house.

CHAPTER 18

Abby

The guesthouse was hot and quiet. Papi hadn't returned, and the air inside was humid and suffocating. Abby turned on both fans and opened the windows to let the sea breeze in. Barana had told her to figure out the poacher mystery herself, but all she wanted was to forget the whole thing. The afternoon had been one big failure. María hadn't told them anything new, Luna's eggs had been taken, and Tulu was keeping secrets from his own sister. Abby had just wanted to help, and all she'd gotten in return was Barana yelling at her and leaving her alone in the guesthouse.

At least she was used to being alone.

Barana's refusal to even consider the possibility that Tulu was involved irritated Abby. She felt guilty for accusing him, but it would be foolish not to at least examine the idea that he was involved. He was an obvious suspect. Their only suspect.

Abby didn't have a brother, but if she did, she would've confronted him immediately.

I should just focus on my photography.

I'll spend the rest of the trip taking perfect pictures.

I'll email Mom every day.

I'll read and relax.

The heat had made Abby's denim shorts stick to her legs. She rubbed off some of the sweat, set her bag down, and pulled out her camera. She hoped that looking at her photos would help get her mind off the disappointing afternoon (and the unbearable temperature). She moved the mosquito netting aside and hopped onto the bed. She lay on her stomach and put her feet up as she turned on the camera.

The totem in her pocket poked her hip, reminding her of its presence. She leaned sideways and pulled it out. Setting her camera down on the pillow, she held the small turtle with both hands and examined it once again. The wood had been whittled by expert hands. The leatherback's ridges were finely carved, and the moon etched on its back was hypnotizing.

But for the first time, the charm was ice-cold.

As she thought of Barana and how much she had wanted to help her, it warmed a little and began to glow.

What are you trying to tell me?

She placed the charm on her white pillow and, looking through the lens of her camera, focused on its moon.

Tap, tap, click.

She sat up and took more photos of the totem from a few inches away. As she focused, the crescent moon seemed to sparkle even more. The wood looked different too. It was almost as if the little turtle would become real at any moment. After taking another picture of the mysterious object, she tucked it under her pillow and patted it down.

Abby lay back on her belly and scrolled through her pictures. The ones from the cemetery were her favorites, hands down. She'd captured the plant-covered tombstone of R. Durón perfectly. A big tree with round leaves stood a few feet behind the gravestone. Though most of the area was overgrown with weeds, the words at the top of the stone were clearly legible. She couldn't explain it, but she felt an odd connection to the cemetery, and especially to this gravesite.

She scrolled left to the photos of María and her family, then left again to the manatee. The pictures took her back to that first time she rode on a boat through the mangroves of La Mosquitia. The photos were unlike any Abby had ever taken. There were dozens of pictures of people, close-ups of Papi, and tropical landscapes bathed in Honduras's warm light. But more than that, each individual photo, while standing on its own as a unique image, was part of a greater tapestry— a collection of interconnected people and places that together made a perfect, more beautiful whole.

Abby decided to ask Papi for his laptop as soon as he got back to the room. She wanted to download her pictures and keep them safe, maybe try her luck at emailing some pictures to Mom, and perhaps even Fiana, on his computer.

She kept scrolling. The pictures of Luna and Barana were almost too magical to be real. The enormous leatherback who shared the same moon-shaped scar with her friend was like something out of a movie, and yet there she was, captured in her camera. Abby admired the ridges on her back, the softness of her carapace, the strength in her flippers—she was an amazing creature! Luna was not only majestic, but there was also a wisdom about her, a feeling that she was from a different time and place.

Ugh. Why had they gotten into that fight?

Was Barana still her friend?

As she thought about how to handle the fallout with Barana, Papi walked through the door with a beaming smile. His beard was starting to grow in, and he looked like a scruffy, Latino version of Indiana Jones.

"Abs! Coneja, you won't believe the dive we had."

Before she could get a word out, Papi started telling her about all he'd seen underwater. The barracuda, the shrimp, the schools of fish. He babbled on about the invasive lionfish and how important it was to control their population. And of course, the new trap-like casitas, dive equipment, and how much safer the fishermen would hopefully be. He was so excited that she could barely even say "Cool!" without him interrupting. Finally, he took a breath, and Abby had a chance to speak.

"Did Barana's father dive?"

"Not yet. Tomorrow's his day, though. He's ready. Sorry, Coneja—how was *your* day with Barana? I'm surprised you're not still out exploring together."

Abby considered telling him about Tulu, María, the poachers, and the stolen nest, but she didn't dare. It was too much information at once, and Papi had enough things on his mind. Besides, he was happy in Honduras. She didn't want to spoil his mood with her drama.

"It was good! We went to the beach after school and . . ." She paused. *Focus, focus.* "Her brother hung out with us a bit. He's nice too. But we all got hot and tired. Plus, I wanted to look over my pictures."

Her dad nodded. "You must have dozens by now. You've seen a manatee, a monkey, a sea turtle. Bet you'll see a jaguar next." He did a cat growl and put his hands up in the air as if they were claws.

Papi could be a real dork sometimes.

Abby wanted to take him to the cemetery and show him the gravestone she had found. She thought it was cool that their last name was etched in stone thousands of miles from where they lived. He'd been so busy that they hadn't even gone swimming together yet. Then again, it had only been a couple of days.

"I want to go to the cemetery with you tomorrow." Abby put her hands in a prayer position, as if begging him. "It's seriously not even creepy. It's right by the canal that goes out to the ocean. It's close!"

"This weekend, Abby. I have to be on the dive boat first thing tomorrow, and then I'm preparing for my presentation on Friday."

"You promise we'll go?"

"I promise." He breathed out so loudly he sounded like Abby did whenever they asked her to do the dishes or take out the trash. Like going to the graveyard was a chore he didn't really want to do.

"Tell me more about school." He grabbed a T-shirt and shorts from his suitcase, stealthily changing the subject back to her. She went along with it, but she wasn't letting the cemetery outing go. The graveyard by the beach was one of her favorite parts of Pataya, and she wasn't leaving without taking Papi there.

"The classrooms all face a big patio, like a courtyard in the center of the building. And the rooms don't have air-conditioning. It's not bad, because all the walls have these square bricks with holes in them like mini-windows. And the tops of the walls are open so air can flow in."

Papi smiled and nodded. "What about the lessons?" He grabbed his water bottle and took a huge gulp.

"Math was weird. I had to learn division the other way around. Like, the box is backward here."

Papi laughed and almost spit the water out of his mouth.

He wiped his lips. "I remember that." To Abby's surprise, he walked to her bed and sat next to her, looking her straight in the eye. "These experiences you're having are special. Experiences like these . . . they make us who we are."

Abby nodded. She could feel in her bones that this trip would prove to be a life-changing experience.

"Abs? Did you hear what I asked? About the camera?" Papi said.

"Oh, sorry," she said. "I spaced out."

"How are you liking it?" He picked up the camera and pretended to take a picture of her. "Can I see more of your pictures?"

Abby didn't want him scrolling through her images yet, not with the picture of the magical totem right smack at the end. She snatched the camera back.

"Not yet! I want to edit them and pick through my favorite ones before I show you. It's seriously the best present in the world, Papi. I love it. I've been trying to take more risks with it too—you know, following Ms. T's advice and incorporating more portraits in my portfolio."

"You sound like a pro already." He got up and walked toward the door.

"It's still a little hard asking people for their picture, but it's gotten easier," she said.

"You just need to be polite; most people love having their photo taken."

"Not all people! Like that first family I photographed here, the parents didn't seem very happy about it, even though they said it was okay. The dad didn't even smile."

"It's okay if not all your subjects smile. Makes the art more real. Matías, the gentleman in that picture you took the first day—he was one of the hardest-working divers before he got sick."

"Do you think he'll ever be able to dive again?"

Papi shrugged as he opened the door. "Possibly. I think he's a little scared, to tell you the truth. He's lucky it wasn't worse. He still has some pain in his legs, but with continued physical therapy, I think, he might be able to dive again. Fortunately, with the new traps, nobody will have to dive as much anymore."

Abby couldn't imagine what it was like getting the bends. If she ever went diving, she was resurfacing as slow as a turtle.

"Well, since you won't show me more pictures, I should go shower and get this salt water off my body. I have a meeting in half an hour. Let's meet at Bela's for dinner? I promise we'll get more time together soon. The first few days here are always the busiest. But don't worry, kiddo. We have this weekend plus all of next week for me to make it up to you."

"Can I at least borrow your laptop and download my pictures while you're gone?"

"I need my computer for the meeting, and it needs to charge while I shower. But I'll be back before dinner, and you can borrow it then."

"Actually, can we get our dinner to go and eat here

tonight? I kind of want quiet time the rest of the evening."
Abby didn't want to risk seeing Barana again. Not tonight.
She wasn't ready to confront her after their disagreement.

Papi kept his hand on the knob and paused, thinking about
it. "How about *I* go over to Bela's, say hello for both of us,
and bring you back a plate? You can download your pictures
while I'm there."

"That's perfect!"

"I know it's been a lot, Aberdeen, and I'm so proud of you
for how well you're adjusting to being here. Outdoor bath-
rooms, new food, speaking Spanish *all* the time . . ."

Abby smiled. She was proud of herself too.

She was glad she hadn't told him about her argument with
Barana or about her suspicions of Tulu. Papi was relaxed.
And happy. She'd share her turtle detective drama another
time. Still, she was keeping things from him, and that didn't
exactly feel good in her stomach. She probably wouldn't eat
much for dinner, but at least she'd gotten out of having to
see Barana before she was ready.

She lay back down, closed her eyes, and tried to forget the
parts of the afternoon that had been less than stellar. No time
with Papi, a poached nest, a fight with her new friend, and
the suspicion that Tulu was behind the stealing. She reached
under her pillow and placed the turtle charm over her heart.

It was warm again.

CHAPTER 19

Barana

There were stones in the ocean, and Barana was a scarlet macaw fly-
ing above them. As she dipped closer to the surface of the water, she
realized they weren't stones at all. They were sea turtles, hundreds of
them: hawksbills, greens, loggerheads, and, the biggest ones of all,
leatherbacks.

But the ocean was not blue. It was fluorescent and glowing like
something from outer space. She descended through the pitch-black sky
to get a closer look and admire the ancient turtles from above. If only she
could swim with them.

Suddenly, the waves and sand rattled, as if the earth were shak-
ing. Barana rose way up above the roaring surf and headed toward the
beach. A row of identical tall figures stood along its edge. Hundreds of
men were waiting for the turtles, for their meat, their shells, and their
eggs. They were mirror images of each other, standing like towering coco-
nut palms where land met sea.

"No!" she tried to scream, but nothing came out, not a single squawk.

She had no voice. She wanted to warn the turtles to keep them from coming onto the beach. The only thing waiting for them was danger. Maybe even death.

She flew down and pecked at their shells with her beak, flapping her wings violently. "Swim away!" she wanted to cry.

The row of men stood their ground, unmoving and patient.

Their faces were a blur. The only hint of color was their identical red ball caps. She wheeled around to get a closer look, but no matter how she angled her body, they were always facing away. She was flapping in place.

The full moon rose in front of her, and almost instantly the pounding stopped and the figures on the coast disappeared. The moon blinked on and off like a flashlight. One second, it lit up the ocean, and the next, darkness.

She saw the turtles sinking into the water's deep abyss, until they disappeared completely. All that remained was the twinkling sea, which shimmered and shone from plankton that glowed like neon stars.

The moon was gone. Barana was finally able to start moving again, and her body took off as if she'd been flung from a slingshot. She reached the beach, where only one red cap lay abandoned in the surf.

She landed on the wet sand and picked it up. Underneath it was her turtle totem.

She flew with the totem in her beak, its light illuminating the way home.

Her family was gathered around a bonfire. As she flew down to them, nobody could see her. It was like she was invisible. She dropped the bright totem on the ground and squawked as loud as she could.

"Barana! Wake up! You're having a nightmare. Wake up!"

It was Mamá. Barana sat up in her bed, confused and disoriented.

"Where is Tulu?" she asked.

"He stayed over at Jason's."

"Mamá, does Tulu have a red cap?"

"I don't know. What does that matter? Here, toma un poquito de agua."

Barana took a sip of water. Mamá kissed her on the forehead and went back to her room. At least Mamá was no longer upset at her for being late that afternoon. She'd gotten into trouble for skipping the store, and that was on top of her first fight with Abby.

She wondered if Abby had skipped dinner at Bela's to avoid her.

As soon as she was alone again, she reached under her pillow. She needed to see if her totem was still there.

It was. The crescent moon on the turtle's back glowed, and it was no longer cold. Barana held the charm over her heart and let its magical warmth ease her back to sleep. As she lay there holding the wooden leatherback, a new verse popped into her head.

Secret in his pocket,
Betrayal of family bonds.
Trust is lost in seconds.
Siblings torn apart.

She would confront her brother tomorrow.

CHAPTER 20

Abby

Abby slept through her alarm on Wednesday morning. The fight with Barana, the confrontation with Tulu, the stolen nest, the sad state of María's situation, plus the energy-sucking heat of the last few days had finally caught up with her. Papi's meeting had gone late yesterday, but as promised, he'd brought her back a plate of dinner from Bela's: fried plantains, refried beans, salty cheese, and fresh tortillas. At least she'd managed to download most of her photos before they'd gone to bed, lulled by the sound of waves and the thrum of insects.

She got out of bed and went straight to the outside sink to brush her teeth and splash cool water on her face. The sun beamed down on the palm trees, and the leaves' shadows danced over the sand where Abby stood. She was getting used to the whole outdoor-bathroom situation. Chickens roamed under Bela's house, and it was nice to awaken to an already risen sun. Bela's monkey was hanging out with Papi while he sat on one of the lawn chairs, writing feverishly on a yellow legal pad; he looked up and blew her a kiss.

"I didn't want to wake you this morning. I figured you needed the sleep," he said.

Abby spit out her toothpaste and rinsed her mouth. "That's okay. It'll be nice to have a day to myself. I want to go back to the cemetery and beach to take more pictures. You *have* to see the ones I already took of that place. They're on your computer." Abby had made sure not to download the pictures of the poached nest or the mysterious totem. Those would stay in her camera for now, out of Papi's sight.

"Actually, I want you to join me on the dive boat. You can take pictures and snorkel. And we can get quality time together between my dives."

Abby considered his proposition. They hadn't done much together so far, and while being on the rocking boat might make her nauseous, she *was* curious. If she wanted to be a wild-life photographer, she needed to get used to being out on the water. She approached her father and knelt to pet Pitufo. The monkey climbed onto her shoulder.

"Who will I snorkel with while you scuba dive?" Abby said.

"The guys who stay on the boat will keep their eye on you. We have snorkel flags to swim with, and you'd hang on to a rope attached to the boat."

"What are snorkel flags?"

"Little triangular red flags that poke out from the water to alert people that a person is there."

Abby thought about it. *What's the worst that could happen?*

"Okay. I'll come. But I'd better not get seasick." She figured it was worth risking nausea to get her mind off Barana and the turtle drama. She still wanted to convince Barana they needed to get to the bottom of whether Tulu was involved. But since she'd already missed the school boat, she couldn't do anything about it until Barana got back. Might as well join Papi.

"I've got something in my bag to help with seasickness. I'll show you at Bela's," Papi said. They walked across the yard to Bela's for breakfast, with Pitufo following closely behind.

Bela's welcoming face greeted them from the kitchen. Papi helped himself to a cup of black coffee and joined Abby at one of the dining tables. He took a sip and savored the hot Honduran coffee like he was in a commercial, closing his eyes after his first gulp. Then he gave her a double thumbs-up and grinned so big that every one of his teeth showed.

"Remember what happened when we went whale watching in Massachusetts?" Abby really didn't want to relive that experience today.

"How could I forget?" He did a barfing face.

The last time she was out on the open seas was when they went whale watching outside Boston, and she'd spent most of the ride leaning over the boat's railing with a paper bag in her hand.

They never even saw a whale.

As they laughed about the infamous excursion, Bela came over with a tray of mangoes and bananas all neatly cut up. She placed it in front of them and crossed her arms over her huge chest.

"I'm making some eggs for my guests. How do you like them, muchachita?" she said to Abby.

"Revueltos, por favor." Abby liked her eggs scrambled.

"¿Y usted, Doctor?" Bela smiled at Papi and raised an eyebrow.

"Also scrambled, Bela. Gracias." He took another sip of his coffee.

Bela nodded and smiled before going back inside.

Papi reached into his backpack, removed two bracelets, and fastened them on Abby's wrists. They were blue and made of a thick rubbery material with a plastic circle on the underside of both.

"These will keep you from getting sick."

"How?"

He pointed at the little plastic stud on the bottom of one of the bracelets. "This little thing will apply pressure to a specific part of your wrist. That pressure point has been proven to relieve nausea."

Abby regarded the two bracelets. "Huh," she said. "They'd better work, because I'm about to fill up on scrambled eggs."

Just then, Bela walked in with their eggs and a basket of fresh tortillas. They smelled like warm corn and butter.

"So, what is your plan today, Abby?"

"I'm joining Papi on the boat, but I'm a little nervous about getting seasick." Abby wondered if she would be better off staying home with Bela and exploring Pataya by herself. "Maybe I could stay here with you instead?"

Bela's belly jiggled as she laughed. "Nah, you go on with your father. You'll be surprised at what's out there waiting for you."

Abby couldn't help but think that the only thing waiting for her out there was nausea and a bad sunburn.

"Bela's right, Coneja. You'll love the experience. Besides, the bracelets will work."

Abby held her wrists up and tried to convince herself that Papi was right. More important, being out at sea was part of a wildlife photographer's job.

Bela put both her hands on Abby's shoulders and gave them a squeeze. "Be brave, my girl. You will have fun—you'll see."

Something inside Abby stirred. It was as if Bela's warm touch had given her the courage she needed to embrace the adventure. She remembered Ms. Tenley's words. *Take risks.* Perhaps her stomach would cooperate after all. She could take beautiful photos and maybe see a dolphin or two, to make up for the failed whale sighting from a few years back. She'd never snorkeled before, but after four years of swim lessons, what could go wrong?

AFTER THANKING BELA, they trekked away from her house and over to the lagoon dock, where a group of men were waiting at the boat to get their workday going. The bright sun had already started working on Abby's skin. She pulled out a bottle of sunscreen and applied it to her shoulders and face while Papi talked to the fishermen. When she tucked the bottle back into her bag, she felt the totem's warmth and remembered Luna. She remembered Barana.

Despite their disagreement about Tulu, she didn't want to fail Barana or the turtles.

She hopped onto the boat and took a seat near the front. Oxygen tanks sat all along the center of the boat, secured inside round wooden frames. A handful of what looked like oversize butterfly nets and mesh bags lay on the deck.

Papi handed her a life vest. "Put this on. You'll need it on the boat and for snorkeling."

"Seriously?" Abby considered herself a good swimmer, and a clunky life vest wasn't exactly comfortable to wear on an already scorching day. But her dad nodded, so she put on the vest and immediately felt like a wrapped-up hot dog. She hoped this puffy thing wouldn't get in the way of taking good photos.

They sped off in the opposite direction from the school, toward the small canal that connected Pataya's lagoon to the Caribbean Sea. She couldn't help but look back in the direction of Barana's school. Her stomach felt icky. She was still upset at Barana for being so stubborn, but she also felt a tinge of guilt for bailing on her that morning, even though it was accidental.

The canal was shallow at low tide, so the captain slowed the big boat down to safely make it through the narrow passage. With a jolt, Abby realized she knew exactly where they were—in the part of the canal that ran by the cemetery.

"Papi! There! Just over the shrubs and sea grapes! You can see a few of the tallest gravestones!"

Papi stood next to her as she focused her lens on a tall white stone at the graveyard's edge.

Tap, tap, click.

Abby managed to shoot the quiet shoreline with the cemetery in the background. Only a few gravestones were tall enough to make it into the frame, but it was cool to see it from a different angle. The engine gurgled once again, and they took off toward the northern reefs.

There were close to a dozen men on the boat, and Barana's father was one of them. He looked terrified. His eyes seemed glued open, and his mouth was tense. Abby hoped he'd be okay.

She sat at the bow and looked out at the horizon to avoid feeling ill. If it worked in a car, she hoped it would work on the boat. Almost half an hour later, they anchored at the first buoy that alerted them of the casitas below, and Abby was nausea-free. *Mercy!*

Papi got to work. He and the divemaster guy double-checked the tanks and regulators—big black mouthpieces they'd be breathing with. They handed each of the divers a waterproof board and pencil and went through a safety checklist. Abby was blown away by what a good doctor Papi was. She'd never seen him in action like this before.

She pulled out her camera. "Papi," she interrupted. "¿Puedo?" She did a clicking gesture to ask if it was okay to take pictures. He nodded and continued his speech.

She pretended to be a professional journalist—instead of the wildlife photographer she dreamed of becoming—and took pictures of the hustle and bustle before the dive. Papi reminded the divers exactly how long they'd be down and how many casitas they'd visit, and he reviewed the instructions for resurfacing.

"We'll make two decompression stops on the way up. I don't want a single diver taking any risks, not on my watch. Not ever. We come up slowly and carefully, stopping at thirty feet, and then again at fifteen. Safety first!"

The men nodded.

Barana's papá put on a weighted belt and a tank. Today was his first dive, and Papi would be his diving buddy.

Abby's stomach churned, and it wasn't because she was seasick. She thought of her abuelo, and that reminded her that things could go wrong underwater. She couldn't imagine the conditions Abuelo had had to endure when he was a diver. Papi said that back then they didn't even use oxygen tanks. Instead, they would free-dive for several minutes as they searched for their catch. Once or twice Abby had tried to hold her breath to see what it would feel like to be underwater for that long. The longest she'd ever lasted was fifty-two seconds.

She reassured herself that Papi was a pro. *They'll be fine.*

She reached into her bag for her water bottle. As she felt around for it, her fingers brushed the turtle totem. Its warmth calmed her down, and she remembered to breathe. But the mixed emotions of anger and regret bubbled back up into her belly. She was still upset that Barana had angrily dismissed her suspicions of Tulu, but she also regretted accusing him so persistently. She was holding the totem in her palm when Papi interrupted her thoughts.

"Coneja, here's your gear," he said, handing her a mask, snorkel, and flippers. Then he showed her the waterproof "dry bag" near the back of the boat. "Keep your camera in here when you're not using it." Finally, he explained how to safely use the ladder in the stern to step into the water. There was a long rope with a doughnut-shaped floatie attached to it. He instructed her to hold on to the rope when she went snorkeling.

"Ateliano and Matías will keep an eye on you. If you need anything, let them know. Ateliano loves the water, so I wouldn't be surprised if he joins you."

Ateliano wore a New Orleans Saints T-shirt and smiled a toothless smile at them. He looked ancient. Abby assumed that, like Matías, he could no longer dive. Then she remembered Barana's warning about Matías's temper and hoped she wouldn't have to witness it.

Papi and the divers each had a mesh catch bag in their hands for the spiny lobsters. Only a handful of the men wore proper dive suits; the rest of them dove in the shorts they were wearing. At least Papi's grant had ensured they could dive with brand-new oxygen tanks and BCDs, a term Abby had recently learned stood for "buoyancy control device." One by one, they stepped off the boat and into the water, disappearing beneath the surface. Abby took photos from the side of the boat as the oxygen bubbles coming out of the divers' breathing devices got smaller and smaller. Papi looked up from beneath the clear water and blew ring-shaped bubbles at her, waving with one hand as he descended.

Tap, tap, click.

Pretty soon they'd swum far enough away that she lost track of them.

The boat remained mostly steady, but now and then it shifted and moved with the waves. Abby hobbled over to the stern, where she could sit on the floating ladder and let her feet cool down. She took pictures of the turquoise sea. After several shots from the boat, it was time to snorkel and get a view of what lay beneath the waves. She stood, stowed her camera in the dry bag, and adjusted the mask and snorkel over her face.

Then, as she dipped her fin-covered toes into the water, something glistened at the surface.

A leathery black head poked out a few feet away from the boat's edge.

Startled, Abby lifted her feet out of the water, pulled off her mask, and squinted to make sure she wasn't seeing things. The sea was as clear as an aquamarine glass window, and the mammoth sea turtle's body floated just an arm's length away. She stood and leaned over the back rail to confirm what she'd seen, still in disbelief.

The current brought the leatherback a few inches closer, and Abby could make out the moon-shaped scar between the two center ridges of her back. It was Luna.

She couldn't believe it. She pulled her camera out of the dry bag and started taking pictures. *Tap, tap, click. Tap, click. Click. Click. Click.*

Matías and Ateliano sat on two overturned crates playing cards. Abby called them over to see. "¡Una baula!" she said.

Only Ateliano bothered to get up.

His gums glistened in the sunlight as he grinned from ear to ear when he saw what Abby's commotion was all about.

"Nos está diciendo hola," he said.

Ateliano was right. It *was* like Luna was saying hello to them. For some reason, though, Abby felt that Luna's visit was more than just a friendly greeting. The massive sea turtle was visiting her for a reason.

Ancient, wise mama.

Matías yelled over at Ateliano to come finish the game and said he'd seen enough baulas in his lifetime. Barana hadn't exaggerated. That man was a grump.

Luna floated for several minutes in front of her, like an aquatic dinosaur, waiting. . . .

"I'm going to get in with her," Abby said to Ateliano. "Will you keep an eye on me, like Papi said?"

He nodded and smiled his toothless smile.

After tucking her camera away, Abby hurriedly adjusted her mask and snorkel back on. When she gingerly stepped onto the ladder and into the warm Caribbean Sea, Luna was still in the same spot. Abby breathed into her snorkel and submerged her body, holding on to the thick white rope with one hand.

Cautiously, she swam away from the boat and a little bit closer to the leatherback, careful to respect her space. Careful not to get too close. The turtle seemed even bigger underwater. Luna glided closer until her glistening eyes met Abby's. It was like she knew the truth and wanted Abby to find it. Or maybe it was more than that—maybe the turtle was delivering a message that she and Barana had to work on the mystery together. A sign not to give up.

After a few minutes, Luna turned, churning against the water with her huge, powerful flippers, and disappeared into the blue beyond. Abby stayed a little longer, admiring the coral and the schools of angelfish and minnows in the distance. It was like she was flying above an alien world, her body weightless and free.

Abby watched the world beneath the waves until her fingers looked like raisins. Finally, she turned back toward the boat, excited for the divers to return safely so she could tell Papi what—and who—she'd seen.

CHAPTER 21

Barana

The nightmare had shaken Barana so much that she drank two full glasses of water as soon as she awakened. Papá would dive for the first time today, and she didn't want to wake him up, so she tiptoed around their small kitchen the way she'd done the night she snuck out. Normally, he was gone fishing by the time she got ready, but this week was different—for many reasons.

She grabbed a banana and two sweet buns to eat outside. Breakfast by herself on the porch would have to do. The sky was pitch-black to the west, but the eastern horizon had started turning orange and pink. Since Tulu wasn't home, she whispered to herself while she washed her face and teeth, just to make sure she still had a voice. The bird in her dreams had scared her into thinking she might not.

She walked down the stairs and sat on a hammock, waiting for Abby. The sky lightened some more, but her American friend was still nowhere to be seen. Abby hadn't shown up at Bela's for dinner the night before, either, and Barana feared that she'd upset her more than she'd meant to. Not only that, but their disagreement about Tulu had angered her brother to the point of spending the night at Jason's house. Both of them were mad at her. She'd been ditched. Twice. But she was mad too.

She got up from the hammock and walked to the guesthouse, trying to put her pride aside. She stood outside the door and considered knocking. Her chest tightened, and she couldn't bring herself to do it. She wanted to apologize for yelling at Abby about Tulu. She went around the side of the guesthouse and peeked through an open window. Both Abby and her father were still sound asleep.

There was a faint light coming from Abby's bed. Barana squinted to get a better look but couldn't make out what it was. Did she have a flashlight under there? The mosquito net made it impossible to tell.

The sun continued rising, and Barana needed to get going or she'd miss the school boat.

Walking by herself to the lagoon dock was depressing in a way it had never been before, and her backpack felt heavier than usual. Everything looked gray.

Tulu was already at the palapa when she arrived. He looked at her with cold eyes and ignored her as they boarded the school boat. He made himself busy, acting like nothing had happened, joking around with Jason and their cousins and laughing way too loud for so early in the morning. Barana wanted to confront him, to demand that he tell her what secrets he was keeping, but there were too many people nearby. She needed to do it in private.

It was weird sitting in her favorite spot at the front of the boat without Abby. The vacant space to her right was like a reminder that she'd messed up. She put her bag where Abby would've sat and pulled out her notebook, pencil, and turtle totem. The small pocket of her shirt was the perfect place to hold the charm, right by her heart. Then she wrote:

Like phases of the moon,
A friendship grows.
Darkness shrinks.
And light expands.
The reflection of a bigger star.

The charm warmed up when she finished; she pulled it out and kept it hidden between her palms the rest of the ride to school. When they got to Paraíso and deboarded, she waited for Tulu on the dock, but her brother didn't even look her in the eye as he got off.

"Tulu," Barana said.

He kept walking on the dock toward the shore, like she was invisible.

"Tulu!" she yelled. She ran and reached for his hand. "Hermano, why are you ignoring me?"

"I'm going to be late to school, Barana, and I have a huge test today. Not everything is about you. Where's your friend, anyway?"

"She stayed home. You and I need to talk."

"About what?"

"Why didn't you sleep at home last night?"

"You think I was out poaching?" He shook his head. "Primo and I studied together for the test. We can talk at home."

"Or right after school."

"No puedo. I'm staying after school to plan the beach cleanup." He kept walking. "I'm taking the late boat. Plus, I have a soccer game after that."

Tulu hadn't taken the late boat in weeks, and Barana wondered if he was telling her the truth about his beach cleanup plans. "Fine. I'll see you at home, then."

Barana didn't know what was true and what wasn't anymore. She marched to school, defeated and alone.

The day's lessons felt unbearable. Every class was endless. Her mind wandered, and her nerves rattled around through her body like speeding boats.

Finally, the recess bell rang, and she ran outside for air like she'd been holding her breath. At least now she was halfway through the school day. As she walked toward the bench she and Abby had sat on the day before, her scar began to tingle.

Was Luna nearby? She'd never felt the prickle in her back so far from home.

Maybe Luna had a message for her.

She pulled out her notebook and started drawing. To her surprise, something told her to draw Abby and Luna in the water, gracefully floating next to each other beneath the waves.

As her scar's tingle intensified, she knew.

To solve the mystery, she would need Abby's help.

That was the message.

They had to catch the poachers before her special turtle came ashore again to lay another clutch. And they needed to do it together.

CHAPTER 22

Abby

The boat rocked gently over the teal waves as Abby waited for Papi and the crew to return. She dried off and put on her favorite oversize vintage T-shirt, which she'd packed in the bag she brought on the boat. She sat on a center bench by a row of oxygen tanks and showed her pictures to Ateliano. He peered over her shoulder as she zoomed in. Not even the best of her photographs fully captured Luna's magic. She wished she could've taken photos underwater. Like Paul Nicklen and his crew did. Still, Barana would appreciate the photos. That is, if Barana ever talked to her again.

Ateliano whistled to Matías to come see. Ateliano's smile lines were like cracks snaking through a dry desert. His skin was so leathery and tanned that Abby couldn't tell what color it might've been when he was born.

Matías finally got up. He hovered over them and took a

puff of his cigarette, blowing smoke in their faces. Abby tried to hold her breath to avoid inhaling the poison fumes.

"Apaga ese cigarrillo," Ateliano said. "You know the doctor doesn't like anyone smoking on the boat."

"Your camera's fancy," Matías said, ignoring him. "Let's see that picture you took of me and my family."

Abby tried not to show her irritation at Matías. She scrolled back in her files and displayed the portrait for him. He leaned over the side of the boat and spit into the water. He tilted his head with the cigarette in his mouth as he judged her work. Abby examined the photo too, realizing it was a decent composition.

"It's good. You like Pataya, then, gringa?"

"Sí," Abby said. "It's beautiful."

He grumbled and returned to his seat. Ateliano joined him and they continued their game while Abby went back to minding her own business at the bow of the boat.

As Abby waited for Papi, she thought of Abuelo, and imagined him diving at this very spot years ago. She pictured him swimming with Luna too—a younger Luna, before she'd gotten her scar.

What felt like eons later, Papi climbed into the boat, dripping seawater, and much to Abby's relief, Barana's father followed closely behind. They high-fived on the deck, and Papi praised him for resurfacing calmly. "You're a natural, amigo," Papi said.

One by one, the divers brought in their catch, filling the

enormous saltwater cooler with dozens and dozens of lobsters. Papi let Abby watch as they double-checked that all of them were male. Females were not up for grabs—especially the ones with eggs on them. Every single lobster they caught had to be a dude.

"How can you tell?" Abby said.

"You flip them over and check their bellies." He held the lobster's pincers steady and showed Abby what the male's belly looked like. "You make sure there's only *one* pair of these little swimming appendages on each of the segments on their bellies. Females have two pairs on each, and they're feathery."

Tap, tap, click.

She needed to capture the funny-looking lobster before Papi released it into the box. It was one of the best science lessons she'd had.

Papi said that after they returned to New Jersey, this same group of men would continue diving together. The longer they stayed out at sea, the more money they could make to support their families.

The divers decompressed for almost an hour to give their bodies the rest they needed before returning for their second dive. They ate and talked about the new casitas initiative and how hopeful they were for the future.

While they took their break, Papi sat with Abby.

"Guess what I saw?" She pulled out her camera and showed him.

"Again? A leatherback? Wow, what are the odds? She's beautiful!"

"*The* leatherback. Seriously, Papi, she was awesome. Big, beautiful, and silky! I'm positive it was the same one we saw on the beach."

"Will you snorkel again? Maybe you'll see her one more time."

"I'm definitely jumping back in . . . but I have a feeling she won't be making another appearance today." Abby had seen the look in the leatherback's eye. Luna had delivered her message and had gone back in search of jellyfish to munch on—she needed strength before returning to Pataya's shores.

Abby was ready to see Barana again. They needed to make amends and come up with a plan to catch the poachers before Abby left Honduras. And they only had a little over a week.

Papi gave Abby a mini-lesson on diving and showed her how to read the gauge on the regulator. "Maybe I'll take you on a shallow dive next week. And maybe you start saving up for an underwater case for your camera for the next time we visit."

"It's like you read my mind," Abby said, smiling.

Papi and the divers went back for their second dive, and Abby snorkeled above them as far as the rope would let her. There was no sign of Luna, but she wasn't surprised.

She floated on her back and stared at the sky. It was broad

daylight, yet the moon was out too, big and white and bright. Yup, Luna's message was loud and clear. Her friend's turtle with the moon-shaped scar needed protection from both of them. All the leatherbacks did.

WHEN THE DIVE boat returned to the dock, Barana wasn't back from school. Abby would have to apologize and tell her about Luna later. Papi needed to unload the equipment and have a debriefing with the divers before the boat went back to Lempira for more oxygen tanks.

"You head over to Bela's without me, Coneja. Unless you want to stay and watch. I've got a few more things to do before I head back."

"Okay. See you later, then."

The way to Bela's was simple, and Abby was too hungry to wait. She wished Barana was back from school, but it wasn't yet one-thirty. They'd been gone for five hours, and it was still early in the afternoon.

She'd eat her lunch and then wait for Barana at the house.

Abby waved at María on her way up the hill, but María never looked up from where she stood hanging laundry. Abby wondered if the baby would come before she left Pataya. With about ten days left of her trip, the odds were looking good. María's belly was enormous.

The sea turtle office was just ahead, beyond the bend. Abby realized she hadn't taken a picture of it in full daylight. She approached the front of the building for a closer look. A rusty lock prevented her from pushing open the door. As she stepped back for a picture, she wondered what the now-faded mural had once looked like.

She photographed the door and stepped even farther back to get a full view of the structure and its surroundings. Tall coconut palms leaned over the building, as if standing guard, and bright pink hibiscus flowers created a natural fence on one side. Perhaps someday things would go back to normal and the sea turtle project would be revived.

As always, Bela welcomed her into her home with a warm embrace. Barana's grandmother was like a big soft pillow, and she smelled like flowers and pineapple. She wore her salt-and-pepper hair in a long braid, and her apron was yellow with little white polka dots. Maybe if Abby's own abuela were still alive, she would've cooked for them and hugged her the way Bela did.

"Where's your father?"

"He's unloading stuff and talking to the divers. He'll be here soon. The ride was incredible, Bela! I didn't get seasick, *and* I saw a leatherback!"

Bela laughed and put her hands together in a prayer position on top of her enormous chest. "¡Alabanza! People here live an entire lifetime without ever seeing a baula out at sea. And how did my son do? Did he survive his first dive?"

"He survived. Papi was his buddy. They even caught a

few lobsters together." Abby took a seat at one of the tables. Her legs were tired from swimming.

"Que bueno. The doctor is a good man. ¿Tienes hambre, muchachita?"

"I'm starving."

"I made ceviche de pescado. Have you had it before?"

Had she had it before? Despite the traumatic memories of that infamous fourth-grade potluck, her mouth still watered at the thought of ceviche. She could almost taste the lime juice, cilantro, and tomatoes. She gave Bela two thumbs-up, and her lips puckered in anticipation. "I love ceviche!"

Bela smiled. "Good. I'll bring some out for you. First, tell me about the turtle. Was she beautiful?"

"She was like a mythical creature. I took pictures of her, if you want to see. It was Barana's special turtle. The one with her same moon scar."

Abby turned on her camera and found the pictures. Bela's eyes sparkled as she flipped through the images. It looked like she was about to cry. She put both her hands on Abby's cheeks and thanked her for showing them to her.

"What else have you photographed?"

"So much! The kids at school, seabirds, the ocean, and even the cemetery."

"Barana took you to the cemetery? Ay mi nieta, probably trying to scare you with tales of El Cadejo."

"Nah, she didn't scare me. I loved it. There was even a gravestone with my last name on it."

"Very special place, that cementerio," Bela said. She disappeared into the kitchen and came out with a big bowl of ceviche.

Abby helped herself to two servings. She would've had a third, but she didn't want to be greedy. After she finished, she thanked Bela and went outside to wait for Barana. As she rocked herself in a hammock, she reached for the turtle totem and held the warm, soothing charm in her hands. Before she knew it, she was dozing off.

∽∾ ∾

"ABBY? ARE YOU sleeping?" a familiar voice whispered in her ear.

When Abby opened her eyes, Barana was standing above her.

"What time is it?" Abby said. She was confused, and her head felt heavy.

"Almost three! Where did you get this?" Barana asked. She was holding Abby's totem.

"It was under my pillow the night I arrived." Her heart gave a lurch as she braced herself for Barana to say it belonged to her.

Instead, she said, "It's beautiful."

Barana reached into her pocket and pulled something out. "Look." In her hand was another wooden leatherback, carved in the same likeness as Abby's. Its moon sparkled like diamonds, and her hand trembled as she held it.

"You have one too?" Abby said.

"Yes. It was also under my pillow."

Barana tucked her charm into the pocket of her shorts and gave Abby's totem back to her.

"These totems are a sign," Barana said.

"What do you mean?"

"A sign that we can't give up yet. We're closer to catching these poachers than we think."

Abby nodded her agreement. "Hey, Barana?"

"Yeah?"

"I'm sorry I accused your brother. I was just trying to help." As she spoke, the moon on her totem glowed golden. They looked around to make sure nobody had witnessed it. Then they looked at each other in amazement. It was as though the totems responded to *them*.

Abby quickly tucked it in her pocket.

"See? Told you. They're a sign," Barana said.

"I'm starting to believe they are." Abby smiled, feeling the totem's warmth.

"And I'm also sorry. I shouldn't have been so mean to you. Plus, you might be right. It feels like Tulu's hiding something. My parents are worried about money, and maybe he thought selling the eggs would help. I hope you're wrong, but we need to make sure."

Abby was relieved that they'd found a way to work out their disagreement. She reached for her new friend's hand. "Did you talk to him this morning?"

"No. Tulu didn't sleep at our house and was as cold as ice to me on the ride to school. He won't be home until dinner. Mamá said I should spend the afternoon with you since you missed school. By the way, I don't blame you for skipping it."

"I didn't mean to skip, but I overslept," she said.

"Oh," Barana replied.

"It ended up being a surprisingly good morning, though," Abby said. She couldn't wait to surprise her with the pictures of Luna.

"Let's promise each other we'll work together from now on."

"Pinky promise," Abby said.

"What's that?"

Abby taught Barana how to "pinky swear," and they immediately agreed that the next step was to spy on Tulu at the soccer field and follow him wherever he went after that. They let Bela know they'd be exploring the village and would be back before sundown.

"You won't believe who I saw," Abby said as they walked to the field.

"Who?"

"Luna . . . She came up to the boat! I snorkeled next to her!"

"I knew it!" Barana said. She reached her hand behind her and touched her scar. "I sensed something this morning, like Luna was nearby. I think deep down I knew she was with you. I've never told you, but my scar . . . it tells me things about Luna."

Abby wasn't quite sure what Barana meant, but she nodded anyway.

Some things don't have a logical explanation.

They stopped in the middle of the path, and Abby showed her the pictures.

Barana beamed. "I've never seen her out at sea like that," she said. "She looks so peaceful!"

"I wish you could've been there."

"Thank you for caring about the baulas," Barana said. "Especially Luna."

"You're welcome, but it's because of *you* that I care. You've taught me to see the turtles through a whole new lens."

Barana gave her hand a squeeze, and Abby felt her heart expand as they walked on in silence.

When they got to the soccer field, Tulu and his friends were nowhere to be seen. The only kids there were a bunch of nine- and ten-year-olds running around burning off energy.

"Que raro," Barana said.

"It is odd. Do you think their game ended?"

"Maybe there was no game. He's got to be somewhere else."

The girls looked everywhere: Pulpería Gloria, the primos' house, Tulu's friend Jason's house, the beach, the church, the community center, and finally the clinic, where Papi was still in a meeting with a group of fishermen. No sign of Tulu. Pataya wasn't very big, but Abby's feet were sore anyway.

They retraced their steps back to the soccer field. From there, Barana suggested they go to the lagoon and wait on the main dock. Maybe staying put would offer them some answers.

They sat on the dock's edge, watching pipantes rock back and forth with the wind. The tiny canoes, each made from a single piece of wood, were tied to crooked posts all along the shore. Barana dangled her feet into the water. Abby joined her. The blazing sun burned her nose, and she wished she'd worn her hat.

Without saying a word, each of them pulled out their favorite objects: Abby, her camera, and Barana, her journal. They sat in silence as they let their creativity soar like the birds that flew above them.

"You really like taking photos, don't you?" Barana said, breaking the silence.

"I do."

"Why?"

"I don't know. Lots of reasons. I love remembering moments, and places . . . and people. I guess pictures help me do that. I also love how I can make the light show up a certain way or play with angles to make reality appear different."

"I think you take pictures for the same reasons I like to draw and write."

"Want to see some of them?"

Barana nodded, and Abby scrolled through every image she'd taken in Pataya.

"I want to make a video collage of this trip, to connect the individual images and show how they are a part of something bigger," Abby said. "Plus, it'll make it easier to share with my photography classmates and teacher if they're all in one file."

"How do you do that?"

"You stitch photos together on a computer and make a video. Like a slow-moving slideshow. You can even play music in the background."

"Will you put pictures of me in that video?" Barana asked.

"Not if you don't want me to."

"It's okay with me." Barana nodded and looked inside her notebook. She put her chewed-up pencil back in her ponytail and turned to Abby. "I've never shown anyone these drawings, except maybe Tulu because he sneaks up behind me and tells me how to fix them. But you showed me your pictures, so . . . Promise you won't laugh?"

Abby promised.

Barana held out the journal and opened it to a drawing of Luna. Abby was mesmerized by the shading, the fine details, and the movement of the sea in the background.

"Barana, you're seriously talented. I'd get that turtle tattooed on me if my parents let me."

Barana blushed. "En serio?"

"Seriously," Abby said.

"We should both get one," she said, laughing. She turned

to the drawing she'd sketched that morning, the one of Luna and Abby in the water, and held the page open for Abby to see.

"No way! You drew *me* swimming with her? How did you know? Wait—*when* did you draw that?" Abby said.

"Today. At recess." Exactly when Abby had encountered Luna. Neither one of them could believe the coincidence. Barana had drawn exactly what Abby had experienced.

"Barana? Would you mind if I took some photos of your drawings?" Abby didn't want to pass up the opportunity to photograph Barana's art. Her drawings were an important part of the story that Abby was beginning to see take shape in her collection of images.

Barana paused, then gave Abby her journal and said, "Claro."

Abby took great care as she flipped through the pages. She selected a few of her favorite sketches and took pictures of them, with the graying wood of the dock as the backdrop. She switched the toggle to portrait mode and used a black-and-white filter. Her new camera finally felt like an old friend.

Tap, tap, click. The drawings looked magical.

Barana exhaled and put her head in her hands. When she looked up again, she spoke softly. "It's like Tulu disappeared, or he's purposely avoiding me."

"Do you really think he would do it? Take the eggs?"

"In my heart, I don't believe it. But the clues fit. He's tall. He could have a cap I've never seen before. He's keeping secrets. He wasn't home the night I saw the poachers. *And* he was the only other person who knew where Luna's nest was."

"What do you want to do?"

"Wait here a while longer. Then go home and wait some more. He has to come back at some point."

From the far end of the lagoon, a motorboat approached the dock. There were four figures in it. As the lancha got closer, the tallest one turned his head away, avoiding both girls' eyes.

It was him. Tulu was on the boat.

CHAPTER 23

Barana

The purple sky and neon-pink clouds framed the approaching boat like one of Chiqui's paintings. The air left Barana's body like she'd been hit in the stomach by a soccer ball. She looked up at the colorful sky and asked God for a sign. She felt for a tingle in her back, or a burning. But nothing came. Focusing on the boat, she tried to match its silhouette with the one from the night she'd snuck out, but her mind would not cooperate. Tulu and his crew got closer. Her brother stood next to the pilot of the boat and another young man.

"Is that really him, or am I seeing things?" Abby said.

Barana nodded and stood up. "It's him."

Inhala, exhala.

The boat was several feet from the dock when her scar spoke up. It began to throb. The boat's engine revved before the pilot shut it down, and the lancha skimmed the dock's edge. Tulu hopped off and began tying the rope to a post.

"Where were you?" Barana needed answers from him. She needed to know he was innocent.

"Have you been looking for me, hermana?" he said, securing the boat with a cleat hitch knot.

"Just answer the question." Barana searched his eyes for the truth.

"Plans changed. Profesor Erazo had us make posters for the beach cleanup, and then Ernesto, Jason, and I hitched a ride with Santi."

Barana recognized Ernesto as the mysterious young man from the turtle office. She eyed him suspiciously as Santi tossed a big bag to her brother. Her scar continued to burn.

Tulu fist-bumped his friends. "I'll catch up with you guys."

The chavos grabbed their belongings and walked up the dock. Barana kept an eye on them, memorizing what they were wearing.

"What's in the bag, Tulu?" she said, wincing from the pain in her scar.

Tulu placed the bag on the dock and untied the knot at the top. He put his arms out dramatically, like a heron drying off its wings.

"See for yourself. Obviously, you still don't trust me. And I see you're hanging out with her again, which explains why you're still doubting your own blood." Tulu gave Abby a glare that said more than words ever could.

"Her name is Abby." Barana slowly stepped forward,

grabbed a corner of the bag, and peeked inside, praying that its contents would prove her brother's innocence.

"What's in it?" Abby asked.

"Just junk." It always amazed Barana how much litter Tulu collected. Inside the bag were straws, water bottles, soda cans, and even an old bike tire and a straw hat. How could someone who cared so much about cleaning the beach harm the turtles who called it home?

"*Now* do you believe me?"

Abby shook her head. "It still doesn't explain how the poachers found Luna's nest. *And* you weren't home the night Barana snuck out. How do we know it wasn't you out stealing the eggs that night?"

"You want me to prove it to you? Let's sneak out—the three of us. We'll hide and wait for the poachers, and you'll see I'm not one of them."

"When?" Barana said. She was always ready for the beach, especially at night.

"Tonight," Tulu answered.

"And what if nobody shows up? Then what?" Abby said.

"Then we go back tomorrow night and every night until we see them," Tulu replied.

Barana hushed them both. Abby was right that the trash proved nothing. They needed evidence, and a stakeout sounded perfect.

"The sun will set soon," Barana said. "Let's get home and

make a plan." They had to map out every detail for their mission to work. They had to be prepared for *anything*.

"Abby, you'll have to set an alarm. We'll meet outside your cabin at midnight and go to the beach from there," Barana said.

They started walking. Barana's scar still throbbed lightly, but it was no longer on fire.

Abby stopped and clasped her hands together nervously. "Okay . . . If Papi sees me sneaking out, I'll say I'm going to the bathroom. If he wakes up when we come back from the stakeout, I'll say I'm coming back from the bathroom. It's the perfect cover. I went the other night, and he never even budged."

Tulu and Barana nodded in agreement.

"But more important, what if *you* two get caught?"

"We'll need a good excuse, especially since I've been busted for sneaking out before. If we don't have a solid story, we'll both be in the deepest trouble ever," Barana said.

They crested the hill and passed the sea turtle office.

"What if you said I begged you to take me to the cemetery? Papi knows I love graveyards. Bela too. We can say I convinced you to take me out at midnight for a photography shoot! Nothing like a spooky picture of gravestones lit by moonlight, right?"

Tulu and Barana looked at each other. Tulu turned to Abby and stopped walking. "Not bad, gringa."

"They'll still be furious we were out, but at least they'll think we weren't looking for *real* trouble," Barana said.

After dinner the three of them laid out their plan: which path they'd take, where they would hide, what supplies they would need, and an emergency retreat. They even left a few bottled waters under Bela's house in case they came back parched. Barana drew a map of Pataya in her notebook—the canal, the cemetery, the beach, Barana's house, and all major landmarks. They made sure Abby knew exactly where they'd be going and how they'd make it home safely. The plan was to take the long way back, since it had more plant cover.

As Barana lay awake in bed waiting, her totem glowed through the pocket of her shorts. It was as bright as the full moon. She held it for strength and hope. She would need it. In a few hours the three of them would face whatever monsters were out there, together.

CHAPTER 24

Abby

At 11:57 p.m., Papi's breathing was steady and loud. Abby grabbed her totem for courage, tucked it in her pocket, and slowly sat up. In three minutes, she'd slip out the door and join Tulu and Barana. She'd decided against setting an alarm. Her nerves were on such high alert that she wouldn't have been able to fall asleep if she'd tried. She had gotten into bed in her clothes and had left her camera by the door.

Fortunately, the floor was not creaky. Sometimes, though, if her feet were sweaty, they'd stick to the fibers of the two petate rugs that lay by their bedsides. When that happened, her steps made a squishy sound. She would avoid walking on them and step directly onto the floorboards instead.

Unfortunately, the crickets weren't singing as loudly as they usually did, and Abby could barely hear the wind and waves. She stood like a statue for a few seconds before tiptoeing across the room.

Where was the natural background noise when she needed it?

Focus.

After taking two small steps, she stopped to see if Papi had moved. He hadn't. She took two more steps and looked again. Still breathing heavily. Her heart raced and her stomach was about to come out of her throat, but she kept going.

Then Papi made a snort-like noise and turned over. Abby froze and waited to see if he was waking. She counted five deep breaths before taking the last three steps that got her to the door. *Okay, now move the lock slowly up and to the right and release the latch.*

Her hand was shaking wildly as she turned the knob. The idea of being outside while armed criminals lurked made her want to puke. She wanted to go back to bed, forget the whole thing, call it a night. But Tulu and Barana were already waiting outside her door.

"I don't know about this," Abby whispered, gently closing the door behind her.

"Vamos," Barana said, not giving her a choice.

Abby's hands continued to shake as they walked. They stopped behind the first row of palms, using them to hide and scan for the ladrones before skittering to the next tree. Cautiously they inched their way toward the cemetery.

They had agreed that the safest place to hold their stakeout was the western edge of the beach. It was next to the canal, where they would have a wide view of the playa, with several big trees and a scattering of sea grapes and grave-stones for extra cover.

Barana walked close to Abby. "If you can get a good photo of the ladrones or their boat, take it."

"No way!" Her hands were way too wobbly, and her nerves were racing like electricity through her body. "I already want to throw up, and we're not even there yet."

Why had she agreed to do this? Why had she brought her camera? If Tulu was telling the truth, there were real, grown-up bad guys out there. The possibility of dangerous thieves on the loose was terrifying. They could actually *die*. "Barana, I think we should head back."

"Shh! We're almost there. Stick to the plan and we'll be okay," Barana replied.

The cemetery was a few yards away, and much to Abby's relief, they made it without running into any bad guys.

The waves rolled in quietly, there was no wind, and the sky was cloudy. Abby could tell the moon was growing round behind the clouds, but it wasn't a clear night. She reached into her pocket and hoped her charm would calm her nerves. When she pulled it out, it was so bright that it illuminated the sand at her feet.

"Put that away!" Barana said.

"Was that a flashlight?" Tulu said.

Abby gulped. "I'm sorry!" Close call.

They sat behind the biggest gravestone three rows into the cemetery. Tulu took a separate spot by a slightly bigger stone in front of them. They crouched on their knees and tucked their heads behind the relics.

And they waited.

The clouds moved across the sky, the waves remained still, and the air got chilly. Abby hadn't been cold the entire trip. But this evening was different. Her teeth chattered. Her digital watch said 12:21 a.m. To pass the time and distract herself, she thought of other palindromes she knew.

Mom

Noon

Kayak

Racecar

Madam

Wow

She couldn't think of any more.

Now it was 12:22 a.m.

She read the gravestones around her and realized that she was two tombstones away from R. Durón's. Maybe this distant relative would keep an eye on them tonight. Keep them safe. Abby didn't pray often, but tonight she prayed to the spirits and angels of her ancestors to watch over her and her friends.

Tulu gestured toward the water. Abby squinted and could barely see anything. It was foggy, and the other side of the canal was hidden by the white blur. Her eyes adjusted. Far in the distance and coming through the mist was a boat. The lancha approached the shore of the canal, and its motor sputtered and coughed as it revved.

It floated eerily toward the coast, and toward them.

Two men sat inside. It was pitch-black and difficult to see more than their silhouettes, but a faint orange light glowed next to the head of one of the men. A cigarette. She could tell that he wore a cap, just as Barana had described.

Abby's stomach clenched, and she had to swallow to keep the sour taste from coming up into her throat. Bad idea. This whole thing was a bad idea. She hoped they would push the boat through the narrow passage into the ocean and disappear beyond the waves.

Instead, they drifted to shore with the engine off. . . .

The capped man flicked his cigarette into the water. He stepped into the shallows and dragged the lancha onto the sand.

Both men pulled something over their mouths and noses. Handkerchiefs. To cover their faces.

"Let's get out of here," Abby whispered. "If we crawl over to the tree, we can take the long way back without ever crossing their path."

"Take the picture," Barana hissed.

No way. Abby wasn't moving a millimeter until those guys were out of sight. Besides, the shaking of her hands had only gotten worse. The men would probably kill them if they saw her.

She showed Barana her camera and gestured a big fat "No" with her hands, informing her that she would be taking *zero* photographs.

Barana pointed to the boat. "Boat! Take a photo of the boat," she mouthed.

Abby shook her head hysterically. "No! It's too far! And there's not enough light!" she whispered. There was no way she was going to risk getting killed for one measly photo of a boat. Besides, the picture would be nothing but a black blob. There was no light to speak of.

It was too far away.

It was too dark.

It was too foggy!

Tulu turned to them, his face suddenly long. The men had started walking toward the beach. Barana once again pointed at the boat and gestured for Abby to take a picture. Abby shook her head violently for the second time.

"They're far down the beach now," Barana whispered. "Do it. It's our only hope for getting any evidence."

The men were far—but not far enough for Abby to relax.

"Let's just go home," Abby said.

"Just do it! We need proof," Tulu said.

"I'm too scared."

"Let me do it, then! Hand me your camera," Barana said.

"No!" Abby mouthed.

"Just crawl on your belly until you reach the first row of tombstones. Then take the picture," Tulu whispered.

Abby trembled. Her hands were so sweaty they could barely hold the camera. She felt the totem in her pocket and tried to summon the courage to get the proof they needed. *Take risks!* She crawled with shaking knees and leaned against a gravestone in the first row. She moved aside a shrub and pointed the camera in the general direction of the boat, but it was so dark and overcast, and she was so nervous, that she couldn't tell if the boat was even centered in her lens.

She had the camera pointed toward the canal and her finger on the shutter when Tulu spoke up.

"Wait," he whispered. "They've stopped. Maybe they found turtle tracks."

Abby panicked. She hit the shutter. The flash went off, and a bright white light erupted from the device. She immediately crumpled to the ground and put her hands over her mouth to keep herself from screaming. And vomiting.

Her friends motioned for her to crawl back to them.

What had she done?

A sharp gunshot echoed loudly in the air.

That's it! They were done for!

A flashlight shone in their direction.

One of the men waved it around frantically as if searching for movement. Abby could tell he wasn't sure where to look. His flashlight was too weak to reach them, but if he got closer, it was all over.

They had seconds to get out of there.

Boom! A second shot.

A final warning. It was now or never.

Tulu crawled toward the back side of the graveyard, where the giant gumbo-limbo tree cast darkness above the stones. Abby and Barana followed. Abby's knees burned as they rubbed against cracked seashells.

They didn't look back. Dashing around palms and shrubs, she understood the meaning of "run for your life." Finally, they could no longer see the poachers or the waves. They stopped behind a large sea grape with big round leaves and caught their breath. From there, they ran across the western edge of Pataya until they reached Bela's.

Once they were safely underneath Bela's house, tears started streaming down Barana's cheeks. Abby hyperventilated and sat against one of the stilts. She hugged her stomach to prevent herself from hurling.

"Lo siento, amiga," Barana said.

"It's not your fault. We're safe now, right? They didn't follow us, did they?" Abby said.

"I don't think so," Tulu whispered. "Do you think you got a picture of the boat?"

Abby shook her head. "I'm not sure. I panicked. I have no idea what I did."

"It's okay," Tulu said. "Let's all calm down before we check. And keep your voices down. We don't want to wake anyone."

Abby's heart was pounding at three million beats per minute. Tulu grabbed the bottles of water they'd left behind—

the only part of their plan that had worked. As Abby held the bottle, her hand shook and some of the water spilled in the process. She was so thirsty she chugged it all in one gulp.

"Focus on breathing," Barana whispered, her face still flushed. "Inhala, exhala."

As Abby tried to breathe, it sank in that she'd been wrong about Tulu. "I'm sorry I accused you, Tulu."

"It's okay. I was sorrier that my own sister thought I was capable of something like that."

Tulu looked over at Barana.

"I'm sorry too," Barana said. She hugged her brother tightly.

Abby's breathing steadied, but she was still sick to her stomach. She dried her sweaty palms on her jean shorts, turned on her camera, and found the picture of the boat. It was blurry and mostly out of the frame, but the flash had captured part of the stern. They could tell the boat was mostly white, with a stripe near the top, but it was difficult to make out the color.

Tulu suggested looking at it again in the light of day, after their shock had subsided. They had to be ready for school in five hours.

"I hope Mamá and Papá didn't wake up while we were gone," Barana said as they walked toward Abby's cabin.

"If they did, we'll say Abby begged us to take her to the cemetery, remember? That's the story," Tulu reminded them.

"Exactly. Blame me. American kids love graveyards," Abby said.

"Hopefully, they're still asleep and we won't need to explain anything."

They quieted down as they arrived at the guesthouse. Outside the cabin's door, Barana hugged Abby. "It'll be okay," she said.

Tulu waved warmly as he turned to go home.

"Buenas noches," Abby whispered.

"Buenas noches," the siblings replied.

She entered her cabin as quietly as she'd exited.

She couldn't see a thing, so she pulled out her sea turtle totem and used it to find her way to bed. She needed to sleep off the events of the night, but she was too mad at herself for leaving the flash on and endangering their lives. The one time she tried to "take a risk," like her teacher suggested, her nerves had ruined everything.

She didn't want to use her cursed camera again for the rest of the trip.

At least not for playing detective.

Things had gotten way out of hand. If they hadn't solved the mystery by now, they weren't meant to solve it at all.

The poachers had won, and they needed to accept it.

Their lives depended on it.

CHAPTER 25

Barana

Barana slept zero hours, zero minutes, and zero seconds. Her eyes were itchy and dry, and her lungs felt like a rusty, empty oxygen tank. She couldn't take a deep breath even if she tried. Her scar had been silent during their stakeout, and she hoped this meant that Luna was safely grazing on jellyfish miles away. At least they'd come home to sleeping parents.

It was still dark outside, but the promise of day was in the purple hue on the eastern horizon. Tulu and Barana got out of bed before their parents and went through their morning routine as if nothing had happened. They exchanged a few whispers and agreed to be as calm as the waves on a day without wind.

Much to their surprise, Papá woke up as they ate. When he prepared the water to make coffee, Tulu requested that he make a bigger-than-usual pot. It was nice having Papá home in the morning. As he boiled water on the small gas stove,

Tulu poured the coffee grinds into a brown cloth filter, and Barana sat and prayed. She hadn't prayed in a while. But today it was necessary. She prayed for protection for her turtle, her friend, and her family.

Papá poured her a small cup of coffee and placed it on the table in front of her.

Barana hadn't asked for it, but she figured it couldn't hurt. She sipped it slowly and a jolt ran through her veins. "Gracias, Papá."

Her father smiled a tired but hopeful smile. It had been a while since she'd seen it. She looked over at Tulu, and neither of them could help but quietly grin at the fact they were bonding with Papá over coffee.

After their caffeine boost, Tulu and Barana hurried down the steps and across the yard to pick up Abby for school. She was already outside waiting for them. The three of them were in it together now.

As they walked down the camino toward the lagoon, the hauntingly quiet sea turtle office beckoned Barana closer. Its faded walls were an empty shell of the past. A turtle shell without the turtle.

She resisted sneaking inside the office. She needed to think before acting impulsively. She had tried coming up with a plan while she lay awake in bed, but the only things that kept coming to her were the images of the boat and the cigarette being flicked into the water and the deafening sound of the gunshots. Something about the boat had been familiar, but she hadn't been able to put her finger on what.

They sat on the dock and waited underneath the palapa, half asleep and heavy-eyed despite the coffee. More schoolchildren arrived, and their chatter and giggles were like loud marimba music in Barana's ears.

In the distance, she finally heard Nati's motor.

The engine sounded like a smoker's cough.

It revved and gurgled loudly before coming to a stop.

She opened her eyes and stared at the lancha as it approached.

It was white. It had a faint stripe.

The closer it got, the more Barana knew in her bones what she was seeing and hearing.

This was the boat. How could she not have seen it earlier?

Tulu's mouth gaped open, like he'd just realized the same thing.

Abby's eyes were like a lechuza's—an owl's—wide and focused.

All three of them knew.

Nati got closer. His body type matched that of the shorter poacher. He knew the local waters like the back of his hand. Then Barana remembered the way he had spoken up at church when María made her announcement. He had made the biggest fuss of all and insisted that everyone stay away. *He* had suggested the poachers were outsiders from far off the coast.

It all made sense.

They climbed into the boat along with the rest of the schoolchildren. Barana tried not to make eye contact. Her chest felt tight, and she wasn't sure she'd taken a breath in over a minute. Nati didn't say good morning. He didn't have mini-bananas to offer them, either. He was not himself today.

Did he know it was them at the cemetery last night?

Barana hoped nobody could tell how hard and fast her heart was beating. For the first time in years, she kept her gaze on the horizon the entire ride to school. No sketching, no chatting, nothing. Abby and Tulu did the same.

At least she had her totem. She gripped it tightly until they were safely off the boat.

As they marched up the hill to school, Barana whispered, "Were you thinking what I was thinking?"

"Yes," Tulu and Abby replied at the same time.

"I've heard Nati's engine for six years. I should've recognized it last night," Tulu said.

"Let's look at Abby's picture again, to be sure," Barana said.

Abby held up her small satchel and shrugged. "I left my camera at home. It was nothing but bad luck last night, and I didn't want to drag it with me today."

"We'll check later," Barana said. "I'm sure the picture will be a match."

"We should follow Nati after school," Tulu said. "Maybe he'll lead us to the other guy. We only have half the answer right now."

Barana liked how her brother was thinking. Nati was one of the poachers. The other culprit was taller, wore a baseball cap, smoked, and likely lived nearby.

María had said the poachers went north the day they threatened her. Was Nati working with an outsider?

No. Something didn't feel right. Barana feared there were no outsiders involved in the poaching scheme. That realization was the scariest part of it all.

Someone else from Pataya was in on the crime.

THE AFTERNOON BOAT ride was no different from the morning's. Nati was still not himself. Barana was no mind reader, but she could tell he was distracted. She tried to act normal, even forcing a smile when she boarded the boat. He did not smile back. Instead, he glared at her with a threatening look on his face until she took her seat.

It was the longest twenty minutes of her life.

They arrived in Pataya and walked the path as if heading home. Rather than continuing, however, they went off the camino and found an avocado tree they could climb to spy on Nati. Finally, after chatting with a group of fishermen, Nati began his trek up to the village.

Their hidden perch in the tree was successful. Nati walked right past them, unaware that they were watching from behind a screen of leaves.

They waited until he was far down the camino before they hopped off and followed him.

Much to Barana's surprise, Nati stopped by María's house. María was in her yard and approached him slowly. When María got close, Nati gave her something, a small object that María then placed in the front pocket of her light green apron.

"Stay here. I'll get closer and try to listen to what they're saying," Tulu said.

The girls agreed.

They watched as Tulu neared the back of María's house and hid behind a short palm. Its leaves were huge, and its trunk was wide, providing a decent hiding spot. He stood there for a few minutes before turning to come back.

"Vámonos, rápido," he said. "I'll tell you what they said on the way home. We need to get out of here."

None of them dared turn their head back to find out if they'd been seen. They bolted up the hill and took a different route home.

"What did they say?" Barana finally asked.

"It was hard to hear everything, but I read their lips and I think Nati said something was 'safe in the office.'"

"What does that mean?" Abby said.

"Beats me. Money? Eggs? Who knows," Tulu answered. "But either María's in on this thing or he's fooling her."

Barana felt like she'd just been tumbled over by a huge wave. "He's got her fooled," she said. She knew that María would never hurt the turtles. But why would she trust Nati with the office? Had he been lying to her and making her think he was helping? "We need to get into the office and get to the bottom of this."

"Hold on," Tulu said. "We can't be breaking into buildings the day after we were threatened with gunshots. We need to see that picture Abby took first. That might be enough. If we can match the boat to Nati's, we'll have proof it's him and can tell María and our parents that he's behind all of it. We might not even need to break into the office."

Abby nodded in agreement. "You're right. We need to get my camera and check that photo."

"Fine. But I'm breaking into the office as soon as we've looked at it," Barana said.

They sped home and went straight to Bela's guesthouse. Abby went inside while Barana and Tulu waited by the door. When she came back out, her eyebrows were up, and her mouth was agape. She looked like she'd seen a dead body.

She glared at them with two empty hands stretched out in front of her. "My camera . . . it's gone."

"Are you sure? Could your father have taken it somewhere?"

"No way. He wouldn't. Someone stole it. I'm one thousand percent positive."

CHAPTER 26

Abby

Abby had heard of panic attacks, but she wasn't sure she'd ever had one until that very moment. The stakeout had been terrifying, but now she felt like the earth beneath her feet was opening, like she was falling and her insides were about to come out. She had alerted the poachers to their presence at the beach last night, and now her brand-new camera had been taken from her room—most likely by the same criminals!

"Do you think it was *them?*" Barana said.

A shiver crawled up Abby's spine. "If it was the poachers, it means we're dead meat. It means they know we were the ones on the beach last night."

Tulu made a sound like a bomb had exploded in his head. "Maybe *that's* what Nati meant was 'safe in the office.' Maybe he hid your camera there."

"But why would María ask about that? She can't possibly be involved in this," Barana said.

"Who knows? But it doesn't matter. It's worth going to look. We have to at least try," Abby said. Her heart was pounding so fast she could practically see it straining against her chest. Their lives were in danger, her brand-new camera was gone, and the world was spinning. She needed to do something. But first, she had to focus.

"Inhala, exhala," Barana whispered.

"We should go. To the turtle office," Abby said. There was no time to waste.

Barana sat and pulled her notebook out of her bag. "Too many people walking around. It's the middle of the afternoon. We need to wait until it's dark."

"There's *no* way I'm sneaking out again at *night*! Not after what happened yesterday. We need to do this now, or I'm not doing it at all," Abby said. "Papi will be furious when he finds out my new camera was taken."

Tulu agreed and suggested that one of them break in while the other two guarded the perimeter. If any witnesses walked by, they could distract them somehow. They decided Barana would be the one to enter. She knew the contents of the office better than either of them, and she'd fit through the window easily.

As they prepared to go, Barana and Tulu's mother came down the steps of their house in a fury. She held a piece of paper in her hand and waved it like a test with a bad grade on it or a note from the principal.

"Can either of you explain this?" she demanded.

She shoved the paper at them.

TELL YOUR KIDS TO STAY OFF THE BEACH. OR ELSE.

Abby stood in silence as Tulu and Barana lied to their mother's face.

"That makes no sense," Tulu said. "We haven't been on the beach."

"Except for the one time you let us go," Barana said. Her voice was shaky.

"Mentira. Don't you dare lie to me. Why else would someone leave a threatening note at my store? Do you understand that this is real?"

"Mamá, we didn't do anything," Barana insisted.

Abby could tell their mother wasn't buying it, and she wanted to help.

Then, as if reading Abby's mind, their mother turned and said, "Well? Do *you* know anything about this? You've been hanging around with my kids all week."

Abby looked at her friends. Barana made a ghostly face and Tulu mouthed, "Uuuuuu!" Ghosts. *Ghosts!* They wanted her to use their backup lie from last night!

She took in an exaggerated breath and tried to act embarrassed. Then she let out a louder-than-normal exhale.

"Actually . . ." She paused. "We went out once. But it's my fault. I begged them to take me to the cemetery last night. I love graveyards, and I'm obsessed with this one gravestone that has my family's name on it . . . and . . . well, I wanted to see it under the moonlight! Lo siento. Tulu and Barana aren't to blame." She tried to act naive, like she'd been busted for a childish excursion.

Barana and Tulu nodded at her in approval.

Their mamá shook her head in disapproval. "My children should know better than to be taking a visitor out into the night when there are poachers out there." She glared at Barana and Tulu, grabbed both their hands, and tugged them along.

"You're all going to Bela's until dinner. You hear me? Watch your sister and help your abuela with whatever she needs. Chiqui and I need to bake for tomorrow, and I can't have you sneaking off again. We will talk about this at dinner. With your fathers. And you can expect consequences." She untucked baby Marisol from her sling and handed her over to Tulu. "*You* watch Marisol."

Tulu held the baby in his arms as all three of them slowly and shamefully marched up Bela's steps. Barana's mother scowled at them from below.

They went inside the kitchen and told Bela they were there to help until dinner.

"Very good," Bela said. She was happy to see them.

It was nice to not be in trouble with her . . . yet.

"You girls go through this bowl of beans and get rid of the wrinkled and damaged ones." Bela reached in the bowl and pulled out a bean that looked more like a gray raisin. "See, like this one."

The girls got to work while Tulu held Marisol on his lap. Bela brought him a basket full of cotton diapers. "Fold," she instructed.

Pitufo sat on the edge of the deck's railing with a smirk, like he was checking their work.

The afternoon dragged on, and with Marisol to care for and Bela popping in to issue new tasks, there would be no breaking into the office until morning. Papi had his big presentation tomorrow afternoon at the community center, and Abby didn't want to upset him before then. She had to make sure he didn't notice the camera was gone.

At dinnertime everyone gathered on the dining deck: Papi, Barana's father, Bela, and her husband, Juan. Lastly, Barana's mother arrived with a basket of fresh bread.

Abby's stomach churned as they all took their seats, but it wasn't from hunger. She braced herself for the big announcement about their forbidden escapade, and for the punishment that would surely follow.

As soon as everyone had a plate and was seated, Barana's mother let it all out. She wasted no time.

"I have news." She glared at the three of them. "Estos muchachitos thought it would be fun to visit el cementerio last night. And apparently those poachers saw them, because I got a threatening note at my pulpería saying to tell my kids to keep off la playa." She waved the paper in the air like a flag.

Papi's eyebrows rose a whole inch, and he swallowed his bite in one gulp.

Barana's father made two fists with his hands and banged on the table. "Barana! Tulu! What were you thinking?"

Papi looked over at Abby. "Aberdeen? You snuck out?"

Don't puke. Breathe. Focus. Abby tried to stay calm. She reached in her pocket for the turtle totem. It was hot as embers.

"It was stupid. I wanted to see the graveyard under the moonlit sky. And the tombstone with our name on it . . . I, uh, I wanted a dark, sort of creepy photo. I know it was childish. Lo siento."

"Abby, do you realize how dangerous that was?" His voice was so loud Abby had to fight the urge to cover her ears.

The grown-ups erupted into lectures and speeches about how reckless they'd been, and how irresponsible of Tulu for being the oldest and going along with the idea.

Barana's father looked at his daughter suspiciously. Abby remembered he'd caught her once before coming back from the beach. She hoped her cemetery story would be enough to convince him they weren't out to see Luna or catch the poachers.

As the lectures died down, she remembered her camera.

Please don't ask why I don't have it with me.

Please don't ask where it is.

Please. Don't. Notice. It's. Gone.

She repeated these three wishes in her head until the words were so jumbled that they got tangled in her brain. She ate quietly and without appetite. Afterward, they bolted to the kitchen to do the dishes before anybody asked them to.

"Well, no soccer for a month, and I have to alternate baby-sitting duties with my sister," Tulu said.

"And I get the pleasure of working at the pulpería every afternoon. Including weekends," Barana said. "At least Tulu finally has to help with baby duty."

Papi hadn't specified a punishment for Abby yet, but his disappointment was enough of a consequence. And he didn't even know about the camera.

"When should we do the thing? You know . . ." Abby mouthed the word *office* and gestured like she was climbing through a window. She didn't want Bela or anyone else hearing them.

"Before school tomorrow. It'll be dark enough, and only a couple of students walk by there on the way to the dock," Barana whispered.

It was risky. Getting caught would be the final straw; if their parents had been harsh about the cemetery, the punishment for breaking into the office would be ten times worse. But if they were going to prove without a doubt that Nati was the poacher, they needed to recover Abby's camera. They needed evidence. Until they did, Abby just had to hope Papi didn't get curious about her pictures.

CHAPTER 27

Barana

I am from a village,
Once peaceful and safe.
From a land by the Atlantic,
Where hurricanes of doubt
Meet courage and hope within.

Barana closed her notebook and left the poem unfinished. The ending would come later. She had no appetite, so getting ready for school took less time than usual. Mamá and Papá were still in bed with Marisol when she and Tulu walked out the door. She packed an extra uniform blouse snugly inside her backpack in case she ripped or dirtied the one she was wearing now. La directora was strict about the uniform policy.

Abby was already outside brushing her teeth when Barana and Tulu crossed the yard to the guesthouse.

"Lista?" Barana said.

Abby gave her a thumbs-up while splashing her face with water from the pila.

Barana got close enough to whisper. "Did he notice your camera was missing?"

She hoped her friend hadn't gotten into more trouble. They'd had enough of that to last them several decades.

"No, but keep it down. I've tried to act normal, but I can't keep it up for much longer."

"Don't go back in your room; let's just wave and go." Barana's chest was aching. She didn't mean for her friend to lose her camera. They had to find it. It was the only way out of this mess.

"I already kissed him goodbye. The sooner we leave, the sooner my stomach will finally settle." They started down the moonlit path and hurried toward their fate. Barana paused to look up. The moon had a way of giving her perspective. She breathed in its magic and gathered the courage she needed to follow through with their plan.

The sea turtle office stood before them like an impenetrable fortress. A rusty lock held the door in place. They went around the back, where the window was missing a few of its horizontal wooden panes. The panes could be moved up and down to let in the sea breeze, and with a little wiggle, Tulu pulled the first one out of its slit. He gently extracted another pane, creating a big enough hole for Barana to fit through, while Abby kept watch near the front of the building. They had about ten minutes before the sun rose completely.

Tulu gave his sister a boost, and she pushed herself through the opening, headfirst. Her knee was shaking.

"Just breathe, hermana," Tulu said.

There was a table under the window she could hold on to for balance. As her chest and arms made it inside, she pushed off the table and bent her right knee, slowly pulling her leg through. She rolled her body onto the table—and made way too much noise in the process.

She felt as heavy as a six-hundred-pound baula. Every movement seemed difficult. Even breathing.

Inhala, exhala.

She looked at the door and prayed that nobody would come to the office this early in the morning. Barana hadn't seen a soul there for weeks. No. No one was likely to come. Abby and Tulu would warn her if they did. She needed to trust them more than ever right now.

The turtle totem glowed bright, and she used its light to search for Abby's camera.

There were papers and supplies everywhere: nesting logs, pens, wooden stakes, rope, and the collection of signs they used to mark off nests. Barana missed those days. Now the office was dusty and crawling with insectos.

Tulu whispered through the window, "Hurry! Sun's coming up."

The sky was turning a faint lilac color outside, and the school boat would be arriving soon. Her scar began to burn.

She worked faster, opening filing cabinets and desk drawers and shuffling papers and equipment around in search of something—anything.

Was it even there?

She'd searched everywhere.

Then, out of the corner of her eye, she saw a small gray trash can underneath the desk. She got on her hands and knees and reached for it. As she dragged the wastebasket toward her, she could immediately tell there was something heavy inside.

Her heart gave a jolt. It was Abby's camera.

Barana had no time to get emotional. She wanted to scream! Kick! Jump! But she didn't have time to make sense of it. She needed to get out of there. *Now.*

She hung the camera around her neck and clambered onto the table. As fast as she could, she slipped her body through the window, this time legs first. Her stomach got badly scratched on the way out, but the pain was nothing compared to the relief of knowing she'd found what they were looking for.

Tulu wasn't there to catch her when she dropped out of the broken window to the sand below. Nobody was.

She landed on both feet, caught her breath, and wiped down her clothes. Abby was by herself, pacing in front of the building, holding both of their bags.

When she saw what Barana had in her hands, she ran up and hugged her.

"I can't believe it was in there! So, it *was* him."

Barana gave her the camera. "Hurry up. Put it away and let's go. We can't miss the boat."

Abby tucked it safely inside her backpack. "We'll check the pictures when we get to school. We can't risk Nati seeing it."

"Where's my brother?"

"Some kids started asking him questions. He managed to get them walking again; they must be down the path."

"Were they wearing uniforms?"

"Yes."

"Okay, good. Come on, let's catch up with them."

Then Barana stopped dead in her tracks. "Wait—I have to put the windowpanes back."

She ran to the window and turned to look around the palm trees that surrounded the building, making sure nobody was there. She carefully slipped the two wooden windowpanes back inside their grooves as the sun peeked above the horizon.

When she finished, she ran toward Abby, and they walked briskly to the dock, where they met up with Tulu under the palapa.

Nati must have been running late. Which was odd. He was never late.

"Did you find it?" Tulu mouthed.

Barana gave him the slightest of nods.

They needed to get to school and find a private spot to look at Abby's pictures.

Then the unmistakable sound of the lancha approached.

"Act normal," Tulu said. "He has no idea we found the camera."

Barana wasn't sure she could pull it off. She wanted to yell at him, call out his betrayal, and tell the entire village he was guilty. Abby squeezed her hand.

Inhala, exhala.

Barana tried to breathe. She knew they had to be patient.

The lancha reached the dock. Tulu and the older students helped Nati tie it to the post. Nati smiled a tight, fake smile as they boarded, and Barana said buenos días before quietly taking her seat. She held Abby's hand in one of hers and the turtle totem in the other. Clouds covered the sky as they rode over the water. Barana closed her eyes and let the salty air, her friend's hand, and her totem calm her nerves.

Once at the school dock, they hopped off the boat and speed-walked uphill. Tulu joined them on a quiet bench at the end of the courtyard.

"It's okay if I'm a little late," he said.

Abby pulled her camera out of her bag and turned it on. "Here goes nothing." She pressed some buttons, and Barana waited with her stomach in her throat to see if she'd found the photo. "It's here."

"Show us!"

They examined the image of the blurry boat by the canal on that terrifying night.

The match was undeniable. This was the evidence they needed to prove their suspicions about Nati. Though the picture was out of focus, Abby zoomed in, and they could match the dent on the boat in the picture to Nati's. And though the faded blue stripe was faint, it was there.

"We need to know what María's involvement is in all of this. Why would she trust Nati with a key to the turtle office?" Abby said.

Barana shook her head. "There's no way she's involved. He must be lying to her. Or using her."

"Hold on. I think I might have another piece of the puzzle," Abby said.

She held her camera out for them to see. On the small screen was a picture of María and her family. "I took this portrait on my first day here. Look at what Matías is wearing."

It was the red ball cap. And it was the same one they'd seen the poacher wearing on the night of the stakeout. The same one in Barana's nightmare.

"Also, remember one of the men was smoking when they came onto the shore?" Abby said. "Matías was smoking on the dive boat."

Barana thought back to the shadowy figure behind the palms, to the night she snuck out, to the cigarette butt left behind at Luna's empty nest, and to the look in María's eyes when she made the announcement at church. In her heart,

Barana knew the answer. Matías was guilty. He'd lost the ability to scuba dive, he'd lost his ability to provide for his family, and he'd lost his integrity.

The man had become the thing his very own wife hated most—a *poacher.*

"They need to pay for this. They lied to our faces. They lied to María. They lied to everyone," Barana said.

"But María told us the masked poachers threatened both her *and* Matías," Abby said.

"Maybe it was too dark for her to recognize Nati. Matías must've played along that night and there's a *third* man involved," Barana replied.

"Or maybe María knew the truth all along, but there was nothing she could do about it," Tulu said. "Maybe she was too scared."

Barana needed answers. There had to be an explanation for all of it.

"All we know for sure is that Matías and Nati are involved. We saw them. María's involvement is still a big question mark," Abby said.

"Either way, we need to tell everyone right away," Barana said.

"Papi's giving a presentation at the community center after lunch today. He's presenting stuff about how diving accidents have gone down over the last two years. A lot of people will be there, even your father and probably Matías. Maybe we can go straight there after school?" Abby suggested.

"Perfecto," Tulu said.

Barana nodded. They had a plan. They'd be safe at school, and then they'd speak their truth at the community center.

The only problem was the ride home.

If Nati happened to go back to the office to check on the camera, they were in deeper trouble than ever.

THE FINAL BELL rang. It was time to bring the poachers to justice. Barana untucked her school shirt as they walked out of the school's front gate. She could feel the droplets of sweat dripping down her face and stomach. Still, Barana refused to believe that María knew what her husband and Nati had been up to. María loved the leatherbacks. She was a good mother. She was innocent in all of this.

"Ready?" Abby said. She also looked concerned. She hadn't even taken her camera out all day. Abby usually took pictures during recess—and even in class, if the teacher let her. Today, it had remained tucked away inside her backpack.

Barana shook her head. "No. What if Nati went back to the office and realized the camera was gone?" Her voice was shaky.

"It won't matter. We still have to tell everyone," Abby said.

Barana wasn't so sure. "Also, what if after telling everyone, nothing changes? What if the project disappears anyway? What if nobody cares anymore?"

"That will never happen. *You* care. Even if things don't go back to normal right away, speaking out is the first step. It's the only thing left to do, and what happens after that will depend on everyone, not just you and me."

Tulu caught up with them a few feet from the dock. His chest was puffed like he was ready for battle.

They stood in a row at the end of the dock and waited.

The school boat appeared across the river. Now that they knew the truth, its shape and sound was even more recognizable as the poachers'. Barana pictured Nati and Matías loading turtle eggs onto it, and her blood boiled.

Both of Luna's nests. Gone. Because of those ladrones. Barana knew she would never be able to look at Nati and not think of Luna's babies.

Nati glowered at them as they approached. He knew they knew. There were daggers in his eyes. The girls and Tulu boarded quietly, taking their regular seats and looking straight ahead at the horizon.

Barana's scar throbbed, and her heart quickened. Nati was onto them, and every cell in her body knew it. They needed to get to the community center as fast as possible. And yet the boat churned along the canal as slow as a sloth. Was Nati purposely keeping them from getting back to Pataya in time for the presentation? Or was the snail's pace of the lancha a coincidence? Kids squealed at how sluggishly they were moving and leaned over the side to touch the water.

"Maybe we'll see a manatee!" one of the youngest riders said.

Barana knew she needed to distract herself; otherwise, she'd do something she'd later regret. She pulled out her journal and drew a hatchling. It was how she imagined baby Luna. She drew her moon-shaped scar, her beady black eyes, and her long, powerful flippers. She wanted to continue her last poem about the truth she was seeking, and about the poachers. She chewed her already bumpy pencil and looked out at the slow-moving landscape as they made their sluggish way through the canals.

The second verse came to her line by line, and she wrote:

I am from a place
Of palms and drumbeats,
Of fishing boats and hatchlings.
Where community meets the sea,
And turtles of the midnight moon come home.

By the time she looked up, they had arrived.

"We need to hurry," Tulu said. He grabbed Barana by the hand brusquely and motioned to Abby. "The meeting started an hour ago. If we run, we'll make it there before it's over."

As they jumped onto the dock, Nati didn't take his eyes off them.

Barana felt like a boiling pot of water with the lid on tight.

The moment she let go, the steam would escape and shock everyone around her with its heat and pressure. She wanted to scream at Nati.

They ran like jaguars, and none of them dared look back to see his face.

INSIDE THE COMMUNITY center, Abby's father was speaking on the raised wooden platform in the front. Two local doctors and Pastor Pablo sat with him. Barana quickly scanned the room and saw Matías. Papá was across from them, and a group of men, women, abuelos, and abuelas sat on benches around the room.

Half the village was there. But not María.

Barana, Abby, and Tulu charged to the front and spoke all at once, telling Abby's father they had something urgent to say. They were so loud and talked so quickly that he hushed them.

"Stop, you're all talking way too fast. Take a breath, and only one of you speak." He stepped back and apologized to the audience.

"Barana can explain," Abby said. She looked at Barana expectantly.

Barana's hands were shaking. She wasn't sure she could do it. What if nothing came out of her mouth? Like that bird in her nightmare, frozen with fright. She'd yelled along with Tulu and Abby, but speaking by herself in front of this crowd? That was terrifying.

"Go ahead, Barana," Abby's father said.

Barana nodded nervously.

Tulu placed his hand on her shoulder and mouthed, "Tell them!"

This was it. Matías had his eyes on her, the townspeople were waiting, and she knew her life and her turtles' lives depended on this moment. After days of searching for answers, they'd finally gotten to the truth. Her chest tightened as she met Matías's eye. He looked like he was about to lunge forward and choke her.

Instead, he crossed his arms, lowered his gaze, and shook his head in threatening silence.

Barana reached into her pocket and grabbed the turtle totem that had given her hope and strength all week long. It almost burned her palm.

Inhala, exhala.

Abby took her hand, and Barana closed her eyes, searching for the right words in her mind. When she opened them, María was standing in the back of the room, with Nati by her side. They looked at each other and then at Barana. Then she slowly started walking toward the front.

Nati must've followed them and alerted María.

It was now or never. Barana had to speak.

"Barana?" Abby's father said.

"It's about the poaching," she began. *Inhala.* "The turtles, their eggs—it wasn't outsiders!" *Exhala.* Her voice was so loud she startled herself. The words came out like a shout. Her knees were shaking, and her scar burned. María and Nati kept walking toward her. Slowly. Deliberately.

"They're *here.* It's been someone from our village all along. We saw them. You have to believe us." Tears streamed down her face.

"We want justice," Tulu added.

"And for the poaching to stop! The hatchlings are a part of Pataya. It's their home too!" Abby said.

"What are you saying?" Pastor Pablo interrupted. "You *know* who the poachers are?"

Abby nodded. "The three of us know."

Barana couldn't bring herself to say their names, but she had to.

She remembered her totem. Warmth. Courage. Hope.

"Matías Morales." She pointed to the back of the room. "And Nati Zelaya."

Roars echoed through the large room like the night of the storm. Everyone had questions.

"Matías, Nati—is this true?" the pastor asked, getting up from his seat and glaring at the accused.

Papá got up too. He walked toward Barana and grabbed her shoulders, arms, and face as if examining her for wounds or bruises. "Mija, how did you find out? Did they hurt you?"

He stared icily at Matías and clenched his fists like he wanted to punch him.

Barana shook her head and embraced her father as if she'd been a lost child reunited with her family. "Lo siento, Papá. We weren't out taking photos that night at the cemetery. We were searching for answers." The truth released the burning. Her scar no longer hurt, but she couldn't stop the tears. Papá held her tight as Matías and Nati scrambled forward.

"¡No es cierto! It's not true! Ask them if they have proof!" Matías said.

Now María stood by his side, her face pale.

Nati stood next to them with his arms crossed, shaking his head. "They can't prove it."

They don't know we recovered Abby's camera.

"It *is* true! It was them!" Abby yelled.

Barana was furious. The nerve these men had. To lie, to deceive them all. And why wasn't María saying anything?

"They fired their gun, Papá!" Barana screamed. "And they're wrong. We *can* prove it."

Papá stared at Matías and lifted his fist. "You poached from our own beach *and* threatened my daughter's life?"

"I told you, they're lying!" Matías insisted.

Barana was about to tell Abby to show everyone the picture of Nati's boat when a familiar voice interrupted the congregation.

"¡Silencio! Todos."

The crowd immediately quieted.

María held her big round belly and turned to face Matías. "I can't do this anymore. It's time to tell everyone the truth."

María had their back. María would admit to her husband's wrongdoing.

"It's all true," María confessed. "Barana is right about—almost—everything."

Almost?

The entire crowd held its breath waiting for María to continue.

Inhala . . .

"Before the storm, they froze our funding. I fought to convince the government to continue supporting our small conservation project, but to no avail. After the storm, it was useless to ask. Everything went to rebuilding."

Why was María talking about the project's funding?

"The poaching was my idea. Matías could hardly work. Our project had been forgotten. We were desperate. I thought . . ." Tears streamed down María's round cheeks. "I thought if we could show everyone that the beach still needed patrolling, maybe we could convince them to keep funding our efforts. The patrolling. The education. The outreach. The tagging and the observation. I thought maybe we could even get enough to finally build a proper hatchery."

Exhala . . .

"María, basta," Matías said. "Enough."

"No. They need to know. *I* told my husband to go out

there. But only temporarily. The plan was to use the money from the eggs to get us through for a while, or until we secured our project's funding again." Her voice cracked. She covered her face with her weathered hands and let out an anguished sob. "I'm so sorry!" she wailed.

Matías continued for her. "I knew a man who would give me cash for the turtle eggs. I convinced my cousin to help me transport them on his boat until the end of the season." He glanced over at Nati. His cousin.

María was sagging on her feet, her tear-filled face still hidden behind her hands. She shook her head and mumbled, "I'm so sorry, I'm so sorry." Barana feared she'd go into labor right then and there from all the stress. Pastor Pablo invited her to sit, and someone from the crowd brought her water. Barana realized just how much María had been struggling. As a wife, as a mother, and as a member of their community.

María gathered herself with the pastor's support. And piece by piece, she filled in the gaps in the story: how her husband couldn't dive anymore after his accident, how he'd entered a deep depression and the storm had only worsened his mood, bringing with it a dimming of his spirit and desperation to make ends meet. That it felt like everything had fallen apart.

Barana's chest softened, but her hands kept shaking.

María was still the same woman who had taught her how to measure the carapace of a leatherback, the same woman who'd shown her how to identify a mama turtle by her markings. She'd cared for the baulas since before Barana had even been born. That woman was still there, even though she'd made a horrible choice that carried dire consequences.

In that moment María was like a turtle without a shell. Exposed.

Barana had wanted consequences, but something inside her changed. No punishment could bring back the stolen eggs.

"How many eggs did you take?" Abby's father asked.

"Three nests. About three hundred eggs," Matías replied. "María begged us to stop after the first one. She regretted her idea immediately."

"Why didn't you?" Barana asked.

"We needed the money." Now he was the one blinking hard to stop the tears from escaping, rubbing his cheeks with balled fists when the lágrimas fell anyway. He looked over at Abby's father and lowered his head in shame. "I shouldn't have done it," he said. "I knew it even then, but I did it anyway." He placed his hand over María's belly and turned to face the crowd. "We made a bad choice, a shameful one." He stretched out a corner of his shirt to dry his face. "I don't deserve your forgiveness, but my wife does. Nobody, *nobody* cares more about the baulas than she does. I beg you to please . . . forgive her."

María wiped her face and breathed in once more. "After

the third nest, they finally agreed to stop, but we decided to keep the lie going. We wanted to make it *seem* like the poachers were still out there until we secured the funding to bring back the conservation project. I wanted nothing more than for our efforts to grow—for our good work to continue."

"We were going to relocate a nest when the kids saw us on the beach," Matías said. "We were done poaching by then."

"So, the heroes and the villains are one and the same," Abby's father said. "Clever."

"No," María replied, tears streaming down her cheeks. "There are no heroes here."

And in that moment, Barana knew that no punishment could come close to what María already felt.

Dozens of conversations broke out across the room. Pastor Pablo and Abby's father hushed them. Then the pastor turned to Nati.

"Would you like to say something as well?"

Nati nodded. "We will make this right. I am sorry for frightening you three," he said, looking at Abby, Barana, and Tulu. "My cousin should never have fired that gun."

The pastor turned to them. "Thank you for having the courage to come here. This is, of course, a great offense to our community and to the sacred sea turtles that have been here for centuries before us." He paused and looked into the thieves' eyes. "Threatening our children and deceiving this community will not be condoned in Pataya, but we recognize your remorse. I can see this pains you deeply—especially María. Now we must all come to an agreement about how to rise from this."

Barana wondered what he meant. Would there be consequences?

"Our Lord teaches us that the only way to move forward is through love, forgiveness, empathy, and compassion. María and her family deserve a second chance."

The crowd nodded and murmured in agreement. A few people clapped softly.

Pastor Pablo continued. "We must lift each other up in our darkest hour. While there is dishonor in what you three did, there is honor in what you've confessed today. We will stand by you as your neighbors and rely on our collective strength to rise from these events, making our beach safe and peaceful once more. And yet . . ." He turned to face María, Matías, and Nati. "This is possible only if you promise to mend the damage you have done, especially to these three children."

Barana reached for Abby's hand, still trying to make sense of what had happened. María hadn't wanted to harm the turtles. She'd been caught in a web of hopelessness and desperation.

What she needed was understanding and support. What they needed was an opportunity. Her husband's inability to work as a lobster diver, plus the slashed funding for the conservation project, meant they felt like they had no other option but to take what was not theirs.

María approached Pastor Pablo and asked to address the crowd once more.

"I can speak for the three of us. We vow that this will never happen again. In truth, all I wanted was to resurrect our project. I think we still can. And I promise you all this: we *will* repair the damage we caused."

Matías reached over and held his wife's hand.

There were nods and smiles and hands clasped in prayer.

Barana's heartbeat and breathing steadied. Her heart was as shaken as a storm-tossed sea, but through the tumult she felt a sliver of hope. Like the first sliver of the crescent moon after the darkness.

CHAPTER 28

Abby

It was Saturday morning, and the first time in days that Abby had woken with the sun already high in the sky. She and Papi lay in bed reading, letting the golden glow of the late morning wake them up slowly. Papi didn't have to work all weekend, and they had an entire week left in Pataya after that. Seven. Whole. Days.

After yesterday's announcement had shaken the town, Papi promised to spend more time with her. Pastor Pablo, Papi, Barana's parents, and a group of town leaders had stayed to have a closed-door, grown-ups-only meeting with María, Matías, and Nati. Abby, Barana, and Tulu had been escorted home by a young local doctor. Bela had been waiting for them with a smile and a feast. There was horchata to drink and fresh-cut mangoes for dessert. A sense of peace rounded out the evening. Barana and Abby agreed to spend

Saturday with their families. Their parents insisted they had "a lot to talk about."

Cozy beneath the mosquito net, Abby felt her stomach churn as she remembered that she had yet to come clean about the camera theft. She pulled the turtle totem out from under her pillow and held it snug between her hands.

"Papi," she said.

He put his book down on his lap. "Yeah?"

"The night we caught the poachers . . . There's something we left out."

He sat up some more and put his reading glasses on his lap, waiting for her to continue.

"My flash went off. That's how they knew we'd seen them. That's why they sent that scary warning to Barana's mom." Abby looked down, ashamed.

Papi got out of bed and sat on the edge of hers. Abby couldn't bring herself to continue. She still hadn't told him they'd *stolen* her camera after that.

"You think it's your fault they threatened you?"

The totem warmed up. Courage. Hope. Strength.

"They never would have known if my flash hadn't gone off. But there's more. The next day when I got back from school, my camera was gone."

"They stole it? How did you get it back?"

"We found it in the turtle office. That was the clue that confirmed it was them. The final straw."

Papi put his hand on her shoulder. "Don't ever keep something like this from me again—okay, Abby? No more secrets."

Abby nodded. She would keep that promise. "Papi? Have you ever told a lie? Or kept things from people you loved?"

Papi looked away and didn't answer. Then he said, "Sometimes we keep things from those we love for so long that we forget what the truth is." He paused and pursed his lips. "Let's start our morning with a walk down to the community center. We need to call your mother."

"Can we go to the cemetery after?"

Papi ran his hands over his face, as if massaging himself. He took a deep breath in and finally nodded. "A promise is a promise."

They got ready and grabbed a couple of tortillas stuffed with queso fresco and beans from Bela on their way out. At the center, they connected Papi's laptop to the network and video-called Mom. Abby was nervous. She didn't know if Papi would want to tell her about the poacher fiasco.

"Hello? Abby!" Mom said. "Oh my gosh, I miss you guys! You look so tanned! And look at your hair! How's it going down there?" Mom was overjoyed.

"It's awesome, Mom. Seriously. We have to come back together. The ocean, the people, the food!"

"Are you taking tons of pictures?"

"*Tons*. And this afternoon I'm making a video collage of them on Papi's computer. I'll send it to you when I'm done. My friend Barana, she's a great artist. I even took pictures of her drawings to put in my video." Abby's plan was to create a social media page for the Pataya Sea Turtle Conservation Center, post pictures, and raise awareness about it. Maybe even start a GoFundMe. It would be her way of helping from afar.

She wanted to share her photos with the world.

"Barana's your host's granddaughter, right?"

Abby nodded.

"Papi said you went to school with her!" Mom went on. "What was that like?"

"Great!"

"So, all that Spanish came in handy?"

"Sí," Abby said, smiling.

"Can't wait to see your pictures, honey! You know, I got a very nice email from Ms. Tenley . . . about a contest she says she told you about. Something about a summer exhibit. Seems there's still time. She asked me to remind you to send her a special photo."

"Oh. *That.*" Abby thought Ms. Tenley had suggested the contest out of pity. Maybe she'd been wrong. Maybe Ms. Tenley really *was* trying to push her as an artist *because she believed in her.* "Tell Ms. T she'll get a picture by tomorrow. I need to decide which one to submit. . . . And, Mom?"

"Yeah?"

"Thanks for letting me come." Abby's smile was genuine and bright.

"You're welcome, kiddo." Mom paused on the other end

of the line, and Abby could hear her breathing. "Abby?" she finally said. "It's nice to see you smiling again."

Abby wasn't sure what to make of that comment, but she had to admit it was accurate—she *hadn't* smiled much over the past year, and it was time to change that. Ever since Fiana moved away, Abby had felt completely out of focus. She'd depended so much on her one friend that she'd closed herself off to others. "You noticed?" was all Abby said.

"Of course I noticed. I'm your mother. Papi and I know what Fiana meant to you. I was just worried you'd never see how many other friends were out there waiting for you to open your heart to them."

Abby nodded and blinked back tears. "I guess Barana helped me with that," she said. By welcoming Abby into her world, by encouraging her creativity, and by trusting her, Barana had become the friend Abby didn't know she'd needed.

"I can't wait to go down there with you guys and meet her myself," her mother said.

Abby did an air hug and blew her mom a kiss. "I can't wait, either!" she said.

"Te amo, hija," Mom said.

"Love you too!" Abby replied.

It was like the time apart had made everything clear. Of course, her mom would freak out when they told her about the stakeout, but that was for another day. . . . First, Abby needed to send Fiana a quick email and begin the process of letting go. It was okay if they only chatted a few times a year

and liked each other's social media posts to "keep in touch."
They'd always be special to each other, but Abby knew that
it was time to stop clinging to a sinking lifeboat—it was time
to see what happened if she kicked her legs and swam into
the unknown.

Papi talked to Mom for a while longer, and Abby hopped
on one of the local computers. She kept it short:

> *Dear Fi,*
>
> *Hope London is great. I know it's been weird trying to
> stay in touch while in different time zones. And it's been
> hard, going from seeing each other every day to texting less
> and less.*
>
> *Even if we don't talk as often, maybe we can arrange
> for a monthly call? Like, first Fridays or something?
> Anyway, I'm writing to you from Honduras, which has
> been a life-changing trip! I'll share pictures with you
> next time I have a chance to write, or I'll upload them to
> Instagram soon so you can see them.* ☺
>
>
>
> *Love,*
>
> *Abby*
>
>

There, that did it. Abby had a hunch they'd drift apart,
but that was okay. Not all friendships were meant to last
forever.

THE CEMETERY WAS tranquil. Little butterflies and bees buzzed around the bushes, and the gravestones glistened in the sunlight. In the background, the sea was bright turquoise and still as the stones.

Even Mother Nature was at peace.

"I remember coming to this place when I was five," Papi said. "There were fewer gravestones, but not much has changed."

"What else do you remember?"

"Pataya was smaller, and maybe a little more rustic, if you can believe that. Our house didn't have running water. I loved the beach. Your abuelo would take me fishing out on the lagoon. I enjoyed that too."

He paused, reading the names on the stones.

"After we left, my mother worked a lot, and she only had two weeks off each year to come back for the holidays. That's when I'd see my father."

"And after he died, you left Honduras for good," Abby said.

Papi nodded. "I was nine when we arrived in New York."

Abby knelt and picked up a beautiful round seashell.

"That's called a moon shell," Papi said.

Abby held the pink seashell as they walked. A *moon* shell. Go figure.

They walked to the grave of R. Durón, and Papi stood still. He crouched down and pulled away the overgrown vegetation that surrounded the tombstone. He used his hand to brush sand and dirt off the engraving.

"Papi? Do you really not know who this gravestone belongs to?" Abby crouched next to him and placed the shell by the stone.

Papi sighed. "Why are you so perceptive?"

"Photographers have a keen eye. You told me that yourself."

Papi nodded and smiled.

"I've never visited my father's grave. Losing him when I was young was very painful. I was angry and sad at the same time. When I come to Pataya, I avoid this part of the beach, afraid of how I might feel. Abuela and I weren't here for his burial, and I'm not sure she ever forgave herself. Maybe I haven't forgiven myself, either."

Abby reached over and grabbed her father's hand.

"It feels good to be here now. I guess I needed you to come to Honduras to give me the courage to visit him." Papi squeezed her hand, and his eyes got watery.

Abby imagined Abuelo's spirit embracing them both from above. Though the grave was just a big chunk of limestone, and Abuelo wasn't literally *here*, his spirit was always with them, like a totem you carry in your pocket.

She walked around the cemetery in search of wildflowers. Papi didn't move or turn to see what she was doing. She grabbed some yellow and purple ones and brought them to him. He lay the bouquet by his father's grave as his eyes glistened with unshed tears. Abby gently placed the flowers next to the moon shell and stepped back.

Tap, tap, click.

She took a picture of him in front of Abuelo's gravestone. Papi's silhouette stood in stoic silence as the sea beyond gently sprayed its salty breeze. This would be the picture she'd send to Ms. Tenley.

Their walk on the beach could wait. Right now, everything was perfect.

Everything was in focus.

CHAPTER 29

Barana

Barana had never looked forward to church before, but this Sunday was different. Today's service was like a new beginning. Even the air smelled of possibilities. Pastor Pablo had come to visit Barana the day before and asked if she'd share a few words with the community after mass. He told her he thought she could be "an inspiration." She'd reluctantly agreed, but it wasn't until Sunday morning as she lay in bed that she'd decided exactly what she would say.

As the family got ready, Barana noticed Tulu wasn't around. "¿Y mi hermano?" she asked her father.

"Está en la casa de Bela. He said he needed to get something." He smiled a suspicious smile at her.

Barana was already dressed, so she stepped out into the warm air and ran down the steps and across the yard to her grandmother's. A noise was coming from underneath the house, where Tulu kept his junk.

"Tulu?" she said.

"Don't come any closer. I'm working on something."

Barana stood still. He was in the far corner with his back to her. "Okay . . ."

Moments later he walked over with a sculpture in his hands. "This is for you."

It was a leatherback sea turtle made of recycled materials. He had glued the pieces together and used a rubber tire and rope to make its ridges.

"You made that?" she said in disbelief.

"I used black and white boat paint. It's finally dry. What do you think?"

"It's beautiful!"

"Feliz cumpleaños, hermana. I wanted to give it to you before mass."

Barana went up and hugged him tighter than the tightest life vest.

With all the drama of the poachers, she'd forgotten about her birthday. She was thirteen today.

"Is this the secret you were keeping? Did that guy outside the turtle office have something to do with this?"

"Yeah—his father owns a hardware store in Paraíso. He got me the special kind of glue I needed. I've made more sculptures. Animals, mostly." He showed her a few other works of art. He'd made a monkey and a manatee and had started on a bird. This entire time her brother was working on something good for himself and their village, recycling junk and making art, and she'd mistakenly blamed him for the poaching. Tulu had even painted a crescent moon on the turtle's back.

"Gracias, Tulu. This is amazing."

"Come on—let's go show Mamá and Papá."

ON THEIR WAY to mass, Barana and her family walked hand in hand, and baby Marisol giggled and swayed on Mamá's back. Their parents had loved Tulu's surprise, and the mood felt like Christmas in June. The only problem was Barana's nerves. Even her skin was clammy despite the heat. As if reading her mind, Mamá said, "You're going to do great, Barana."

After the reopening of Pulpería Gloria yesterday, Barana's parents had given them an earful about their irresponsible actions. Both Barana and Tulu had gotten diaper-washing duty for the rest of the summer, on top of their punishments for lying about the "cemetery excursion."

But their parents were also proud of them.

They said that "No more secrets" would be their new family motto.

Barana didn't feel invisible anymore. When you hold in a secret, it's like the people you love don't really see you, because they don't see the real you. Now her parents understood just how important the baulas were to her. She didn't have to sneak around anymore.

They sat in their pew, and Barana took out her notebook, rereading her words. As she chewed on her pencil, Abby and her father scooted into the pew in front of them. Barana pulled the pencil out of her mouth and smiled at her friend.

"You got this!" Abby mouthed.

During the sermon, Pastor Pablo spoke about the importance of community and protecting not only each other from the "storms of life" but protecting the natural world too. The congregation sang at peak volume, with more people joining in the singing than usual. It had been two weeks since the storm, and it finally felt like Pataya was beginning to heal.

After the service the pastor invited Barana to speak. She trembled on her way to the altar and tried not to panic. She looked out onto the crowd and focused her gaze on her family and Abby.

Inhala, exhala.

"Buenos días. Thank you for this opportunity. I'd like to share a poem I wrote.

> *"We are from a village,*
> *Peaceful and warm.*
> *From a land by the Atlantic.*
> *Where hurricanes of doubt*
> *Meet courage and hope from within.*
>
> *"We are from a place*
> *Of palms and drumbeats,*

Of fishing boats and hatchlings.
Where community meets the sea,
And turtles of the midnight moon come home.

"From a house above the sand,
Built by family and love.
Where storms come and go,
And people rise and fall,
Till truth sets them free.

"Somos el futuro de Pataya.
Guided by strength of spirit,
Moonlight on our backs,
And glowing sun in our hearts.
We are not alone."

When Barana raised her eyes to look up at the congregation, everyone was clapping and smiling. One lady in the back even stood up. They cared.

"Thank you, Barana," the pastor said. "I'd like to formally ask all of you to support Barana, María, and our town's conservation efforts. We can all do a small part to bring it back to life. This is our beach. Our project. Our future."

The crowd stood and clapped.

Pastor Pablo spread his arms wide. "You may go in peace."

ABBY AND BARANA held hands and left their shoes by the steps of Bela's house. Barana couldn't remember the last time her entire family had gone out on the beach together. The moon was full, hanging low above the sea, and it reflected back like a magic mirror. Her birthday couldn't get any better.

Then she felt it. She almost didn't recognize it at first. The tingle in her moon scar had returned. She had to close her eyes and focus to make sure it wasn't her imagination.

Would they see Luna tonight?

There was a slight breeze, and the sand flies weren't biting. Papá carried the food, Abuelo Juan carried a radio for music, and Tulu carried a cooler with sodas. Of course, he'd also brought a spare bag for the litter.

"We have a surprise for you," Bela said. "A celebration is in order!"

As they walked through the lines of palms and onto la playa, Barana saw what Bela was talking about. Everyone was there! María and her family, Nati, Pastor Pablo, Chiqui, Jason, the primos, neighbors and their children, all gathered around a huge fogata. Barana worried the bonfire was too close to the tide line. It was still nesting season, and a fire that size could be a hazard for the sea turtles.

As they approached the blaze, María walked up to her, gave her a big hug, and reassured her that there were no nests nearby; they'd chosen that spot for the bonfire precisely because it was far from where any baulas might reach. Knowing the leatherbacks would be safe, Barana allowed herself to exhale and celebrate.

"¡Feliz cumpleaños! To you, Barana, I dedicate this fire. It is a new beginning." María opened her hand and gave her a key. "It's for the office. I'm going to need your help the next few months."

Barana wasn't sure what to say. She was still conflicted about how she felt, but she accepted the gift and allowed herself to start trusting María again. "Gracias," she said. "You can count on me."

"It will take a village to keep things going when the baby comes," María said. She explained it would be a community effort, as Pastor Pablo had suggested. There was only a month or so left before the sea turtles migrated back to the open sea, and by the time they returned next year, María would be able to take on the work again, with her baby tucked in a sling.

"People approached me after mass and asked what our plan was. Your poem inspired everyone, Barana."

"It did?"

María nodded. "Chiqui will paint a brand-new office mural, your grandfather is going to fix the windows and the door, and apparently your friend created a video that has already gotten hundreds of views on the internet. It seems to be going . . . viral? And I met with almost a dozen volunteers this afternoon. The project will be a way for us to empower our people. Even the children of Pataya. We will work on a proposal to get funding from international and national conservation organizations."

"What about your husband?"

"Dr. Durón says he might one day dive again. That's his passion, so I think he will do as the doctor says, help on the boat, and slowly get back to going into the water."

María said volunteers had already started signing up for patrol shifts to monitor nests and hatchlings. To collect data just like scientists while she focused on writing grants. What began as a small effort by a village by the sea could one day provide Pataya with more than a hobby for its nature lovers: it could be a source of ecotourism for years to come.

Barana wished María had thought of all this earlier, but there was no looking back now. Only forward, like the pastor said.

"I always knew there was something special between you and the turtles," María said, with a note of solemnity in her voice. "I hope you know how sorry I am. For everything. I'll make it up to you, Barana. We all will."

Barana offered María her hand. They shook to the future. Barana understood the events of the last month had been motivated by fear and desperation, and while it might take her a while to fully trust her old friend, she could forgive her. Her bare feet dug into the warm sand. She felt like she could finally stand firmly on her playa, knowing everything was as it should be.

"Do you think your baby is coming soon?"

"Very soon. Who knows, I may be leaving your party early," María replied.

As the full moon rose higher in the sky, so did the flames, and so did Barana's faith in the home she shared with her turtles. She and Abby sat by the fire while Tulu, Jason, and the primos talked about the latest soccer match.

"I heard you made a 'viral' video," Barana said.

"I was going to surprise you later tonight. It's already gotten tons of views. I think this is just the beginning of something big!"

"Thank you," Barana said. "You're a real friend." She didn't want to get too dramatic on her birthday, but it was true. She would never have gotten to the truth without Abby.

"My totem hasn't stopped glowing tonight," Abby said.

"Neither has mine."

"Do you think we'll ever know where they came from, or how their magic works?"

Barana looked around at everyone gathered by the fire. Her loving grandmother, her artistic brother, her hardworking parents, and her wise abuelo Juan. She couldn't say for sure where the totems had come from, and she realized she didn't need to know. "I don't think so. But I'm okay with that."

"Me too," Abby said.

They sat there quietly as the calming surf came and went. Then Abby reached into her bag and pulled something out. "I have a birthday surprise for you. I saw Tulu at the community center yesterday while I was working on the video, and he told me about your birthday."

Abby gave Barana the object she'd pulled out of her bag. It was the picture of her and Luna on the beach, the day they'd all seen her. "The printer at the community center isn't the best, but it came out okay for being on regular paper . . . and I wrote something on the back."

Barana flipped the photo over and read, "See you next summer, amiga. Love, Abby."

"Really?" Barana said.

Abby nodded. "I think I'll join Papi every year from now on."

"I love it!" Though they still had a week to hang out, Barana couldn't wait to see Abby again next year. She was working on something to give Abby too—a drawing of both of their totems, side by side, glowing beneath a full moon. She'd finish it before Abby went back home.

Barana tucked Abby's photo safely inside her notebook and put it back in her bag, right next to her totem and the key to the turtle office.

Tulu walked up to them and reached out his hands. "Who wants to dance? Abby? Hermana?"

"I don't think so," Abby said.

"Come on," Tulu insisted.

Abby hesitated but finally got up, brushed the sand off

her denim shorts, and started walking toward Tulu like she was about to prove something to the world.

"Wait!" Barana cried. "Show me how this thing works." She pulled Abby's camera out from her bag and pretended to take a picture.

"Oh no. *No, no, no. No* pictures of me allowed!"

"¡Por favor! Show me how, or I'll mess around with it until I figure it out myself."

Abby huffed a little. Then, as if shaking off a fishing net from her body, she said, "Fine. But don't make me the focus."

Barana was surprised at how simple the camera was. Turn it on, point, and shoot. Maybe she'd walk around and snap photos of everyone: Nati chatting with Abuelo Juan; Bela and María discussing breathing techniques for her imminent labor; kids playing by the fire while Mamá kept an eye on them; and Abby's father standing at the break of the waves with his jeans rolled up.

Beneath the light of the bright moon and surrounded by the sounds of tropical music, her lanky brother tried to teach her new friend how to dance. It was nice to hear Abby belly-laugh as she swayed her hips, and to capture the moment forever.

After a while, the flames died down and people started heading home.

But Barana's scar was still tingling. Before, she would've snuck away and tried to find Luna. Now she understood that moments like these, with friends and family, were as important as looking for her turtle. She'd see Luna again, and wherever Luna was, Barana knew she was okay.

The scar on her back told her so.

"Barana," Bela said. "Take your friend for a stroll down the beach. The moon is full, and I have a feeling you might see something special."

"Really? Alone?"

"Yes. We'll be here for a while longer. The night is too magical to go home just yet. Go. It's perfectly safe."

Barana waited for the song to end before whispering in Abby's ear, "Let's go for a walk on the beach!"

"Where are you going?" Tulu asked.

"Just down the beach," she said. "Come with us! Bela said it was okay."

"Nah, you two go. And say hi to the ghosts for me." He did a spooky face and raised his arms in the air all creepy.

Still the same old Tulu. He'd probably hide behind a palm tree and try to scare them later.

Walking toward the cemetery felt like déjà vu. The sea was calm, the moon was brillante, and the tingle on Barana's back had intensified.

Barana and Abby were far from the bonfire when they appeared.

Not creepy poachers.

Not ghosts.

Not Luna.

A parade of miniature leatherbacks, emerging from their hidden nest beneath the sand and marching to the waves.

A forgotten nest.

Survivors.

They were no more than three inches long, and their flippers were almost as long as their bodies. Their leathery black bumps and clumsy crawl made Barana believe that anything was possible.

Barana and Abby stood side by side as the baby baulas crawled awkwardly and determinedly toward the ocean. The moon was high in the sky, and its reflection on the water guided them to the waves. Lagging behind her brothers and sisters, a lone leatherback pushed through the sand. Barana approached her with care to make sure she found her way home.

She noticed the sea turtle was unusual. She shimmered, as if there were diamonds on her back. Barana got closer.

The hatchling had a glowing moon on her carapace.

She was a living, breathing replica of their totems. And she was perfect in every way.

Acknowledgments

I am grateful and humbled by the support of so many talented people who made this book a reality. To my kind and fierce agent, Sara, thank you for always being in my corner, and for trusting that Barana and Abby's story needed to be told. Thank you to my brilliant editor, Katherine, for believing in me and this story, and for your pitch-perfect editorial eye. Working with you has been a dream. To the extraordinary team of copy editors at Knopf—Artie, Amy, Alison, and Jim—I have learned so much from you! Thank you to Michelle and the entire design team for making this book look absolutely gorgeous, and to Zeina for her luminescent art; I couldn't have imagined a more beautiful cover. To Morgan H. and the entire team at Pippin, thank you for all you do! Jennifer, I dreamed of having a map in this book— thank you! Gianna, Lena, Jake, and everyone at Knopf who supported *Turtles* from the start and who worked tirelessly to bring this book to market, ¡Gracias!

Thank you to my Pitch Wars #UnicornMojo mentors who changed the course of my life: Jessica and Julie. You took me under your wing and helped me become a far better writer than I ever imagined. To my entire 2020 Pitch Wars family, what a gift to have found each other in the middle of an unprecedented year. Hannah, grateful for our sprints, chats, and friendship! Heather and Isi, being on this journey with you has been a treasure. #PowerPuffTriplets forever! Thank you to my critique partners—Allison, Leah, and Rachel—for helping me believe I had more stories to tell. To the MGin23 Debuts: riding this roller coaster with you has been unforgettable! To the amazing Las Musas community, thank you for uplifting our voices!

To all my friends (and their kids!) who beta-read those early and messy first drafts, especially to Stella and Tamara, with whom I first shared Barana and Abby's story, thank you! Ruth, Vivi, Alanna, Akiko, Emily, Leigh, Mai, Juan Carlos, Dani, Book Club ladies—near and far, your cheers of support and your genuine joy for this book are what true friendships are made of. Thank you to my teachers at the Escuela Americana and the University of Georgia, especially Mrs. Motz, Mr. Jaén, Mrs. Martínez, Ms. Flores, Dr. Fitt, Dr. Alber—you instilled in me a love of reading, poetry, ecology, marine science, and writing.

To my siblings—Jose, Luli, Pablo, Juanpi, Carol— grateful does not come close to expressing how I feel about having you in my life. Jose y Jorgito, thanks for joining me in La Mosquitia all those years ago. Mama, thank you for teaching me patience, faith, and perseverance. Papa, because of you I appreciate nature, embrace the unknown, and have learned that life is worth second chances (thanks for teaching me to scuba-dive!). To my entire Agurcia and Agüero family, my sisters-in-law, nieces and nephews, primos y primas, tíos y tías, and especially my abuela, Tita, thank you for always believing in me. Bela, Jachi, Lilo, Tito, LaFrenda, Bob, I wish you were still here.

To my daughters, Fiana and Brenna. You inspire me every day to reach for the stars and to be the best version of myself. You are my moon and my sun! I adore you. Sean, thank you for your steady encouragement, for calming me when the seas got rough, for having faith in me and my writing. . . . And, of course, for keeping my computer updated, for granting me the wish of double monitors, and for early-morning coffee. I am blessed to share this life with you.

Lastly, thank you to the tenacious environmental conservation warriors, especially in Honduras and throughout Central America, who, against all odds, fight for our forests, oceans, rivers, and all their magnificent creatures.

Protecting Our
Sea Turtle Friends

Sea turtles have inhabited our world's oceans for over one hundred million years. These ancient creatures fill an important role in keeping the marine ecosystem healthy. But they face threats that could have lasting consequences for our planet. *Dermochelys coriacea,* the leatherback sea turtle, is the largest member of the sea turtle family, growing to over six feet, and ten feet at the longest. They are also the only species of sea turtle that lacks a hard shell—instead, they have a thin, tough, rubbery skin, which is strengthened by thousands of tiny bone plates. Leatherbacks migrate thousands of miles over the course of their lives. What's more, they can dive up to 4,200 feet and hold their breath for as long as eighty-five minutes. This author can barely hold her breath for eight seconds!

Though sea turtles spend most of their time in the ocean, they must come ashore to nest—and ensure the survival of the species. Leatherbacks usually nest in intervals of one, two, or three years, and they lay between six and nine clutches each season. Females lay about eighty fertilized eggs (slightly bigger than Ping-Pong balls) per nest. The eggs incubate for two months, and the temperature of the sand determines the sex of the individual hatchlings. Despite the turtles laying so many eggs, it is estimated that only one in one thousand hatchlings will make it to adulthood.

In the United States, the leatherback sea turtle is classified as "critically endangered," which means it faces a high risk of extinction. Internationally, the species is listed as "vulnerable," although leatherback populations in the Pacific Ocean have declined at alarming rates. Like all species of sea turtles, leatherbacks are primarily threatened by:

Illegal trade and direct consumption: Turtles are poached for their meat and eggs. Hard-shelled species are also captured for their shells.

Bycatch: Animals that are captured accidentally in fishing gear.

Loss of habitat: The development of our world's coastal areas can destroy or disturb turtles and their nests.

Climate change: The warming of our planet could have an adverse effect on sex ratios, resulting in more females.

Litter and pollution, especially plastic: Sea turtles may confuse plastic bags and other ocean litter for food.

Communities along the coast of Honduras are working hard to protect sea turtles and their environment, but there is much more to be done—education, creating job opportunities, and ensuring that those who do this important work are offered a living wage make for a good beginning. In La Mosquitia, children and teachers have already had a great impact—and so can you! We are all part of this one wondrous earth. Whether it is sea turtles or monarch butterflies, no creature is too small or too big to be protected. If you want to help, below are some things you can do:

Be a smart consumer. Try to limit how much plastic you use . . . a lot of it ends up in our oceans!

Purchase sustainable seafood.

Support sea turtle ecotourism. When visiting sea turtle nesting beaches, consider participating in a turtle walk to support conservation efforts!

Adopt a turtle! Many organizations offer "adopt a turtle" programs that support their conservation efforts.

Educate yourself and others. Learn about sea turtles and other marine life.

There are many organizations all around the world that are making a difference. Here are a few, but you can always support those doing environmental work in your local communities as well!

BICA (Bay Islands Conservation Association): bicainc.org

Earth Watch: earthwatch.org

MOPAWI (Mosquitia Pawisa Apiska): mopawi.org

ProTECTOR, Inc.: turtleprotector.org

Roatan Marine Park: roatanmarinepark.org

Sea Legacy: sealegacy.org/tide

Sea Turtle Conservancy: conserveturtles.org

World Wildlife Fund: worldwildlife.org

SOURCES

NationalGeographic.com/animals/reptiles/facts/
    leatherback-sea-turtle

ProTECTOR, Inc.: Protective Turtle Ecology Center for
    Training, Outreach and Research

Sea Turtle Conservancy

WIDECAST: Wider Caribbean Sea Turtle Conservation
    Network

World Wildlife Fund